Nothing can spoil this cat's appetite . . .

Chase poured herself a second cup of cocoa, leaving the marsh-mallows off this time. Besides, there were some wisps clinging to her cup that would melt in nicely. "Did Larry's wife—Elsa?—give you any more details about what happened?"

"Yes, Elsa Oake. We got sidetracked by those two and their butter sculpture history, didn't we?" Anna gazed into her cup.

"Oh, you're empty. Do you want another cup?"

"No thanks, Charity." Anna hesitated, setting her mug aside and rubbing Quincy's right ear. "Elsa told me everything she saw, and it's not good. She was supposed to meet her husband at the food trailers for an early lunch. He'd been doing some preliminary work on his sculpture in the morning."

"And he didn't show up, I'm guessing."

"Right. So she went looking for him. She said she opened the door to the butter room and saw her husband on the floor and Quincy licking the sculpture. When she called her hus-band's name, Dr. Ramos blocked her way. That's when she screamed."

Berkley Prime Crime titles by Janet Cantrell

FAT CAT AT LARGE
FAT CAT SPREADS OUT

FAT CAT SPREADS OUT

Janet Cantrell

BERKLEY PRIME CRIME, NEW YORK

BERKLEY
PRIME
CRIME

An imprint of Penguin Random House LLC
375 Hudson Street, New York, New York 10014

FAT CAT SPREADS OUT

A Berkley Prime Crime Book / published by arrangement with the author

ISBN: 978-0-425-26743-1

PUBLISHING HISTORY
Berkley Prime Crime mass-market edition / June 2015

PRINTED IN THE UNITED STATES OF AMERICA

10 9 8 7 6 5 4 3 2 1

Interior text design by Kelly Lipovich.

Penguin
Random
House

ACKNOWLEDGMENTS

I must thank several people who helped out with *Fat Cat Spreads Out*. I, of course, didn't write this all by myself in a closet without asking anyone any questions. When you belong to the friendly, supportive community of mystery writers, there's always help available. Thanks in particular to the following:

My agent, Kim Lionetti, as always, and my editors, Danielle Stockley and Michelle Vega, as well as every member of the Berkley Prime Crime team.

For synopsis help, Peg Cochran. For pet recipes and sheep consulting, KB Inglee and Bodge. For generous bidding on the name that I gave to the redheaded travel agent, Marisa Young. For taste testing the Harvest Bars, members of Ben Egner's family, mainly Dani, Jack, and Nancy. For being astute and valuable readers, Kathy Waller, Gale Albright, and Paula Benson.

My family gives me all the support in the world, and I'm grateful for every one of them.

I want to mention the late, great rescued feral cat Agamemnon, who lived a good long life, kept us amused, and inspired many of Quincy's antics. Thanks, Erin Rotunno and Jess Busen, for bringing him and James into our lives.

And last, Skott Johnson, the president of the Dinky-town Business Association, whom I forgot to thank in *Fat Cat at Large*. I apologize for this, as the assistance he gave me was a huge help.

ONE

Charity Oliver, usually called Chase, smiled as she handed the bag of dessert bars to the customer and took her money.

"I just love these Hula Bars," the customer said. "My grandkids do, too. I can't keep them in the house."

The satisfied woman left the shop with her pineapple-coconut treat, setting off the tinkling chimes above the door. A bit of brisk October air whooshed in before the door closed.

At last, the shop was empty. The Bar None had done great business today, nearly nonstop. But there was so much else to do right now!

Chase let her cheek muscles relax from all the hours of smiling. They almost hurt. Still, business was good and she couldn't complain. She surveyed her domain—hers and Anna's.

The salesroom design had been handled by Chase alone, and she was so proud of it. The walls were striped the colors of raspberry and vanilla, set off by the cotton-candy-pink shelving that held boxed dessert bars. The glass display case near the rear of the salesroom housed fresh merchandise, dessert bars made by Chase and Anna in the kitchen behind the front area.

"Ms. Oliver," said Inger, the sales clerk, "I can stay out here if you want to get off your feet." Her smoky gray eyes smiled with the rest of her small, pretty face. The standard mulberry smocks they all wore in the salesroom, with pink rickrack and the embroidered Bar None logo, suited Inger's blonde coloring. Her curls bounced when she nodded at the customers, who seemed to genuinely like her.

Chase wondered if Inger's offer to let Chase rest was a veiled reference to the fact that her employee was a good ten years younger than Chase's thirty-two, but decided it wasn't. Inger was a genuinely kind and guileless young woman. Inger had taken a break about two hours ago, so it was Chase's turn.

"Thanks, Inger. Holler if you get swamped." Chase pushed through the swinging double doors to the kitchen, where Anna was working, and took a seat on one of the stools at the center island. The aroma of cinnamon and pumpkin spice wafted through the room.

Chase picked up the cup of tea, now cold, that she'd left there hours ago.

"She's a gem, Charity," Anna said. "You did well to hire

Inger." Today, her periwinkle-blue eyes sparkled, picking up the sapphire tones of her sweater, even though all you could see of it were the sleeves beneath her Bar None apron. The rest of her outfit was her usual plain T-shirt and jeans. Her grandmotherly build and gray bobbed hair gave no indication of the fact that, in her seventies, she could work circles around Chase.

Chase took a sip of the tea, then set it down to redo the clip in her honey-blonde hair. It constantly needed redoing. Since her hair was so straight, her clips slipped easily and allowed her locks to dangle in her face. Not an ideal style for a place that sold food.

"That was pure luck," Chase said. "I had to do something in a hurry when we lost the others. I think all the college kids already had jobs, so she was the only applicant." She started humming "Luck Be a Lady" from *Guys and Dolls*.

Anna slid three batches of Harvest Bars, their new creation, into the oven. "I think we'll have enough of our new dessert bars for the fair as soon as these are done. It's almost time to close up."

Anna and Chase had come up with the idea of pumpkin spice dessert bars especially for the autumn fair. When Inger had tasted them, she insisted they would be a huge hit.

Chase glanced at the clock on the wall. Five forty-five. Fifteen minutes until their regular Thursday closing time of six.

Her cell phone trilled and she saw Tanner's ID. "I'll be back in a sec," she called to Anna, heading for the back door. She answered the call once she was outside. "Tanner, so what do you think?"

"I'll do it. Your offer is good. But when do you want it by? And what exactly do you want?"

"A webpage. Isn't that what we discussed?"

The kid—he couldn't be more than seventeen or eighteen—had designed the website for Dr. Michael Ramos's vet clinic and Mike had been happy to refer him to Chase. "Ms. Oliver, you need a web presence, not just a page. I can do it all if you want. You'll need Facebook, Twitter, a blog—"

"Wait a minute. Let's do this one step at a time. My partner isn't totally on board with this, so we can't go whole hog right now. We just need a webpage for visibility. And a map. And maybe a place where we can take online orders, I think. Those are the main things I'd like to get started."

"Sure." She could almost see him shrug his skinny shoulders. "If that's the way you want to play it. I'll do the page first. But you're going to need to get involved, you know. Can you e-mail me some shots?"

"Some shots?"

"Yeah, the outside of the store and the place where you sell things."

"The salesroom. Yes, I'll take some pictures and e-mail them."

"Cool. We're on."

She was starting to shiver, so she hurried back inside.

"Who was that?" Anna looked suspicious.

"I had to get something from my car."

"Who was on the phone? It was that computer kid, wasn't it? Did you tell him we don't need to be *online*? We sell products at the store, not on a computer."

4

"It would at least be good advertising. People could find us on the web and would know how to get here."

Anna looked doubtful. "Come help me get these boxed up to take tomorrow."

"I'm still not sure if we should have let Julie talk us into having a booth at the Harvest Fair." Julie was Anna's actual granddaughter, though she treated Chase as if she were one, too.

Anna picked up her cup of tea from the granite counter next to the stove and came to sit next to Chase. "I think it's a fabulous idea." Anna's merry eyes crinkled when she smiled.

Chase was glad the subject was changed from the webpage.

Dinkytown, where the Bar None was located, bordered the campus of the University of Minnesota in Minneapolis. The neighborhood, so named after a remark meant to be derogatory, was a miniature shopping district with a few residences sprinkled in. Chase's own apartment was above the shop.

A plaintive mew came from behind the office door.

"I'll go check on him," Chase said. She warmed up a Kitty Patty in the microwave for a few seconds. Slowly, she edged the office door open, putting her foot in position to keep Quincy contained inside.

The butterscotch tabby sat in the middle of the floor, even though the feeding woman was ready to block his escape if he'd been near the door. The treats usually came earlier in the day, and the cat was starting to feel hungry and neglected.

It seemed he was being careful not to look too eager, waiting while she set the patty on a plate before he strolled over to give it a sniff. However, after the meaty aroma reached his pink nose, he dived in. The woman smiled and cooed baby talk to him for a few moments before she left.

❦

Chase returned to the kitchen, where the pumpkin-spicy smell of the baking welcomed her again. She couldn't get enough of it. She and Anna were the co-owners of the Bar None, their pride and joy and joint business venture. Though Anna was Chase's senior by quite a few years, she was also her surrogate grandmother and the woman who had helped raise her after her parents passed away. For the most part, they got along. Anna used to sneak cookie bar crumbs to Quincy, which didn't help his weight problem. But now that Chase had perfected the Kitty Patty treats, Quincy was slimming down a bit and Chase didn't have to always worry that Anna was sneaking things to him. A big source of conflict had evaporated with the creation of the Kitty Patties.

"Ms. Oliver?" Inger's faint voice drifted back to the kitchen.

Chase rushed to the front room, where she found Inger Uhlgren slumped over the glass display case, clutching the edges with whitened knuckles.

"What's the matter?" Chase lifted the hem of her own Bar None smock and wiped Inger's damp forehead. Inger's blonde curls were matted against her wide, usually clear brow, which was now pinched and furrowed.

"Anna!" Chase put her arms around the young woman, and when Anna rushed to their side, the two of them managed to help Inger into the office, where there was a chair with arms and a back.

"Go," said Anna. "Call someone. I'll stay with her."

"Who should we call, Inger?" Chase asked. She knew someone should man the salesroom for a few more minutes, but maybe they needed an ambulance more urgently than anything else.

"I'll be okay." A bit of color was returning to Inger's pale face. "I had a dizzy spell. If I sit for a few minutes, I'll be able to get back to work."

Quincy approached, sniffed Inger's shoes, then jumped into her lap, where she stroked him a few times before dropping her hand into her lap.

Anna fanned Inger's glistening face with a folder from the desktop. "You'll do no such thing. We're nearly ready to close. You're not going back to work. You need to see a doctor."

"No, really, I don't. I get these spells. When it's over, I'll be all right."

Anna and Chase shot each other doubtful looks, but Chase left them, making certain that Quincy was in the office when she closed the door. The rascally cat had a real skill for escaping at exactly the wrong times and getting into exactly the wrong things. In the past, he'd led Chase into some trouble.

Today, though, her problem was Inger, the model employee they'd hired a few weeks ago. She hadn't been feeling well lately and this wasn't the first time Chase had worried about her.

7

As soon as Chase returned from the front, having drawn the shades, flipped the sign, and locked up, Inger stood.

"If you don't mind, I'll go home now."

"Do you need one of us to take you home?" Anna asked.

"No, I can drive. Thanks, though. I feel bad about not staying to help clean up."

"We wouldn't think of letting you do that when you're sick like this. Let us know if you can't make it in tomorrow morning," Anna said. She ran and got Inger's jacket from the hook by the door that led to the parking lot behind the store.

"Thanks, Mrs. Larson. Thanks, Ms. Oliver. I'll be fine tomorrow."

"Call me Chase." Chase studied her as she walked out to the parking lot. Her gait was steady, but she was still pale as she made her way to her old, faded red sedan.

Quincy scooted out of the office, since the door was standing ajar, into the kitchen, to perform his customary countertop prowl. Since he'd been put on a strict diet, Chase took extra care not to leave fattening bits of baking debris for him to find. She thought she had convinced Anna to be careful of his weight, too. Still, he managed to scare up a few crumbs almost every night. When he was finished, one of the women sanitized the countertops as part of their own nightly ritual.

Anna was taking baking sheets out of the dishwasher when the office phone rang, so Chase ran to answer it.

When she heard the deep, rumbly voice of Dr. Michael Ramos, her heart sped up.

"How's my favorite patient?" he asked.

8

"Quincy is doing well. He hasn't gotten into anything he shouldn't have for over a week now."

"Glad to hear it. I have some news. Aren't you and Anna renting a booth at the Bunyan County Harvest Fair this year?"

"Yes, Julie thought it would be a good idea." Julie, Anna's granddaughter, was also Chase's best friend and had been since they'd grown up together.

"I think it's a good idea, too. You'll probably sell a lot of dessert bars, and you'll get valuable advertising. A lot of locals get an early start on Christmas at that fair."

Chase didn't want to tell him that October 18 was too early for people to buy their consumables and have them last until the holidays, unless they froze them. That gave her an idea, though. They would hand out freezing instructions with their wares. If, that is, they were still able to do the fair.

"I don't know if this will work out," Chase said, opening a file on the computer and typing in the freezing instructions while she clamped the phone between her ear and shoulder.

"What's the problem?"

"Inger has been feeling ill for the last two weeks."

"That's a long time. Has she seen a doctor?"

"No, she's usually nauseated in the morning, then feels better by afternoon. Today, though, she felt faint just before closing."

"I'm not a people doctor, but you know what that sounds like, don't you?"

"No. What do you think is wrong with her?"

"I think she's pregnant."

9

TWO

Anna wrestled the clumsy wicker basket onto the display table in their booth with a grunt.

"What are you doing?" Chase rushed to help her, but was too late. "That basket is too heavy for one person."

"Oh, pooh. My laundry basket weighs more than this."

They had stuffed the pretty basket full of dessert bar packages this morning before they left to set up their booth for the opening of the fair and bazaar tomorrow. Anna thought they could use the basket as part of their display. Anna, a seamstress wizard, had lined it with pink-and-purple-striped cloth before they'd filled it. The table was rather small, but Chase thought they could make it work.

"Let's tip the basket and put the dessert bars half in and half out," Chase suggested.

"Oh, like they're tumbling from the basket, right? Great idea, Charity." Anna started unpacking the small boxes onto the top of the table so they could set up the arrangement.

A gust of wind stirred the back tarp slightly, and it flapped against the supporting poles.

The booths were set up along the sawdust strewn midway at the Bunyan County Fairgrounds. They were nine-by-nine tents, each furnished with a five-foot table and two folding chairs for the price of the display space. Chase hadn't looked around yet to see who the other vendors were, but she wanted to take a walk along the entire concourse after they set up and before they left tonight.

The tinkling music of an electric calliope came from the direction of the traveling carnival that was setting up in part of the huge visitor's parking lot. The rides were mostly children's rides, including a merry-go-round (with the electric music), a small roller coaster, a train ride with a fancy old-fashioned locomotive, and, for the brave, a Tilt-A-Whirl. Chase thought they must be trying things out today.

Several booths of carnival games lined up at the edge of that lot. Chase used to be a fair hand at ring toss. Maybe she would get a chance to see if she could still do it. Later, after things were well under way, of course.

The main attractions at the fair were the butter sculpture competition and the pet contests. Chase was glad the booths were set up on the path leading to the exhibit building and close to the butter sculpture location.

She wasn't sure what the sculpture contest entailed, but was eager to find out. Julie had started to tell her, but their phone conversation had been cut short by a wave of Bar None customers. All she knew was that the Bunyan County Fair had held the competitions for years, and she remembered seeing some when her parents took her to the fair as a young child.

A shadow fell across the opening to the booth. Chase turned to find Quincy's veterinarian running an appreciative eye over what they'd done so far.

"I like the banner with your logo. The stripes are eye-catching."

"Mike," Chase said. "What are you doing here?"

"I'm the vet for the fair. That's the news I meant to tell you last night."

"The fair needs a vet? I guess I haven't read up on it enough. Is there livestock?"

"No, not actual farming livestock."

"I thought I saw a man unloading a sheep or a goat in the parking lot."

"There aren't any blue ribbons for farm animals, but there are a lot of pet contests. All the farm animals you'll see here are pets. There's an obstacle course for dogs and a Fancy Cat Contest. You might consider entering Quincy. But how's Inger today?"

"She came in to work this morning," Anna said. "I told her we'll open limited hours all next week, since she'll be there alone. One of those days she can close up early, or completely, and get herself to a doctor."

"Yep, that's what Anna told her." Chase had her doubts Inger would see a doctor. She hadn't seemed eager to do that. "I'll run back to check on Quincy this afternoon, and I'll also see if Inger is having any trouble. If she is, I'll either stay or close the shop."

"Good idea," Anna said. "I can always go back, too. Between us, we'll get Inger taken care of."

No one noticed when the packages that were in the basket began to shift and quake. None of the three even saw the bright amber eyes peer over the top. The cat was able to leap out of the basket, land behind the table, and squeeze under the tarp that formed the back wall. Free of the confines of the basket, though the contents had provided good eating, he waddled along the aisle of booths, looking for something more to nibble on.

"Did you see what I think I just saw?" Mike stepped into the booth and peered at the packed-dirt floor behind the table.

Chase's cell phone trilled. "It's Inger."

"I hope she's okay." Anna leaned close to overhear the conversation.

"Ms. Oliver—"

"Call me Chase, Inger."

"Okay. Quincy isn't here. I just went in to give him his midmorning snack, and—"

"Midmorning snack? Who told you he gets one of those?" Chase frowned at Anna. Was she still spoiling the cat with too many treats?

Anna backed away from the phone and resumed unpacking a box.

"Mrs. Larson said she gives him one every day."

It was a wonder he hadn't been gaining more weight. Chase glared at Anna's back. "Has the outside door been open?" she asked Inger.

"No. We haven't even had any deliveries. I know he didn't go out the front door. The thing is, the office door was closed. I don't know why he's not in here."

Chase closed her eyes and tried to picture the flurry when they were packing up this morning. Had she seen Quincy when she'd latched the office door? She couldn't remember.

Mike turned to face her. "Is Quincy missing?"

Chase nodded, then spoke to Inger. "Maybe I should come back and help look for him."

When she was a child and Julie nicknamed her Chase, no one could have foreseen that she would spend so much time chasing a cat.

"I think I just saw him there." Mike pointed at the tarp that formed the rear wall of the booth.

"Where?" Anna bent down and looked at the floor under the table.

"He left. He slid out under the tent."

Chase told Inger she thought the cat was at the fair and

cut the call short. "Are you sure you saw him?" she asked Mike.

"Not positive. It's dark back there. But it sure looked like a critter jumped off this table and went underneath the tarp."

"Great," Chase said, planting her fists on her hips. "Quincy is loose again."

After extensive exploring, the aroma coming from the cold building was too much for the cat to resist. It was true, he'd gotten a lot of treats up and down the path he'd been roaming, but this was incredible. The whole building was full of butter. After the heavy door was pushed open, he slipped in, unseen by the person entering. Two people started having a violent scuffle, which sent the cat under a table, crouching until the disturbance was over. After the one left and the other lay still on the floor, the cat picked a table with a large amount of the delicious-smelling stuff and sprang up. It was full of the wonderful goodness. He started licking. Butter. An almost infinite amount of it. Yum.

The three split up and Chase trudged past the booths. She bypassed the sturdy refrigerated building for butter sculptures, since the door was firmly shut. A sign hung on it that read "Keep Closed." The jeweler next to it had seen him. He had even petted Quincy and fed him a potato chip from his snack stash. Chase paused at a booth with darling children's clothing featuring colorful bird, fish, and butterfly accents. The two women there exclaimed how cute Quincy was. They had given him some cheese crackers. At a book vendor, she was told that her cat was so clever, he'd tried to open one of the books on the display table. They had slipped him a piece of ham sandwich. Everywhere she went, from the cupcake tent to one selling unique board games and fancy decks of cards, she was told how clever and darling her orange-striped cat was. Almost all of them had fed him. She wondered how he was still able to walk.

She visited the food concessions selling hot dogs and cotton candy and deep-fried concoctions, shuddering to think what they must have fed him. The people selling handmade banjos and the ones selling glass mobiles hadn't given him anything, but had admired the "charming" animal. At a booth that gave out information about planting microchips into pets, she snatched a pamphlet after asking about Quincy. She would talk to them later.

The calliope music reminded her there was another midway, in the lot that held the rides and carny games. She walked past the food vendors and made her way along the line of barkers who were calling passersby to "step up" and "win a prize" for either "the little lady" or "the kid-dies." At each booth, she hoped to see her chubby buddy perched on a ledge or nestled in with the pastel plush tigers and bears. At least these fair workers hadn't handed out any treats to Quincy. None of them had even seen him.

She trudged back toward her booth. The sun was warm and raised a dusty, pleasant smell from the sawdust. She'd covered almost the entire row of vendors twice. There was one she had skipped. The booth to one side of theirs was empty, except for the standard table and two chairs. A cardboard placard read "Harper's Toys." She gave it a cursory search, but it provided no hiding places and held no food.

Two booths away from the one for Bar None, she paused when she saw a familiar figure. Mike stood a head taller than the other two people he was with, a young woman and an older one.

"No, I'm not sure where it is," the younger woman was saying to the older one. An abundance of glossy black tresses tumbled below her shoulders and swung when she shook her head. She sounded stressed.

"Your grandfather will kill you when he finds out you took that collar." The other woman ran a hand up and down the strap to her shoulder bag. "He has enough on his mind right now and he thinks you've quit taking things that don't belong to you."

"I know. Don't tell him, okay? I'll find it." The black-haired woman turned and entered the tent behind her. The sign above the door said "Fortunes Read."

Chase approached Mike and the older woman.

"Hi," Mike said. "I want you to meet my aunt Betsy. She's my dad's sister." So Betsy was a Ramos by birth. She was much shorter than Mike, but had his same deep brown eyes and dark curls, hers cut short to frame an oval face with only a few age lines.

Anna came running up to the group. "Quincy isn't all that's missing, Charity. The Hula Bars—"

"Mrs. Larson." Mike smiled at Anna. "I'd like you to meet my aunt Betsy."

Anna halted and waited a few seconds until her breathy panting slowed down. "Pleased to meet you." They shook hands. "We're very fond of your nephew. But, Charity"—she turned to Chase—"Quincy got into the Hula Bars."

Chase gasped. "Are they ruined? How many? Are there any left?"

"He destroyed ten boxes."

"He ate ten boxes of dessert bars?" Mike's jaw dropped. "I didn't think even Quincy could eat that much."

"No, no. He didn't eat all of them, only ruined them. I can't tell how many bars are completely gone, but those boxes can't be sold. They're clawed to pieces."

Chase's heart dropped toward her sneakers. "Ten boxes? That's almost all of the Hula Bars that we brought here. They've been our best seller since we introduced them. We needed those boxes to sell."

"We do have a ton of Harvest Bars, but you're right. I guess we'll have to make some more tonight." Anna's brow furrowed beneath her silver curls, and her blue eyes grew somber.

"Thank goodness he didn't destroy the Harvest Bars. Where is that rascal?" Chase clenched one fist inside the other until her knuckles were white.

"He'll come back. One of us has to start baking soon." Anna gave Chase a look that said Chase should do it. "If you stay here, you'll worry yourself to death over Quincy. I'll finish setting up and you can look in on Inger."

Chase resisted the notion of leaving with Quincy on the loose, but Anna finally convinced her. She had searched everywhere and didn't know what else she could do. "Okay, Anna. I'll head back in a few minutes. Call me the second he shows up. "

Anna agreed. They said good-bye to Mike's Aunt Betsy and trudged toward their booth, leaving Mike chatting with his aunt. Chase assumed he'd tell her what a terrible cat owner Chase was, not able to control her animal's weight, or even his whereabouts.

Chase glanced back to see if they were whispering and pointing at her. But Aunt Betsy was walking away as Mike ducked into the fortune-teller's booth. She wondered, briefly, what had been troubling the young woman, and how she knew Mike. The man had a talent for collecting attractive females.

Before she left, she helped Anna finish unpacking the goods that weren't ruined.

"Anna, about that midmorning snack that Inger mentioned," Chase started.

"I made sure she was going to give him a Kitty Patty. It wasn't anything he shouldn't have."

"But he doesn't need an infinite amount of those, you know. I usually give him one about midday, not midmorning."

Anna gave Chase a pained look and turned away to arrange their price list on a plastic stand. A stack of the fliers describing how to save dessert bars for the holidays lay beside the stand. Anna knocked a few of them off the top of the pile and Chase bent down to retrieve them.

As she straightened, they both heard a scream. Chase threw the papers onto the table and she and Anna ran outside their booth to see what was going on.

The butter sculpture building was on the far side of the fortune-teller's booth and a jewelry kiosk, four booths away from the Bar None. Several people were running toward it. Anna and Chase followed the gathering crowd.

A young man in a security uniform came up behind them and pushed his way through. "Excuse me," he repeated. "Emergency, let me through."

Within minutes, the onsite ambulance pulled up, lights flashing, the siren giving short burps, and paramedics rushed into the structure. In a few more minutes, two policemen came running and entered the exhibit space as well. That exhibition space was more than a tent, since it had to be refrigerated to keep the butter from melting. It was temporary but had wooden walls and a door. The door was closed and no one could see in, although Chase tried to peek every time it opened to admit someone else. More police arrived. A woman stood sobbing outside the entrance. Her face was red and splotchy.

Chase saw the young woman from the fortune-telling booth, the one Mike and his aunt had been talking to, at the opposite edge of the crowd. She chewed her knuckles with a worried look. She didn't take her eyes from the closed door.

After a very long time, it seemed, paramedics emerged from the butter sculpture building pushing a gurney. The figure on it was covered with a sheet. Chase's hand flew to her mouth. Anna grabbed her other hand and they held on tight. How awful that someone had passed away the day before the fair started.

The woman who had been outside the building now

followed behind the gurney, silently weeping. She was dressed in a long, red, swishy skirt and cowgirl boots and had a stylishly shaped short hairdo. Chase surmised that someone had had a heart attack. Maybe a man, and this was his wife. Did butter sculptors eat a lot of butter? Were they an unhealthy bunch? The crowd parted to let them wheel the body to the ambulance, waiting a few feet away. The woman spoke with the paramedics, who shook their heads at her and closed the back bay doors.

The two policemen were the next to emerge. They led a tall, handsome man to their squad car. When he looked up to scan the crowd, he gave a shake of his head to the fortune-teller. Then he turned toward Chase. It was Mike Ramos!

THREE

Chase felt her knees weaken as she watched Mike being led away toward the police car.

"Ma'am." A policewoman appeared beside her, holding Quincy. "Dr. Ramos said this was your cat. He sure is a handsome fellow."

Taking the cat, Chase tried to speak, but couldn't get any sounds out at first. "What . . . why . . ." She cleared her throat. "Is Dr. Ramos being arrested? What for?"

"He's being brought in for questioning." The woman left abruptly before Chase could ask her anything more. What was going on? It was like he was being . . . What was a good word? Detained?

Anna reached over to give the frightened cat in Chase's

arms a head rub. "Did you look inside there when we were searching for Quincy?" She nodded toward the building Mike Ramos had come from.

"No. I didn't see how he could get inside. The door was closed." Quincy nuzzled against Chase's arm and left a smear. He had something oily on his whiskers. Butter?

"That doesn't always stop Quincy," Anna said. "But what's happening to Mike Ramos?"

Chase shook her head. It was all too bewildering.

Another car pulled up onto the midway as the ambulance drove away with the body, leaving the weeping woman behind. Out of the newly arrived car stepped Detective Niles Olson.

"Uh-oh, look who's here," Anna said. "That dead man must have been murdered."

"Figures *he* would show up," Chase said. She had a strange relationship with the tall, good-looking homicide detective and a checkered history. Now she really wondered if Mike was being detained.

The man's impossibly dark blue eyes scanned the crowd, lingering on Chase for an extra second before he entered the building.

"What should we do?" Chase asked.

"There's nothing we can do. Dr. Ramos can take care of himself. If he needs help, he'll ask. I'm sure they'll let him go soon. He must have been in the wrong place at the wrong time."

Chase stole looks over her shoulder at the female police officer leaning into the squad car to talk to Mike as she and Anna returned to their own booth with Quincy purring in Chase's arms.

"You bad fat cat," she murmured, burying her face in his soft orangey fur. It smelled faintly of butter. He looked like he'd gained at least a pound eating the dessert bars and the handouts during his travels. "If you really think we can't do anything for Mike Ramos, I'll take Quincy back to the shop now and see how Inger's doing."

"And bake some more Hula Bars," Anna said.

"Yes, and that. You'll be okay here doing all the work alone?"

"With the size of our space, it might be easier for me to finish setting up by myself. I'll be fine."

In spite of Anna's certainty about Mike being able to take care of himself, Chase wanted to ask Julie if her defense attorney friend Jay Wright was available just in case. She called her on her way home, but the call rang over to voice mail. Chase hardly ever phoned Julie in the middle of her workday, and it was reasonable that her personal cell was turned off. She decided not to leave a message and that she would try to call again later.

When Chase got back to the Bar None, it was lunchtime. After closing Quincy into the office, she briefly told Inger everything that had happened. Inger had met the veterinarian and expressed concern for him, but Chase repeated what Anna had said. There was nothing they could do for him. Unless, Chase thought, she could get Jay Wright to free Mike from the clutches of the police.

She asked Inger how business had been in the morning.

24

"Slow. Really slow." Inger looked pale again today.

"Can you see a doctor this afternoon if we close up?"

"I don't really have a doctor, but I can go to the clinic."

"I think you should. You've been feeling bad for too long." Chase waited for Inger to tell her she was pregnant. If Inger knew she was pregnant, that was.

"It's crazy. I don't know what's wrong with me. I mostly only feel bad in the morning."

Maybe she really had no clue. "You need to see a doctor," Chase urged. "Right away."

"Okay, okay, I'll do it."

Chase smiled at her. "Make sure you do. It might be important."

Inger looked puzzled. Yes, she had no clue. "How's Quincy after his adventure?"

"He'll live." She didn't want to detain Inger further with the details of his escapades at the fair. She'd tell her later. But Chase did take a moment to wonder how Quincy had gotten inside the building where the man died, and from where Mike Ramos emerged, escorted by the police. She hoped he would be questioned and released quickly.

"How did he sneak into the basket in the first place?" Inger asked.

"How does he sneak anywhere? The cat has skills."

After Inger left, saying she would go straight to the clinic, Chase baked five dozen more Hula Bars. They packaged six bars to a box, so that would make up for the ten boxes Quincy had gotten into.

She tried Julie again with the same result. This time

she left a message to call her back as soon as she could. She also tried to call Mike to see if he had been let go, but he didn't answer either. It was maddening! She had no idea what was going on.

Tanner had sent her an e-mail saying he already had a mock-up of a website ready. She went to the computer in the office to look at it. She hadn't given the young man the office number because she didn't want Anna answering the phone when he called, so he only had Chase's cell phone number.

Quincy stretched, putting his front paws on her lap before jumping up and settling in.

She opened the file and paused, then knocked back against the chair with her mouth agape. Quincy flinched, but didn't jump down. It was stupendous, given what he had to work with. It was just what she had imagined, with placeholders for the pictures she hadn't sent yet. The home page displayed the address, phone number, and a map that could be used to get directions to the Bar None. Across the top was a banner in pink and white stripes, to match the wallpaper, with the shop name and sketches of dessert bars scattered in among the letters. Tabs for "Products" and "Ordering" and "Contact" were empty. She had a lot of material to send to him yet.

Tanner had been more observant than she thought on his one visit, last week, when Anna was out. She could imagine what Anna would think if she saw him, with his nose and eyebrow rings, not to mention the colorful dragon tattoo on the inside of his arm. He had a habit of running his glossy black fingernails through his shaggy brown hair when he was hunkered down at Chase's computer.

The timer in the kitchen dinged and she hurried in to take out the last batch of bars, dumping her cat onto the floor and slamming the office door shut behind her.

While she was waiting for the bars to cool, Quincy made a racket in the office.

"Oh, poor baby," she said, going back into the office. "Sorry I abandoned you so rudely. Do you have a tummy ache from all that sugar you got into today? Such a bad boy." Her actions contradicted her stern words as she swooped him up and gave him a cuddle. He'd missed his customary noon Kitty Patty, but Chase decided to forgo it today.

She and Anna were planning on taking Quincy to the fair in his crate tomorrow, once the fair started, since Chase didn't want to leave him by himself in the office or her apartment all week long. There were things a bored cat could do to express his displeasure, she knew from experience. Of course, being in a crate all day wasn't good either. She'd have to find a place to let him exercise a bit during the days.

When the Hula Bars were cool enough to pack, she toted them to her little Ford Fusion, parked in its space behind the shop, and drove back to the Bunyan County Fairgrounds. Even though the fair wasn't open yet, most of the bright lights were shining tonight, giving the place a festive look. The merry-go-round music still tinkled from the main parking lot. She parked in the exhibitors' lot and carried the bag to their booth. The evening air was turning decidedly chilly.

Anna, pulling her azure sweater tight around herself, gave a shiver when Chase approached.

"We'll need jackets here at night."

"Anna, is that sweater all you brought? It's fifty degrees out here. Here, put these somewhere and let's get you someplace warm."

"I have to finish putting everything else in the storage boxes." The fair had provided large, heavy metal boxes, bolted to rings in the ground and equipped with padlocks, so exhibitors could store their goods overnight. They were expected to take cash home with them but, fortunately, didn't have to schlep the goods back and forth for the whole week.

Chase stuck the ten replacement cartons in one of the metal boxes and clicked the padlock. "There, now you come with me."

"I'll do no such thing," Anna said. "There are still these to pack." She gestured to some dessert bar boxes at the bottom of the basket that Chase had overlooked. "And these." Anna pointed to more goodies that were tucked under the table, where they'd stashed them when they first arrived. "I'll finish up, and I have my car here."

"Well, then come over to my place for a hot chocolate when you're finished."

"That would be lovely. Should I call Julie?"

"Please do. I've been trying to get her all day. I need to talk to her." Maybe Anna would have better luck. Chase rushed home to get the cocoa started.

* * *

Anna and Chase were settled in Chase's homey living room, Quincy in Anna's lap, his narrowed eyes on the marshmallows heaped atop her cup of chocolate, his nose twitching. Chase had just handed Anna's cup to her and returned to the kitchen to get her own mug when the doorbell chimed. There were two doorbells outside the back door, one for the shop and one for her apartment. Downstairs, the back door led into a hallway outside the shop kitchen, where a set of inside stairs went up to Chase's apartment.

She ran down the stairs to admit Julie. Anna had gotten hold of her, and Julie had said she would be right over. However, when she opened the door, two people, not one, stood outside. Julie had her grandmother's periwinkle-blue eyes and wore her brown hair cut short. Chase was an inch or so taller than her friend.

"Chase," Julie said. "You remember Jay, right?" She smiled up at her taller companion.

How convenient. She could talk to both of them now, rather than going through Julie. "Of course. Jay Wright, right? You're the guy who got me out of jail."

Jay chuckled, showing a deep dimple in his right cheek. That only made him more good-looking than he already was, although his supershort haircut was not to Chase's liking. "Yep, that's me, the right Jay Wright. I heard there was hot chocolate available here."

"Come in out of the cold. I have a favor to ask after you get settled."

Chase led them upstairs. Jay and Julie sat on the leather couch, Chase's one extravagance when she'd furnished her nest. Anna and Quincy were ensconced in the cinnamon-and-mocha-toned stuffed armchair, so Chase pulled a seat in from the kitchen after she put a plate of Lemon Bars on the hassock, within everyone's easy reach.

"We're so glad you decided to do the fair," Julie said, giving her hot drink a cautious sip.

"We're glad, too," Anna said. "But why are you *both* glad?"

"Oh, didn't I tell you? Jay's aunt is on the organizing committee. That's the reason I told you to go in the first place. I owed Jay a favor."

"I guess I owe you one, too," Chase said, remembering his kindness when he had shepherded her out of the police station.

"Have either of you heard what happened at the fairgrounds today?" asked Anna.

They shook their heads.

"One of the butter sculptors died," Chase said.

"Murdered," Anna added.

Julie sucked in a mouthful of air through rounded lips. Jay raised his eyebrows.

"You almost made me spill my cocoa," Julie said.

Chase turned to Anna. "I know the homicide detective was there, but are you sure the person was murdered? Or that it was a butter sculptor?"

"I talked to his wife. They wouldn't let her into the ambulance. She was walking down the midway looking lost and I offered her a ride after you left, but she didn't take me up on it."

"So, give." Julie leaned forward. "What did she say?"

Anna hesitated, looking at Chase.

"What?" Chase asked. "I'm not in trouble because Quincy was there, am I? I didn't find his body."

"No. Dr. Ramos did. He's a suspect."

FOUR

"Elsa said she went to find her husband, Larry—" Anna began.

Julie interrupted. "Larry Oake, the famous butter sculptor?"

Anna turned to her granddaughter. "What do you know about butter sculptors?"

"I've been reading up on the featured exhibits." She glanced at Jay.

Chase sensed a chemistry between the two that was a few degrees warmer and cozier than it would be between business associates. Jay and Julie had attended law school together. He was a criminal defense lawyer, while she worked for the district attorney, prosecuting criminals. Chase wondered how that was going to work out.

"Oake is well known in the world of butter sculpture," Julie went on. "He was sent a special invitation to attend and participate in the Minnesota Symbol Contest."

"Okay," Chase said. "First of all, there is a 'world of butter sculpture'? Second, what is the Minnesota Symbol Contest?"

"Bunyan County," Jay said, "always holds a contest to see who can carve the best butter sculpture. We don't carve butter cows, though. Butter cows are a standard in the butter sculpting world, but we like to do it differently. This year we're asking the artists to re-create a state symbol in butter."

"How big is this butter sculpting world?" Chase shook her head. "I can't believe it's a well-known . . . art? Craft? Hobby?"

"Right the first time," said Jay. "It's an ancient art that began with Tibetan monks."

"You're not serious." Anna gave Jay a stern look. The look of a grandmother who does not like to be lied to.

"He's right, Grandma. Jay's told me all about it. Butter sculpture goes back to the times of Babylon and Rome. The Tibetan monks have done butter sculptures for Tibetan New Year for hundreds of years."

"Well, I guess it's cold enough there for it to keep," Anna said. "It's a shame this isn't in history books. It would make history a much more fun subject."

"Anyway," Julie continued, "we invited Larry Oake specially."

" 'We'?" asked Chase.

"I've been helping with the fair. I hate to think of him being murdered just because he came here."

"Where's he from?" Chase asked.

"Not far. Wisconsin." Jay tipped his mug up and drained it.

"More cocoa?" Chase jumped up to take his cup.

"No, we'd better be going." He and Julie exchanged an unmistakable look and stood up.

Yes, Chase thought, definitely warm and cozy. Maybe even smoke and fire.

"Wait a minute," Chase said. "I want to know if Jay could get Mike out of jail, if that's where he is."

Jay turned serious, all business. "What do you know?" he asked.

"Just that they took him away and Detective Olson was there and Mike's not answering his cell phone."

"I'll make some calls. I can't promise anything, but I'll see if there's something I can do. I'm busy on another case with the firm, but I'm sure I can at least find out what his situation is."

Chase felt her shoulders relax a notch. "Yes, that would be wonderful. Thanks so much."

After they left, Chase poured herself a second cup of cocoa, leaving the marshmallows off this time. Besides, there were some wisps clinging to her cup that would melt in nicely. "Did Larry's wife—Elsa?—give you any more details about what happened?"

"Yes, Elsa Oake. We got sidetracked by those two and their butter sculpture history, didn't we?" Anna gazed into her cup.

"Oh, you're empty. Do you want a refill?"

"No thanks, Charity." Anna hesitated, setting her mug

34

aside and rubbing Quincy's right ear. "Elsa told me everything she saw, and it's not good. She was supposed to meet her husband at the food trailers for an early lunch. He'd been doing some preliminary work on his sculpture in the morning."

"And he didn't show up, I'm guessing."

"Right. So she went looking for him. She said she opened the door to the butter room and saw her husband on the floor. When she called her husband's name, Dr. Ramos blocked her way. That's when she screamed."

"He probably didn't want her to see a dead body." Mike was a considerate person. She could easily picture him shielding the poor woman from the grisly sight.

"I think that's probably the case. But she thinks he was keeping her from trying to revive him. So, naturally, she thinks Mike killed him."

"What was Mike doing in there, anyway?" Could he have been looking for Quincy? Maybe he saw the cat sneak in with someone else?

Anna looked down at her lap and poked Quincy's substantial tummy with her forefinger. "Elsa said this guy was on the table, next to the sculpture."

"Devouring it, I suppose. It looked like Quince had butter on his whiskers when that policewoman handed him to me."

"Elsa was bothered by what she saw. She said her husband had a butter sculpture dowel poking out of his ear. She told me how horrible the trickle of red blood was against his brown skin. She can't get the image out of her mind."

Chase winced. "How awful."

"Maybe Jay Wright can find out about everything and can get Dr. Ramos home," Anna said.

"I'll bet he can." She remembered her tearful relief in Jay's car after he had gotten her out of that terrible interrogation room in September. She hoped Mike was in one of those, dismal as they were, instead of in a jail cell. "I have a feeling Mike is going to need a lawyer. I wonder what Jay will charge him."

"He didn't charge you, did he?"

"No, but Mike might need more services than I did. And Mike isn't best friends with Jay's girlfriend." Chase was sure Mike had gone into the building to get Quincy. But how had Quincy gotten inside? Someone must have opened the door for him. Would that have been Larry or someone else?

Chase sighed. This wasn't the first time Quincy had gone looking for food and found trouble. Why did her cat have a talent for discovering dead bodies?

After Anna left, Chase unpacked the satchel she'd carried to the fair. Along with the parking instructions for exhibitors, and the receipt for the booth, she found the pamphlet from the pet chip place. She leafed through it, deciding that Quincy needed a microchip. However, that would only help find his owner once someone located him. What he really needed was a GPS transmitter. She wondered if they made those for cats.

She picked up the phone and called the direct line to Detective Niles Olson's desk. She'd acquired his number earlier in the year when she'd been a suspect in a murder in the Dinkytown neighborhood. That was the first time

Quincy was found next to a dead body. He had been eating the dinner the man had been preparing.

"Chase?" He'd seen her caller ID. He didn't sound irritated. That was a good start.

"Hi. Could you tell me . . . I, uh, I need to know what's going on with Dr. Mike Ramos."

"Why do you need to know that?"

"Okay, I *want* to know. He's a friend. I saw him being taken away in a police car at the fair. Is he arrested?"

"We're questioning him."

"He's been there for a long time. Does someone think he killed that sculptor?"

"How do you know who the victim was? We haven't released a statement."

"Anna talked to his wife—his widow. She said something was sticking out of his ear. Some kind of dowel?"

Niles Olson expelled his exasperation into the phone. "It was a butter sculpture dowel. It's a pointed metal tool, about the size of a nail file. I'm told it's for making small round holes in the butter. I shouldn't tell you that, but Elsa already told Anna all about the crime scene, didn't she?"

"Yes. Was there a reason she shouldn't? Oh, I know! You don't think Mike is really the killer and you want to withhold what you know from the murderer. Am I right? You think Mike didn't kill that poor man?"

"No comment."

"He was in there to get Quincy, I'm sure." She twirled a strand of her hair between two fingers.

"Your cat again. Why would you let him run around the fairgrounds?"

"I didn't *let* him!"

"Let me guess. He got loose."

"We didn't even know he was there with us. We thought he was back at Bar None. He stowed away in our basket."

"Don't bring him to the fair again."

Chase hung up without telling the detective that Jay Wright was on the case. Or that she and Anna planned on bringing Quincy to the fair every day for the rest of the week.

The next morning, Chase, still in her bathrobe, ran outside to the front sidewalk to get pictures of the Bar None's exterior. Then she whipped inside, turned all the lights on, and snapped some more. She didn't know if Tanner would want to show the kitchen, but she took some shots of it as well and e-mailed them to him.

Then she got ready to return to the fair. It was the opening day. After pulling on her best pair of jeans and donning a soft purple sweater that looked good with the suede jacket she would take to wear that evening, she slipped on the silver-and-turquoise ring Anna had given her for her last birthday. She didn't wear it often, since it was a teensy bit too large and tended to slip off. Today, she wanted to wear something comforting to keep her mind from dwelling on Mike every second. He still wasn't answering his phone. She couldn't get Julie either, and she didn't have Jay's number.

What she really wanted to do was talk to Mike and

see how he was holding up and if he had actually been charged. She still didn't even know, though, if he was in jail or at home. Or what she would do if he did want her to help him out. Or why a ring should make her think of him. She decided she had to try Julie again. She was going to worry herself crazy if she didn't get hold of her.

"Chase! Mike is in the news today. They're definitely saying he was held for questioning in the death of Larry Oake."

"That's what I called about. Did Jay have any luck last night?" Chase twirled the ring around on her finger.

"He got him out early this morning, but Mike is on the radar for the murder. He was questioned for a long, long time, Jay said. Do you think there is any way he could have killed that man?"

"No! He was retrieving Quincy. Quincy had gotten into the exhibit and was after the butter."

Julie groaned. "That doesn't necessarily mean that Mike didn't also kill the guy. But I can't imagine him doing that."

"Why would he kill him? He didn't know the victim. Oake is from Wisconsin, you said."

"He is. But his wife is from Minneapolis. He's probably been here a lot."

"So, what does Jay say? Anything?" The turquoise ring slipped past her knuckle and she pushed it back on.

"Just that he stayed there until they let Mike go. And he drove him home. The only information he has is what Mike told him. Jay isn't sure he can take the case himself, but he will find him a good lawyer, don't worry."

"Maybe he won't need a lawyer. We don't know that he's been formally accused, do we? What do you mean by saying Mike is on the radar?"

"That probably means they don't have any other suspects right now, Chase. The morning news reported his name as a person of interest, but Jay says he hasn't been charged."

Yet, Chase thought glumly. Mike was not off the hook, and things weren't looking good.

FIVE

Tanner texted Chase on her way to the fair, saying the pictures were "dope" and he could totally use them. When she got there, lugging Quincy along in his crate, Anna was already at their booth and it looked about ready to go. A short woman with frizzy bleached hair was leaving as Chase was approaching.

"Who's that?" Chase asked.

"You'll never guess. It's Jay Wright's aunt! He told her where our booth would be and she stopped in to say hi."

"Oh, right. He said she's one of the organizers. I'll have to meet her the next time she stops by."

"Right now you can arrange the basket and these fliers."

The ginger-striped cat fidgeted in the confines of his hard-sided crate. Usually, he settled in and stayed still for journeys that took place in the car, but this time the memory of all that butter taunted him. He could smell that he was in the same place as yesterday, the place with the butter. After his crate was shoved under the table, leaving him in dusky darkness, he started working at the latch. He hadn't conquered this new one. Yet.

The kiddie rides were in full swing. Each one had its own music, creating a merry cacophony in the background for those on the midway.

The presence of armed police officers roaming the midway was a sober reminder that a serious crime had been committed. It took some of the shine off the fair, but seemingly hadn't hurt attendance.

"Did you see the news this morning?" Chase asked.

"No," Anna said slowly. "Is there something bad in it? About Mike?"

"Yes, I'm afraid so. Julie said he's not being accused of the murder. But the paper called him a person of interest."

"Oh dear. But Jay did get him out?"

"Jay stayed until they let Mike go. I don't know if he's here yet or not. What's happening over there?" Chase noticed a commotion down the midway.

"It's the parade. The official opening of the fair. We'd better stay put while it passes."

The fair opened with a procession down the midway. A team of horses led the way, pulling Miss Bunyan County in an ornate carriage. The local Shriners drove their silly little bikes, and a Boy Scout troop marched past, somewhat in precision. Next came the Girl Scouts, tossing hard candies and waving. In the distance a high school band could be heard getting louder as it got closer.

"That's going to scare Quincy," Anna said. "All those trumpets and trombones."

"And drums. Should I throw a blanket over his crate?" asked Chase.

"He's not a bird. Maybe we should get him out and hold him."

"Definitely not. He'll bolt. It'll be okay. He'll live."

Anna raised the skirt of the table to peek in on him. His amber eyes stared back, wide and frightened. Anna dropped the skirt, shaking her head.

"I'll take his cage out in back of the booths," Chase said, relenting. He had probably never been this close to so much noise. It was bound to have a bad effect on him. "It'll be quieter there. Just until the parade passes."

Chase pulled the crate out and hefted it up. This hard-sided cage was heavier than the soft cloth one she had used before. But Quincy had proven he was able to get out of that one without much trouble. It zipped shut, and the zipper was easy for him to open by hooking a claw in the pull if it was left even the teensiest bit agape. Or sometimes, Chase swore, even if it wasn't.

She lugged the carrier between the Bar None booth

43

and the next one, still empty this morning, and set Quincy down on the dirt. The organizers had left aisles between every other booth, using common walls for the booths that were joined together. The Bar None booth was connected to one rented by a travel agency.

A large maple with blazing red leaves shaded the area behind the booths. Chase leaned against the rough, solid trunk to wait for the boisterous parade to end.

Voices came from past the travel agents' booth, which was operated by two women, a short redhead and a tall blonde. The next booth down the line was the fortune-teller's.

A conversation from behind the fortune-telling booth floated to Chase, over the sounds of the parade and the band, which was still approaching.

"Yes, Grandpapa. I know I shouldn't have taken it." Chase heard a low-pitched woman's voice. "But I wanted so much to try it on Princess Puffball before the Fancy Cat Contest. Just to see what it would look like if she wins."

Chase's ears perked at the words "cat contest."

A man's voice spoke too softly for Chase to hear.

"No, I told you. I don't know where it is. I haven't been able to find it yet. I'll put it back in the exhibit as soon as I find it, I promise."

The band drew nigh and drowned out the conversation. When it had passed, Chase leaned out and looked around to see who the speakers were. Only one remained: the fortune-teller herself. That is, the person Chase assumed was the fortune-teller. At any rate, she was the young woman who had been at that tent earlier with Mike and Mike's aunt Betsy. She must have a cat. Princess Puffball? And she had taken something and lost it.

Chase wanted to know more about the Fancy Cat Contest. Mike had mentioned it, and this woman seemed to have an entrant. Should Chase enter Quincy?

After the parade passed, she returned Quincy, in his crate, to his place under the table of their booth. A colorful pamphlet with pictures of sleek cats on it lay on their exhibit table.

"What's this?" Chase asked.

"Some woman in a business suit was tossing them out during the parade. She's with a pet food company. I think they're sponsoring something here."

Quincy gave an irritated *mrow* from his crate. He clearly wanted out of it. Maybe the fortune-teller/cat owner would know where to exercise a cat here at the fair.

"Do you want anything from the food carts, Anna?"

"I'd like something cold to drink."

The day was sunny and beautiful. Chase was warm in her sweater, and thirsty, too. "I'll get us some lemonade. I want to stop and talk to the fortune-teller on the way."

Anna raised her eyebrows.

"She's entering a cat in a contest here. I want to know more about it."

"You're thinking of entering Quincy in a contest?"

"Fancy Cat Contest."

"Quincy is lovely and adorable, but I'm not sure he's fancy."

"Anyway, I'll ask her about it. If she has a cat here,

maybe she knows where to exercise them, too. There must be several cats if a contest is being held."

The entrance to the fortune-teller booth was hung in purple gauze that glittered with silver stars and half moons. One swath was pinned back, leaving a narrow entrance. Chase peeked inside, then stepped into the tent. The young woman sat behind her display table, which was draped in more of the same material. It was dark inside, lit only by several electric candles and a glowing globe that sat in front of her. Chase blinked to adjust her eyes to the dimness. She also sniffed. Something gave off a pleasant scent of lavender.

"Welcome. I am Madame Divine." The woman spoke in a creepy low voice. "Step closer. Have a seat and give me your palm." She stood to take Chase's hands and drew her into a seat. She wore a caftan made from more of the purple gauze, and her shoulder-length black curls were tucked into a gold turban. Her deep purple nail polish shone in the soft light from the globe, which was her crystal ball, Chase surmised.

"Oh, hi. Chase Oliver. Our booth is right over there. The Bar None." She pointed her head in that direction, since Madame Divine had both her hands. "I don't really want my fortune told. I just heard you talking about a Fancy Cat Contest and wanted to ask you about that."

Madame Divine frowned. "What did you hear? Where?" Her natural timbre was rather low, but the spooky voice was gone.

"I didn't mean to overhear. I took my cat behind our

booth to get him away from the noise of the parade. It was scaring him. Most of what you were saying was drowned out by the marching band, but I did hear you mention the contest."

Her frown lessened. "Ah. Well, yes. I'm entering my cat, Puffy." Princess Puffball, Chase remembered.

"How would I enter mine?" Chase put her hands on the round table between her and the fortune-teller.

"Have you read the brochure about the fair?"

"Not yet." It was probably the pamphlet she had seen on their table.

"The entry form is in there." Madame Divine reached for Chase's hands again.

Chase looked around for a cat. A shelf to one side held fortune-telling books, tarot cards, and Ouija boards for sale. "Is your cat here?" She extracted her hands and folded them in her lap, where Madame Divine couldn't reach them.

"Not today. The contest isn't until the end of the fair, on next Sunday."

"Oh. I have to bring Quincy here every day, and I was wondering if there was a pen or a big cage where he could get some exercise."

"There might be. You should talk to the contact person. Daisy something-or-other."

Chase rose. "Thanks, Ms. Divine. I'll look her up."

"Madame Divine is just my stage name. I'm really Patrice Youngren. Nice to meet you." She held her hand out for Chase to shake. Her hands were clad in lace

47

fingerless gloves and she wore rings on almost every finger. Chase gripped the gloved hand and wondered if she wore gloves because she wanted to prevent others from reading her palms. Patrice shook with one hand and put the other on top of Chase's. It was an oddly intimate gesture.

"I guess you know Mike Ramos?" Patrice asked. "I heard you talking to him yesterday."

"Yes, he's our vet."

Patrice nodded and Chase got the feeling she was being dismissed.

"Do you know him?"

Patrice nodded again without offering anything further.

Chase persisted anyway, curious now about the conversation she'd overheard. "I heard you say you've lost something. Is it anything I can help look for?"

A fleeting look of panic widened Patrice's brown eyes but was gone in a flash. "No, thank you."

That cold tone was definitely a dismissal. Chase gave her a smile. "I'll see you around."

For a moment, as she walked through the sawdust, she wondered why "Seventy-six Trombones" from *The Music Man* was running through her head. Then she remembered that the marching band had played it when they'd gone past.

As Chase reached the lemonade stand, she spotted Mike leaving with an extra-large cup.

"Why aren't you answering your phone? I've been so worried."

"Chase, thanks for sending Jay Wright to help me out.

I was trying to figure out who to call." He covered her hand with his and squeezed. "I've turned my phone off because I'm getting so many calls from reporters. And some from crackpots."

"Well, I'm relieved to see you here," she said. "I didn't know if you would make it or not."

"Jay said there wasn't enough evidence to keep me, even though I'm their best suspect. They asked me a few questions then they locked me in a cell with some scary types. Then they brought me out and questioned me for hours more. I'm glad to be out of there."

"They really think you could have killed Mr. Oake?"

"I wasn't charged with anything. That was a surprise to me after all the questioning. Detective Olson acted like he wanted me to confess, but I couldn't tell what he was thinking."

"Yes, I've had experience with that. Well, I'm glad you're here." He still held her hand and she squeezed his, then dropped it. "By the way, I just met Patrice Youngren. She knows you?"

"She sure does." He glanced at his watch. "Look, Chase, I'll talk later. I need to be at the vet station now. I was late getting here."

Mike hurried away. He hadn't really answered all of her questions. At least not the way Chase wanted them answered.

Julie showed up late in the morning. "Need some help?"

"Where's Jay?" Chase asked.

"After being at the courthouse early this morning, he had to go into work today. He's defending a state legislator, and his firm wants to do a good job with it. He'll be by, maybe tomorrow. Definitely next Saturday."

"That's great they gave him a big case," Anna said.

"It's not his, by himself. He's on a defense team."

"Sounds like football." Chase laughed.

"I'll bet he wishes it were football. He'd rather be here on a Saturday, believe me. Anyway, I'm here to see if you need me today, since I'm not working this weekend."

Anna put her to work. She had her granddaughter stand right outside their entrance with a small paper plate of samples to tempt passersby and lure them into the booth.

It must have worked because she and Anna did a booming business, especially during lunchtime. Fairgoers seemed to want dessert as much as they wanted meals. That was fine with Anna and Chase. The visitors to the booth slowed to a trickle in the early afternoon, and Chase told Anna and Julie she wanted to try to find Daisy and ask her about the cat contest.

Anna had saved the brochure, and handed it to Chase.

"Didn't you have your turquoise ring on this morning?" Anna asked.

Chase was dismayed to find that her ring was missing. "It must have slipped off. I've been planning to get it resized forever."

"We'll keep an eye out for it," Julie said, already bending down to check beneath the table covering.

The brochure on the fair contests was thick, and Chase leafed through it. Daisy was apparently in charge of all of them. A hamster run was about to begin, from what the schedule said. The pet competitions were held in the large permanent building, beyond the midway with its many booths.

Chase walked through the open double doors into a large entryway that led to a wide central aisle. A big room on the right held homemade quilts and jars of pickles, fruits, and vegetables. A table near the door held dozens of baked goods. Chase nearly detoured into the space, drawn by the aroma of apple and pecan pies, but held her course for the next one, the animal contest room.

A long table, surrounded by cheering people, dominated the right side of the room. Chase wormed her way close enough to see a plastic track with five lanes that ran the length of the table, about fifteen feet long. Each lane held a transparent plastic ball, and each ball held a hamster. Most of the balls were whizzing down the track, but one held a sleeping white hamster, curled up in the bottom. A red-faced man screamed at the stationary ball. "Snowball! Wake up! We're losing!"

A woman with a stopwatch presided over the finish line made of yellow tape. She was rather short, with frizzy bleached hair and a large, bulbous nose. Her head swiveled from hamster to hamster, ignoring poor Snowball, and her huge silver hoop earrings swung back and forth. After a moment, Chase recognized her as the person who had been at the Bar None booth early in the morning, chatting with Anna.

Another hamster, a black-and-white one, decided to quit, and its owner started screeching at her pet.

The frizzy-haired woman clicked her watch and held up her arms as the winner crossed the line. "We have a new champion. Wiggle Piggle wins!"

After the owners had retrieved their furry contestants, the winner toting along a large bag of hamster pellets, Chase approached the timekeeper.

"Are you Daisy?"

She nodded, sending her hoop earrings swinging and her hair dancing on her head.

"So you're Jay Wright's aunt?"

"And you must be Chase Oliver, Julie's friend. I'm pleased to meet you."

After the greeting, Chase asked her for more information about the Fancy Cat Contest. "The brochure doesn't say much beyond the time and place."

"It's a fancy-dress contest," she said with a grin.

"People dress cats?"

"It's not easy. Sometimes the winner is the one who keeps the costume on. We're so fortunate this year. The Picky Puss Cat Food Company is sponsoring the contest. You'll have to take a good look at the cat collar they're using for the winner."

Chase wasn't sure she wanted to enter Quincy in that competition. It sounded like it might be torture.

"You've seen bags of Picky Puss cat food, haven't you?"

Chase had seen them in the pet food store and even the grocery store and had often noticed the lovely felines pictured on them.

"The winner here will be photographed with the collar

and will be featured on their bags, all over the nation. They're even offering a television commercial appearance. We're so lucky," she gushed. "The owner of the company grew up in this county and decided to do this for the fair."

That would be fun, Chase admitted to herself. If Quincy would cooperate with the photographers. "Can I ask you another question? My business partner and I have a booth out on the midway and I'm bringing my cat with me every day, in his crate. Is there a place I could let him out a bit? Keep him from being so cramped all day?"

"I don't think that's a good idea. No, I don't know any place you could turn a cat loose. We'll have a high wire pen for our contest next Sunday, but people just usually bring their pets that day. You might want to check with the veterinarian, though."

Chase thanked the woman and left the room as a Frisbee-catching contest for dogs was being set up. She stepped aside to let a woman lead a handsome Weimaraner into the room. A sign at the far end of the hall caught her eye: "Veterinarian." It had an arrow pointing left. That's where Mike was!

She nipped around the corner and into the room. No one was in the small anteroom, but she could hear Mike's deep voice behind the closed door before her. She sat in a plastic chair and waited for him to finish with his current patient. There was a neat stack of printed cards on the corner of the desk. She tilted her head to read what was on the top one. It was the recipe for Kitty Patties. How nice! Mike had asked for the recipe when she first concocted the treats. He had said he might hand those out, but she thought he meant only in his own clinic, not here at the fair. Mike had told her he had plenty of cat patients that were overweight and could use her recipe.

The red-faced man who had yelled at Snowball came out in a few minutes, carrying Snowball himself—or herself—in a small cage. Snowball lay curled up at the bottom, much as he—or she—had done during the race. The familiar disinfectant smell of a vet's office wafted from the room.

"Chase, what are you doing here?" Mike asked after the man left. "Is Quincy all right?"

"Yes, he's fine. How's Snowball?"

"You know Snowball?"

"I just watched him lose the hamster race."

"Her. There's nothing wrong with her. She's pregnant and doesn't feel like racing today."

"I thought I'd stop in and say hi. I came over to ask Daisy about the Fancy Cat Contest, and if she knew where I could let Quince get some exercise."

"He's in his crate, isn't he?"

"Yes, his new plastic one. If he hasn't figured out how to get out of it yet."

"Come on back here." He motioned her into the next room. Besides an examining table, a small metal desk, and two shelves full of equipment, eight large cages were stacked against the wall to the left. Several even larger ones sat against the back wall. They were all empty. "Do you want to keep him here for part of the day? It would give him more room."

"What are the cages for?"

"I'm not sure." Mike smiled, crinkling his brown eyes.

"They came with the space. Maybe if an animal gets hurt, I could put it here until it's transported somewhere."

"This might be good. He could move around a lot more."

"If I should get a noisy dog, it might not work, but I don't anticipate that. I can give him a big cage and some cat toys."

Chase left to get her cat. As she opened the door from the reception room to the hallway, she nearly collided with a woman coming in. Chase apologized for nearly knocking her over—the woman was quite short—then blinked, trying to remember where she had recently met her. The other woman responded first.

"Nice to see you again. Chase Oliver, right?" She alleviated Chase's embarrassment at not remembering her right away. "I'm Mike's aunt Betsy." She set her purse on the desk and moved behind it.

Oh yes, she had been talking with Mike and Patrice. "So you're working in Dr. Ramos's office?"

Aunt Betsy smiled. "Dr. Ramos? I call him Mike, since I used to change his diapers, but yes, he asked me to help out this week."

Mike came out of the examining room. "Glad you're here, Aunt Betsy. People are already starting to bring pets in."

"I'll get to work, then." She slipped her purse under the desk and seated herself, ready to assume her duties as the receptionist.

The striped cat stepped cautiously from the familiar crate, the place where he'd been for hours and hours, into the strange new cage. He tested the floor with one paw, then

stepped inside. He raised his head and sniffed. Detecting no objectionable odors, he shifted his attention to the jingle bell, the ball, and the Kitty Patty that had been left inside the door just before it shut. As the latch was hooked, he paid close attention to how it worked.

SIX

After Chase left Quincy with Dr. Ramos, she strolled back to her booth, wanting to look at some of the other vendors' wares. People were coming in and out of the butter sculpture structure, which was next to the main building, keeping the door closed as they entered and left.

The crime scene people must have worked all night. She'd noticed them taking the yellow tape from the door first thing in the morning. It was nice they had hurried with their work, cooperating with the fair people and making it easier for them to carry on. That also made it so she was free to see inside the place.

She pushed the door open. It was on a strong spring, so she had to give it a good shove. They were serious about keeping it cold inside, and it worked. The day was fair for October, but Chase wasn't dressed warmly enough for this deep freeze with her light sweater.

A half-dozen sculptors were at work, with stations for several more. Spectators milled about, watching them practice their art. One artist was building a framework out of metal wire mesh, but the others were further along. If there was mesh in their sculptures, it was hidden beneath the thick layers of slathered butter.

Each sculptor had a station consisting of a wooden table for the creation, about five feet square, and another smaller table that held tools. A name tag stuck onto the corner of the larger table identified each artist.

Chase wondered why the floor was strewn with straw. Maybe to absorb dropped butter.

In spite of the chilly temperature, the heavy odor of butter was detectable. Working in the soft substance was a silent task, but the sculptors threw down and picked up their wooden and metal implements in the heat of their creativity, creating a light clatter against the background of the murmuring observers.

A watchful policeman stood inside the door, his eyes constantly scanning the room. Chase wondered if Larry Oake had been murdered by a militant, crazed vegan, protesting the existence of butter. Or by someone in this room.

Some images were recognizable, some were not yet. One man was nearly finished with a gopher statue. The brochure had said the contest was open to carvings of things that symbolized Minnesota. The most familiar moniker was "Land of 10,000 Lakes" (although Chase knew there were more like 12,000 of them). That would be difficult to depict in sculpture, though. Minnesota was also called the Gopher State, so that statue was apt.

Another sculptor, the lone woman in the group, was carving what looked to be a five-foot star. The state motto was actually "The Star of the North." Another good idea.

One tall, hulking man was assisted by a teenage girl. Chase couldn't tell what his carving was yet. The girl smiled at Chase. "Isn't this fun to watch?"

"Fascinating," Chase said. "I've never seen a butter sculpture being created before. I had no idea it was such an art form." Every one of this group could properly be called an artist, as far as she was concerned. Even though the medium was temporary, they were taking great care and creating intricate and, in some cases, beautiful things.

The man turned to Chase, setting down the wooden dowel he was using to make random holes in his butter. "Very much an art form," he said. "And Mara is one of the best designers I've ever run across. Wait until this is finished. You'll see."

"Oh, Daddy," the young woman said, lowering her head. The man's tag said he was Karl Minsky. Karl looked like he was built with larger bones than ordinary humans. He was huge. Next to him, his small, delicate daughter looked even more petite than she was.

"It's true," her father insisted. "Mara has been accepted to North Star Art School. They came to her even before she applied."

"You know I'm not going there, Daddy."

"You will if I can win this competition."

"Is the prize that big?" asked Chase.

"Twenty-five thousand dollars." Mara's father stressed each word. "It's the difference between her going to art school or junior college. And yes, Mara, you're going there."

"Good luck, then." Chase started to move away. The man's intensity bothered her. He was large and strong-looking, but she had to admit that he had a delicate touch with the butter.

"We have a chance now," the man said, picking up his dowel and making more holes. Maybe his sculpture was a land with ten thousand lakes, after all, Chase thought. It looked abstract and was one of the few she didn't completely admire.

As she walked away, she thought the man added, "With Oake out of the way."

An empty station on the other side of the room must have been Larry Oake's, though his name tag was missing. A few wooden and metal tools lay scattered in front of his sculpture, which was still there. His work looked like the bottom third of a bull. A hole gaped in the flank of the animal, as if someone had decided to make a shallow cave there.

The man next to him was obviously doing Babe the Blue Ox. Maybe Larry's sculpture was going to be of the same creature. Babe was Paul Bunyan's famous sidekick. Both Paul Bunyan and Babe the Blue Ox were favorite Minnesota folklore characters. Large statues of those two resided at a roadside attraction in Bemidji, near the headwaters of the Mississippi.

Minnesota children grew up on the tall tales about Paul Bunyan, the huge, legendary lumberjack, and his pet ox. In one of the tales, Paul dug Lake Michigan as a drinking hole for Babe. Another said that it took five storks to deliver Paul when he was born. As for Babe, it took a crow a whole day to fly from one horn to the other. Babe had also straightened out some of the logging roads when Paul hitched him up to them.

The ox carver, who had been smoothing a flank, set his sculpting tool, an instrument that resembled a small serrated spatula, on the table and wiped his hands. He turned away from his sculpture, obviously to take a break, so Chase thought it might not be intrusive to talk to him.

"Excuse me. Is that Babe the Blue Ox?"

The man smiled. "Sure is." He stuck out his hand to shake. "Winn Cardiman, state champ of Iowa two years in a row." He had a wrinkled, flat face, pale as milk. His ears stuck out of his wiry red hair the same way a chimp's does. His smile took up nearly his whole freckled face.

"Congratulations," Chase said, taking his rather soft hand. She looked over at the empty table. "Is that where Mr. Oake was carving?"

Cardiman's face dropped. His scowl was more like a sad orangutan's. "That's it, yes."

"His place doesn't have straw on the floor."

"I'm sure the police took it away. You know, to analyze it or something. Look for the killer's DNA, maybe."

"It looks like he was working on something similar," she said. "Was Mr. Oake carving Babe, too?"

Now Winn Cardiman's wizened face reddened and

scrunched up. "He stole my idea." He spoke through clenched teeth, anger sparking from his large brown eyes. "I started first and he copied me."

Cardiman looked angry enough to kill Oake. Chase wondered if he had.

The orange cat prowled the large cage. He had eaten the treats and even played with the toys for a few minutes. The man in the white lab coat looked in on him occasionally and talked baby talk to him. But he was bored. He studied the latch. It was a simple one. It was, in fact, easy to open from the outside. The cat tried to reach the lever from inside but couldn't quite manage it.

"This is looking more and more like it was a good idea," Anna said, beginning to pack up. "What I mean is that I'm glad we decided to come to the fair this week. When Julie mentioned it—"

"Mentioned it?" Chase said, slipping on her jacket in the evening coolness. "She twisted our arms."

"You're right. When she twisted our arms, I resisted. I'm glad I'm here, but I am dressing more warmly tomorrow." She gestured at the mostly empty table. "Look how many we sold."

"I didn't think we'd do this well in one day," agreed Chase. There were very few unsold dessert bars to pack up. "I hope we have enough in the freezer to last the week."

"I can always bake more in the evening."

"Night, you mean. The fair is open until after dark." The fair closed at nine and the sun had already set at about seven.

"Semantics." Anna grinned. "Whatever. I can bake more. Why don't you go collect Quincy while I finish here? It'll only take a few more minutes."

A woman was leading a pet pig in a harness out of Dr. Ramos's office when Chase got there. Maybe there's some sort of pig contest, she surmised. There seemed to be animal competitions every day. Betsy was gone already.

"Is her pig sick?" she asked Mike, after the door closed.

"You know I'm not supposed to talk about my patients, but no, the pig is fine. You here to get Quincy?" He stood close and she could smell his clean shirt.

"Time to take him home." She tilted her head up at him, looking deep into those chocolate eyes. She wasn't seeing nearly enough of him.

"How are you and Anna doing?" Mike reached out and touched her arm.

He was so sweet to check on them. "We're selling up a storm. But how are *you* doing?"

"With the police, you mean?" Chase nodded. "I had to answer the same questions again today for Detective Olson." Chase hadn't seen the homicide detective at the fair today, but there was no reason for him to drop in at her booth. "I think I'm still the number one suspect." She saw his jaw working as he clenched his teeth.

"That's not fair. I've just talked to two people who at

least have motives." This time she put her hand on his arm. "You were only retrieving Quincy, weren't you?"

He hesitated for two or three seconds. "Yes, I was getting Quincy."

"It was smart of you to look for him with the butter. I do wonder how he got in there, though." When she'd pushed that door open, the spring was awfully stiff. A cat could never open it, even a heavyset one.

"He had to have slipped in when someone opened the door, don't you think?" Mike asked. He got Quincy from his cage and crated him for Chase.

"I guess. I wish he hadn't gone inside there at all."

Driving home with her pet in his crate on the floor beside her, she wondered exactly why Mike had looked where he had. What made him think to check that place? It was true, she knew, that Quincy could not have gotten in by himself. Even though there was the temptation of pounds and pounds of butter, she would not have thought of looking inside that building. Was Mike holding back his reason for being there?

Later that night, Chase was just getting around to drawing a bath and getting ready for bed when her doorbell rang. Glad that she was still dressed, she ran downstairs and peeked through the chain latch to see who was there.

When she saw it was Inger Uhlgren, she unhooked the chain and threw the door open wide. The young woman looked awful. Her gray eyes usually looked huge in her small face, but tonight all Chase noticed were the black circles beneath those pretty eyes.

"Come upstairs, dear. Can I get you something?"

Inger lugged a heavy-looking cloth bag, which Chase took from her as they went up to the apartment. When they got there, Inger asked for a cup of herb tea. While the water heated, Chase fussed over her, settling her on the leather couch with an afghan. Quincy seemed to sense Inger's distress and curled up beside her protectively.

After they both had mugs of peppermint tea, Inger drank a few sips and set hers down. "My parents won't let me stay," she said.

"They threw you out?"

Inger nodded.

"Why?"

"I went to the clinic, like you said. They told me I'm . . . I'm pregnant." She bowed her head. "My parents say I've shamed them."

Chase bit back a retort about parents who should support and love their children, for better or worse. This girl needed support and love now more than she probably ever had in her life. Inger was twenty-two, but seemed so much younger sometimes.

"I'm so sorry," Chase said, feeling her words were inadequate. "Do you have a place to stay?"

Inger shook her head, which was still bowed. Chase moved to the couch and put an arm around her. Inger burst into tears and Chase held her while she sobbed for a good ten minutes. Chase couldn't help but shed a few tears with her.

When Inger seemed to be done, Chase got tissues for both of them.

"Now," Chase said. "What are we going to do?"

When Inger shrugged, Chase continued, casting about in her own mind for what to do next. "Have you talked to the baby's father? Is he going to be any help?"

"Zack was in the army." Her face crumpled and she sobbed once more. "We were going to get married. We weren't careful enough." She patted her stomach, though it hadn't started to bulge yet. "He didn't think he would get sent overseas again, but he did. And he didn't . . . he didn't come back."

Poor Inger was truly alone.

After another brief crying jag, Chase called Anna.

SEVEN

C hase wouldn't have believed it possible, but the fair was more crowded on Sunday than it had been on Saturday. Their neighbor had finally shown up. So far, the man she assumed was Harper had plopped boxes on his table and was stringing up his banner. It was cute, with "Harper's Toys" spelled out in primary-colored capital letters. Some of the letters were in the shape of toys. The A looked like a teepee playhouse, both Ss were jump ropes, and the O was a striped beach ball.

She went over to say hello. The man, older and gray-haired with rather ugly black tattoos on his stringy forearms, balanced on the table and struggled to fasten the string to his banner in the upper corner of his booth. She didn't want to distract him and make him lose his balance, so she waited until he spied her before she said anything.

He finally got the banner up, using a copious amount of soft swearing, and climbed off the table.

He saw Chase. "Hey, what do you want?" His voice was gruff.

That was rather ungracious, she thought. How was he going to sell toys if he frightened small children?

"I want to say hi. I'm Chase and I'm in the booth next door. I'm looking forward to seeing your toys. Are they handmade?"

"Yeah, they're handmade. You'll see 'em when I get set up." He turned his back on her and started ripping his boxes open with a pocketknife. She walked away without seeing any of the toys. Why was he so unfriendly? The travel agents, their other neighbors, seemed nice anyway.

She whispered to Anna about Harper. "Our neighbor is a crabby old toymaker. Don't bother trying to talk to him."

"Maybe," Anna whispered back, "he's harried, being a day late to the fair. His mood might improve."

Chase doubted it. After she zipped over to drop Quincy at the vet's office, she hurried back to help Anna get their booth ready to open. The onslaught of dessert bar buyers was truly phenomenal. Sales rivaled those of their two busiest times at the Bar None, which were freshman move-in week at the U and the holiday rush from mid-November until Christmas Eve.

Luckily, they were prepared, with piles of boxed treats and tray after tray of individual bars.

Anna had thought to bring several packages of wet

wipes for the sticky fingers of customers who scarfed down their sweets right there at the booth. She and Chase had noticed many of them doing that on Saturday. The eager customers couldn't wait to pop the Strawberry Cheesecake Bars, Lemon Bars, Cherry Chiffon Bars, and pineapple-coconut Hula Bars into their mouths.

Anna took a break midmorning to run home and check on Inger.

After Chase called the night before, Anna offered to let Inger stay at her place. She had more room—an actual guest room, in fact. Since it was Sunday, the shop was supposed to be open, following the normally scheduled Bar None business days of Wednesday through Sunday. However, they had decided to close up today, under the circumstances.

When Anna got back, Chase asked how Inger was doing.

"She was having morning sickness when I left earlier, but now she says she's feeling better. She was watching television. I believe she knows that she has to make some decisions about her future and the baby's soon. She had me drop her off at the shop."

"She went in to work?"

"Said she wanted to help out with the baking."

"The poor kid. I wonder if her parents will come around."

"I hope so."

Julie and Jay showed up just before lunchtime to help in the booth. Naturally, as soon as they arrived, there was a lull. So instead, they wandered off together to see the sights.

By noon, both women were starving.

"Charity," Anna confided, leaning her head next to Chase's while ringing up a large sale, "I'm going to drop if I don't get something to eat."

Chase grinned. "We can't have that. I'll run over to the food trailers and get something. Do you know what you want?"

"Surprise me. Anything but funnel cakes. I don't want extra powdered sugar all over our floor."

"Does Inger have lunch?"

"She said she just wanted crackers, but I left some chicken soup for her to heat up."

Chase hurried out of the booth and down the midway. The beautiful, unseasonably warm weather was holding.

She had worn a knit jersey top, rust-colored and lighter than the sweater she wore yesterday. She brought along her suede jacket, which had served her well the night before. In the back of the booth, Chase had spied a heavy cotton dashiki in bright kente cloth that Anna had stashed for herself for later.

For now, the sun bounced off the tarps of the vendors' booths, glinting off the white paint of the closed door to the butter sculpture building. The faintly dusty smell of the sawdust rose from her feet. Fallen autumn leaves had mingled with the sawdust. In places, she could even pick out brilliant reds from the maple behind their own booth.

The armed police guards were still around. Chase was reminded to be aware of her surroundings and keep her guard up.

She slowed a bit when she heard sobbing between the

butter building and the one next to it, that of a hawker of handmade silver jewelry.

The large sculptor, Karl Minsky, stormed out from between the buildings and strode away without noticing Chase. He was followed by his daughter, Mara.

Mara dabbed at her eyes with a tissue and almost stumbled into Chase.

"Is something wrong? Can I help you?" Chase asked.

"Yes. And no. I don't think you can help us."

Chase took Mara's arm gently and guided her toward a seat near the food trucks. "Can I get you something to drink?"

"Maybe a soda," she said between sniffs.

The nearest line for sodas was short, so Chase wasn't gone long. When she got back, Mara seemed more composed. "Do you want to tell me about it? It might help to talk."

"I'm so frightened." Mara sipped her drink. "Daddy had a big argument with that man, right outside the main exhibition room."

"What man?" Chase asked, although she was pretty sure she knew.

"The one that's dead. I'll bet a lot of people heard them arguing. And now he's been killed."

"Just because they had words doesn't mean your father killed him." She felt a need to comfort the poor girl.

"He was so mad." Mara whimpered. She gave a couple of gulping sobs.

Chase wondered if the girl thought her father had

killed Oake. The next time she saw Detective Olson, she would check and see if he knew about Minsky's threat.

"I'm so sorry to bother you with this. Please forgive me."

Given his intensity when she'd met him earlier, Chase could easily picture Karl enraged. It was very possible he was the killer. But she soothed Mara as best she could and hurried on to complete her errand as Mara wandered off, nursing her drink.

Anna probably wondered what was taking so long. Chase picked the shortest line, fried peanut butter and jelly sandwiches, quickly grabbed two, and scurried back toward the Bar None booth.

When she was almost there, she could have sworn she saw Mike duck through the hangings into the fortune-teller's booth.

Julie and Jay strolled by.

"Do you need us yet?" Julie asked.

"Check in with Anna. I'm on my way there in a sec," Chase said, dawdling.

They continued on toward the Bar None booth, stopping to browse at the travel agency.

Mike's mission in the fortune-teller's booth was short because he came out as Chase passed by.

"Love you," Madame Divine called as he left.

Love you! Who was this woman?

"Having your fortune read?" Chase asked with a bright, stiff smile. She really wanted to ask him what he was doing there. "Does Madame Divine think you'll be off the hook soon for the murder?"

"I wish she could know that," he said, and walked past

her toward his office, trailing the scent of lavender. He hadn't returned her smile.

There was one more delay getting the fried sandwiches back to Anna. Julie and Jay and two women stood talking outside the travel agent's booth, which was next to the Bar None. As she neared, she realized the two women were the travel agents.

"Have you heard?" Julie asked Chase. "About the missing diamond cat collar?"

"It's the prize for the contest. The Picky Puss Cat Food Company donated it. It was displayed along with all the other cat items," Jay added.

"It was the most valuable thing there," the tall blonde said.

"I wonder what they'll do now," the redhead said.

"About what?" Chase asked.

"The collar!" The redhead threw her arms out. "It's the whole point. Why have the contest?"

"They have to have it," Jay said.

"We'll be there in a few minutes," Julie called as Chase left them to their speculations and proceeded to the Bar None, recalling that Patrice, aka Madame Divine, had been protesting behind her tent about having borrowed something from an exhibit and having lost it. If Chase recalled the words correctly, she'd been addressing her grandfather and she'd mentioned the Fancy Cat Contest. Had she taken the diamond cat collar? And lost it?

What was Mike's involvement with her anyway? There must be more than a pet connection. She vowed to find out. And to try not to be overly jealous when she did find out.

The toymaker had gotten his booth set up, finally, and

73

was in full swing. Chattering children crowded into his booth, begging their parents to get them a carved wooden truck or a hand-sewn doll. Chase was heartened that the children took pleasure in the simple, non-battery-operated toys. If and when she had children, she would like for them to play with toys like that. Harper remained surly, even with his customers, but they bought the toys anyway.

Midafternoon, a scruffy-looking man walked past the Bar None to Harper's booth. He wore filthy, baggy jeans and a zippered jacket that was stained with what looked like automobile grease. Chase was curious because he didn't look like the typical toy buyer, or even the average fairgoer. Julie, standing at the edge of the booth, wrinkled her nose at his stench. Chase sidled up next to Julie and watched.

The scruffy man waited for the crowd in the toy booth to thin out, then approached Harper.

"Hardin, I heard you were here," he said.

Hardin? Julie and Chase exchanged a look.

"Keep your voice down," Harper whispered. "Get over here if you want to talk."

The man went around to the other side of the display table. Julie and Chase could no longer hear them. Hardin? Harper? Was the man hiding and using a false name?

"What's going on with that guy?" Julie asked.

Chase gave a helpless shrug.

The scruffy man left soon after, and children once more flocked to Harper's.

Whatever the toymaker's name was, he was good for the Bar None because the children, stopping for the toys, were also attracted to the pretty stripes and good smells next door. Or maybe it was the parents who were drawn in. However it worked, families usually stopped at both booths. Anna, Chase, Jay, and Julie, relieving each other periodically, toiled hard all day long.

That evening as Chase dragged herself, exhausted, to Mike's office to pick up Quincy, she reviewed what she would say to him on her way.

How exactly do you know Patrice? No, too direct. *Have you known Patrice long?* That might do. *Have you heard about the missing diamond collar?* That would be good. *Is it the same one that Patrice filched from the exhibit and lost?* Maybe not.

When she got there, the door between the reception area and the examining room was wide-open. Patrice and an older man were talking with Mike inside. Betsy was again gone. Mike was certainly giving her nice hours.

"Hi, Chase," Dr. Ramos said as soon as he saw her. "I'll go get Quincy."

That seemed rude to Chase. "Who are your friends?" She entered the room and said to Patrice, "I know you, of course. I'll be by for my fortune before the fair is over."

Patrice seemed happy about that.

Then Chase turned to the older gentleman. He had a dignified air about him. His wispy gray hair didn't take away from his ramrod posture. Although he was beanpole thin, his casual clothing—a pair of khakis, a long-sleeved pullover sweater, and polished loafers—fit well.

"This is Vik, my grandfather," Patrice said.

"Viktor Youngren." The man held a careworn hand out to Chase. "I'm so pleased to make your acquaintance."

Mike finished containing Quincy and handed the crate to Chase. "Meet more of my Youngren relatives."

"You're related? To Patrice?"

This man was obviously not a Ramos relative. Mike had a Swedish mother, and Patrice must have a Swedish father.

"Yep, she's my cousin, the daughter of my aunt Betsy."

Thank goodness she hadn't gotten a chance to ask some of her idiotic questions about Patrice and Mike's possible romance. The three acted like they were going to stay and chat all night, so Chase said her good-byes and stepped into the tiny reception room, closing the door halfway. She waited, still inside the darkened room for a moment, fiddling with Quincy's carrier and peeking through the opening to see if any fireworks were going to erupt.

"Mikey, I'm so sorry this happened to you." Patrice wasn't keeping her voice down. "It's all my fault you got caught in there." She waved her hands when she talked. Patrice's rings glittered in the bright overhead lights.

Chase stared at the turquoise one on her left hand.

She had stolen Chase's ring when they'd shaken hands in her fortune-telling tent! Chase gaped at the brazen woman.

"At least I could say I was looking for the cat," Mike said. "It gave me an excuse for being there. If not, I'd look even more guilty."

When Chase heard Viktor start to berate his granddaughter for hiding "it" in a butter sculpture, she moved on.

Why did Mike need an excuse to be with the dead

man? Chase was more puzzled than ever, and beginning to have doubts about Mike.

When she returned home, tired to the bone from standing and selling all day, Inger was still in the shop, packing up last week's leftovers to take to the homeless shelter. They usually dropped them off on Sunday night. Inger had also done a good bit of baking.

"Can I go with you when you take these?" she asked Chase.

"Sure. Just let me put Quincy upstairs."

Chase wondered why Inger wanted to go, then remembered she'd been eager to go there last week, too.

"I'll take them in if you want to wait in the car," she said as Chase pulled out of the parking lot at the Bar None.

"That's okay. I'll help." They had less than usual this week, since they'd been taking so much product to the fair and selling nearly all of it each day.

On the way, Chase tried to find out why Inger was so eager to visit the shelter.

"You really like going to the shelter, don't you?" she said.

"It's a wonderful thing you and Anna do. I like to help out with that." Her eyes glowed with her bright smile.

"Do you know any of the people who work there?"

Inger looked away, as if they were passing fascinating scenery instead of going down the streets of Minneapolis. "Not really."

After they parked and went inside, though, and made their way to the kitchen, Inger scanned the dining room with a look of disappointment. They only had to make one trip to cart the two boxes of dessert bars inside.

The burly chief cook greeted them warmly. "Glad to see you again. The folks here always look forward to your desserts."

He chuckled at Inger. "I think your young man's luck has turned. They're not here anymore."

Chase raised her eyebrows at Inger in question, but the young woman turned away and busied herself unpacking one of the boxes.

When they finished unloading, the cook gave each of them a hug, his apron redolent of sausage, the main course for the night.

They walked out past the tables full of hungry homeless people. About half were single men, some old and some young. The others were couples or families, some with children, and one couple with two toddlers. Chase knew they all had to leave during the day and she wondered what people with babies did in the cold winter weather when they had no place of their own.

Inger inspected the diners one last time on their way out to Chase's car.

On the way back, Chase had to ask her point-blank. "Were you looking for someone?"

"Where? At the homeless shelter?"

"Yes. That's the only place we've been."

"Well, sort of. He wasn't there, though."

"A young man?"

Inger shrugged.

"I guess it's good news that he's not there any longer, that his luck has changed," Chase said.

"Mmm."

That's all Chase could get out of her before she dropped her at Anna's for the night. Before she pulled away from Anna's curb, Tanner messaged her that he didn't have product information and pictures yet. No, he didn't. At the next red light she messaged back that it might be a few days before she could get that to him. She would have to photograph each product and write a description. The prices wouldn't be hard; those were already set. How would Tanner set up online ordering for the customers? Or should they all just come to the shop to buy dessert bars, like Anna wanted them to? It might be too complicated right now to set up ordering and shipping procedures. It was a lot to think about. And Tanner had wanted a blog and Twitter and Facebook! No way. At least not in the near future.

Later that evening, she replayed the conversation that had come to her through the vet clinic door. The diamond cat collar again. She looked up the cat food company online and the dazzling collar was featured front and center on their page.

"What do you think?" She addressed the cat in her lap, who had been helpfully batting her arm as she reviewed the online information about Picky Puss. "Do we still want to enter the contest?"

Quincy blinked his large amber eyes.

"That means yes?"

Quincy twitched the very tip of his ginger tail.

"We have to come up with a costume. Honestly, I don't know if you would tolerate being filmed for a commercial, but it would be excellent to get your picture on a cat food bag." She stroked him and he lowered his head, arched his back, and purred his appreciation.

"I wish you could tell me exactly what you saw in that butter sculpture building."

Quincy raised his head. Did he know the word *butter*?

"If only you could testify that Mike didn't kill anyone. I'm sure you'd do that if you could, right?"

He leaned into Chase's hand as she caressed the side of his head. She fingered his silky ear, the one with the notch missing from a fight.

Quincy closed his eyes and continued to purr.

EIGHT

There wasn't much letup in attendance, even though it was Monday, a regular workday for most people. The schools were having their fall break to coincide with the weeklong fair, which helped immensely.

There was a lull in the action at midmorning, however, and Chase took advantage of it to stroll out of the booth. She stopped to chat with the travel agents. The short redhead was gone, but the tall blonde stepped forward and, with a brilliant smile, handed her their promotional pamphlet.

"I don't think I've heard your name yet," Chase said. "I'm Chase Oliver."

"And I'm Sally Ritten."

"You were talking about the missing diamond collar yesterday," Chase said, leafing through it and admiring the pictures of exotic islands and European cathedrals. "Where is it supposed to be? In an exhibit?"

"It was the central exhibit."

Chase said. "Is that in the main building?"

"Oh yes!" the woman gushed. "You *must* go see the exhibit. Absolutely charming. Even without the diamonds. There's plenty more there to see."

Chase noticed that the woman wore rings on almost every finger and a wide choker studded with what must have been faux diamonds. If they were real, the necklace would be priceless.

"You like jewelry?" Chase asked.

"Of course." She smiled and waggled her gem-studded fingers. "But these are just . . . you know. The exhibit, though . . . You have to go see it."

She decided she would. There was no better time than right now. Chase nipped back to the Bar None and told Anna she was going to be gone for fifteen minutes.

"Take your time. If we get swamped, the customers will have to wait in line. It'll make us look good to have a line out the door."

That had already happened a few times over the weekend, even with two, sometimes four, of them there and working as fast as they could.

Chase made her way to the big exhibition hall. An easel inside the door listed the exhibits and their room numbers. She hadn't noticed it before but now saw that the Picky Puss exhibit was in room 3A, down the hallway to her left.

The room was smaller than the animal contest arena across the hall but roomy enough for the three dozen or so people inside to comfortably browse and meander.

Several tables held glass cases full of feline-themed items. The first was filled with cat toys, according to the sign, including some replicas of famous old ones. These were not toys *for* cats, though, they were toy cats. There were modern cat dolls and stuffed toys. Also darling old metal windup cats, a vintage rubber cat, some cloth ones, some with fur. One metal toy was a striped cat, like Quincy, that held a ball between its two front paws. The original ears, which had been made of leather, were missing, but the sign next to it said that it still worked. If you pushed its blue metal tail down, it would scoot across the floor.

She passed by the next case, which held cat sculptures. Some of them were ceramic and some metal. A few pieces even purported to be Egyptian, but they didn't look old enough to be ancient treasures to her untutored eye.

The next exhibit she came to was the one she had been seeking, the cat food company's main table. It held cat food bags and boxes featuring large photos of various pretty kitties. Some of them were from years ago, since the local company had been around for at least twenty years. The bags surrounded an empty blue velvet cushion. The card next to the cushion read, "DIAMOND CAT COLLAR," in large letters. A woman came up from behind, stood next to her, and huffed loudly.

"It's a shame it's missing, isn't it?" Chase said to her.

The woman was overdressed for the occasion, in a dark blue power suit, white blouse with a large billowy bow, and low heels.

"I am Cassandra Sharp, representing Picky Puss. It is not a shame. It is a travesty." She spit out her words as she waved a wrist bearing a flashy watch. Chase wondered if the diamonds on it were real.

"How terrible for you, Ms. Sharp," Chase said, trying to be nice to the rather rude and abrupt woman. "I hope it can be recovered."

"It does not seem to be a priority for the police, now that that man was murdered."

"I'm sure you can understand that. Murder is more important than—"

"This is my job on the line. The company will hold me responsible. Our insurers will have my head. I never dreamed I would need ironclad security at this Podunk fair. When our insurance company hears about this . . ." She clamped her thin lips shut.

"Don't you think the two events are tied together? Maybe solving the murder might find you the collar?"

"Do not make me laugh." The aptly named Ms. Sharp sneered at Chase, then stalked off and out the door of the exhibition room.

But they *were* related, the murder and the theft—they had to be. The wheels in her head started spinning. She ticked off the facts that she knew, or had overheard and assumed were true.

The Picky Puss company, in the person of the rude sourpuss in the blue suit, had put the valuable item on display in a glass case without a visible lock. Chase assumed she could lift the lid to get at the contents. Not a wise move, even in a "Podunk" fair. People were people everywhere.

Patrice was sticky-fingered. She had probably filched the collar from the exhibit. An even sillier move.

Where was the cat collar now?

"I still cannot believe it," said a man behind her. "Do you see this?" He had a heavy accent—Russian?—and his words dripped with sorrow.

"Papa, keep your voice down," said a whispering man.

The man continued in a softer tone of voice, but with the same intensity. "For you, Peter. I want only best for you. Some day you understand that." His last words came through his sobs.

"Papa, let's go. There's no reason they shouldn't do publicity."

"Peter, the money should go to you."

"No, it should not, Papa. It never should have. Stop saying things like that."

Not wanting to be rude and stare, Chase cocked her head, as if studying all the pieces in the case, one by one, until they moved on. Then she turned her head the slightest bit to catch the speakers in her peripheral vision.

They were the same height and looked almost like brothers, but must be father and son. From the back, the two were unremarkable, both wearing jeans and nylon jackets, both with short brunet haircuts. The younger one was pulling the other by his upper arm. She didn't know if she would even recognize them again if she saw them. She knew for sure that one of them was quite emotional.

Was the man with the accent affected by the display? Was he even referring to it? They were standing facing it, but she had no idea what they'd been talking about. They may have just stopped there to have their discussion.

"Ahead we plow, into the darkening night," she sang under her breath. She continued singing "Autumn" from *Titanic* as she exited the building.

Chase returned to their booth to find Anna deep in serious conversation with a woman who had a stylish short hairdo. Chase recognized her as the weeping woman who had been denied a ride in the ambulance with the dead man. What on earth was she doing back at the fair? Chase thought that if her own husband, which she didn't have now, but might someday, had been murdered here, she would stay far away. Maybe never visit another fair again.

The widow looked up, startled, when Chase entered the booth. She wore long spiral earrings that twirled when she moved her head.

"Hi, Chase." Anna's voice was bright, in contrast to Elsa's glum expression. "Have you met Elsa Oake?"

Chase shook her head. "Pleased to meet you," she said.

"Yes. Same here." The woman sniffed, as if she had been crying. She dabbed at her eyes, but they were dry. She swiped at her nose with the same tissue that she had dug out of her large shoulder bag, then walked out of the booth.

"Is she all right?" asked Chase.

"Of course not, Charity. Her husband has been murdered."

"Well, yeah. But I meant, should you go after her?"

"She's meeting someone official from the fair, or maybe the police, to collect the rest of Mr. Oake's things. They're releasing some of his tools. The things they're not holding for evidence."

"I saw his workstation."

"Poor Elsa is especially distraught because of the situation between her and her husband when he died."

Chase helped herself to a Lemon Bar. She couldn't be around them all day and never eat any. "What situation?" She held the tangy goodness on her tongue to savor it as long as possible.

Just then a chattering family came in and bought so many dessert bars, they seemed to be stocking up for a famine. The rush continued until closing time. The two women worked nonstop, except for brief forays for sustenance when they got so hungry they were ready to drop.

Finally, it was time to pack up. Chase spied something shiny on the floor. She stooped to pick up a spiral earring. "I think Elsa Oake must have dropped this," she said.

Anna took it and held it up to inspect it. "I think you're right. This looks like hers. Looks like a nice one, too."

"We should try to return it. She didn't give you her phone number or address, I don't suppose."

"No, but she said she's staying at the Crowne Plaza

downtown. If you want to run this stuff to the shop, I'll stop by there and see if I can give it to her."

"Anna, what were you saying earlier about her situation, when her husband . . . died?" Chase hated to say the word *murder*.

"It's tough. She had been going through some papers of his—I'm not sure why—and she found a stack of real estate ads he'd cut out. I think she's naturally snoopy. She confronted him before they came here, and he said he was going to buy a live-in studio in Madison and carve butter full-time if he won the prize at this fair."

"He thought he could retire on *that* prize?"

"How much is it?" Anna asked.

"It's twenty-five thousand dollars, which is a nice amount, but that's not enough to live on for the rest of your life."

"Apparently, he's done well with other business ventures, and this would be enough for him to acquire the property and retire. However, his plans didn't include his wife."

"He was going to leave her?"

"If he won," Anna said.

"According to Julie and Jay, he would have won. I don't think anyone here could have beaten him. Not if he really was the best butter sculptor in the Midwest."

"Elsa said she was livid about it. They've been arguing ever since they arrived, but she finally blew her stack."

"Did that happen in the sculpture building?"

"I'm not sure. I got the feeling that the confrontation

was here at the fair, somewhere. The argument was the last time she spoke with him."

After Anna left with the earring, Chase twirled her hair and wondered exactly how angry Elsa had been. Angry enough to commit murder?

NINE

Julie called Chase at eleven, after Chase had arrived home, taken a bath with heavenly rose-scented salts, and gotten her flannel PJs on. The nights were getting colder and colder. She would have to break out her long johns soon so she could be warm and toasty while she slept.

"Chase, can I come by to talk?" Julie asked.

"Sure. I was getting set to watch television for a while before I go to bed."

Julie had sounded somber. Chase wondered if there was trouble between her and Jay. She hoped not. She hadn't yet seen that much of him, but she liked what she'd seen. Julie hadn't been serious about anyone for so long. In law school, her time was taken up with studying and graduating at the top of her class, plus interning. After graduation, she landed the job with the district attorney's office, and they kept her even busier than she'd been in school. Her schedule seemed to be easing up a bit the last few weeks. At least she had time to date.

After Chase let Julie up to her apartment over the shop, she made cinnamon-sprinkled cocoa for both of them.

"Mmm, this is exactly what I need right now." Julie cupped the mug with both hands. "It's getting downright chilly out there. I think a new cold front went through while I was on my way here from the office."

"Is everything going okay, Jules?" Quincy rubbed against Chase's flannel pajama–clad leg, leaving ginger-hued hairs on the black watch plaid.

"I guess," Julie said. "But I, well, I'm not quite happy with what I'm doing."

Chase waited. Not happy with her job? With her boy-friend? When Julie didn't continue, Chase voiced those two options.

Julie laughed. "Not with Jay. Everything is super with him. No, it's my job."

"Has something changed?"

"Not really. I think that I've been working so hard I didn't have time to notice whether or not I liked what I was doing. I'm getting a better handle on how the system works as time goes on and as I work there longer. I have a tiny bit more time to think lately."

Quincy jumped into Julie's lap, purring, and she adroitly saved her chocolate from spilling.

"I've noticed that. And? What do you think?"

"I think I don't want to work in the public sector."

"Why not? I thought you enjoyed it."

"I do, sometimes, but prosecuting has such negative connotations. I think I'd rather do something positive. And it's not enough pay for such hard work."

"Do you want to move to the private sector because Jay works for a private firm?"

"Maybe. I know he works just as hard as I do, maybe harder, and it's basically the same field. Being a defense attorney is the other side of the courtroom from prosecution."

"That's what you want to do? Defense?"

"Not really. Maybe. I'm not sure yet. That's what's making me so edgy lately. I really don't know what I want to do. I thought I did when I took my job, but this isn't it."

"Isn't it good to discover that now, before you spend years and years doing something you don't enjoy?"

"I'm sure you're right. But I don't know what I *do* want to do. It's an unsettling feeling. It makes my stomach hurt."

"Have you talked to Jay about it? I'm not a lawyer, so I don't know what your other options are. He might know better."

"I haven't talked to him. He knows something's wrong, but I didn't want to tell him."

"Why not?"

Julie looked at Chase's ceiling for the answer. "Maybe I don't want him to think I'm flighty. Or a person who doesn't know how to run her own life."

Quincy abandoned Julie for Chase and got a neck rub for his trouble.

"If he's noticed something's wrong, he probably assumes it's about him. Don't you think?"

They both sipped their chocolate in silence for a moment. Then Julie spoke with a decisive air. "You're right. That's not fair, is it? If our relationship is good and is going anywhere, I have to share this with him."

Chase nodded, thinking of how she felt when she thought Mike was keeping something from her and then it turned out that Patrice was his cousin. She and Mike weren't even serious. Not that Julie and Jay were yet either.

"I'll talk to him." She drained her mug and stood to leave. Chase jumped up to give Julie a good-bye hug.

Quincy, lapless, meowed and stalked off, stiff-legged.

"I'm so glad you talked some sense into me," Julie said, giving her best friend a good hard squeeze.

"No problem, girlfriend. It might be that I let you talk sense into yourself. But I expect you to do the same for me when I need it."

After Julie left, Chase wandered over to the glass doors that led to her balcony. It was too cold to sit out there, but she stared through the panes at the streetlights below, glowing like soft lighthouse beacons in the cold, crisp air.

She regretted she hadn't been able to bring the conversation around to asking Julie to look up information about the case against Michael Ramos. Well, Julie wasn't leaving her job tomorrow. There would be plenty of time to try to figure out how to get Mike off the hook for the murder. It was a good thing the mills of justice ground slowly. An unwanted picture of Michael Ramos nearing a grindstone flashed into her mind. She shivered and wrapped her robe around her a little tighter.

The next morning, at the Bar None booth at Bunyan County Fairgrounds, Chase arrived well before Anna. In fact, Anna slid behind the table as the first customers wandered in.

"Good news," Anna said when she arrived, breathless. "Inger's parents took her back. I dropped her off this morning."

"Good grief, Anna. They should have picked her up. Did they apologize for all the trouble they've put you to?"

"I didn't actually see them. Inger asked me to drop her off in front of the house. I made sure she got in, though. Frankly, I didn't feel like talking to them. I might have been tempted to say something I shouldn't. But look. I stopped off to get this." Anna held up a small space heater. Each booth had been provided with an electric power strip so they could plug in lights after it got dark. A pole lamp stood in the back corner of each booth, but there was no provision for heat.

Chase, who hadn't taken off her wool coat yet, was glad to see the heater. "It won't blow out the power, will it?"

"The man at the hardware store said it takes the least power of any of their heaters. Since this is such a small space, it should work well here."

It did. Soon the booth was toasty warm. Anna shed her down parka and Chase took off her heavy coat. Fairgoers were ducking in to warm up, especially those who hadn't bothered to check the weather before setting out and weren't dressed warmly enough.

When a break came for them, Chase asked how it went last night with Elsa Oake.

"It was her earring, all right." Anna perched on the edge of the folding chair to rest her feet.

Chase poured hot cider for both of them from her thermos. She was glad she had thought of that when she woke up. "Did you have any trouble finding her?" She took the other chair and sipped, savoring the cinnamon and nutmeg.

"Nope, no trouble at all. I walked right up and asked the clerk at the front desk of the Crowne Plaza if they could dial her for me. Elsa gave me her room number over the phone." Anna lowered her voice and bent close to Chase. "I will say that she was a little tipsy."

"Mourning her husband?"

"I'm not sure. She doesn't seem too sorry he's gone."

"Surely she's not *celebrating* his death?"

Anna shrugged as a group of teenagers meandered in.

When the lunch rush was over, Chase said, "This morning Mike asked me if I'd meet him for a late lunch today at the clinic. Do you mind?"

"Not at all. It doesn't sound like the most appetizing place to dine."

"I'll get to see Quincy an extra time. He seems lonely when I pick him up at night. He purrs so loud and nuzzles so hard."

"It's good for him. Makes him appreciate you more."

Chase laughed. "I'm not that hard up that I need my pet to pine for me."

The truth was, she hadn't seen much of Mike either since the fair started. Just dropping Quincy off and picking him up, and maybe an odd other time or two. That trick of not seeing much of Dr. Ramos was working on her, making her want to be with him more.

"I have yet to ask Julie if she can get any info from the police on the case against him," Chase said.

"Do you want me to ask her? She's coming over to my house late tonight. You're welcome to come, too, but we're planning our shoe thing."

Anna and her granddaughter both loved shoes—and boots. Every fall, they planned their shopping excursion for days. "You're going next week?"

"Yah. Now that the weather has turned cold, they'll start selling out."

Chase knew, from listening to the plotting that the two of them did, that there was a fine line in timing. A smart shopper couldn't go too early or too late. They'd want the shoes to be on sale, but for the stores to still have a good selection. Anna and Julie both came back from their Fall Shoe Safari with more than they could wear. That was Chase's opinion. She was more of a minimalist, shoe-wise.

"Did I tell you what Elsa said about that little Winn guy?" Anna asked as Chase slipped into her coat and wound her scarf around her neck to leave their cozy booth.

"No. Winn Cardiman? When I spoke to him, he seemed upset that Oake was carving the same thing he was, Babe the Blue Ox."

"Yes, that's the one. Elsa said he and her husband had

a loud shouting match the day they were moving into the sculpture place. Cardiman saw Oake's sketches, according to Elsa, and accused him of copying his idea. Oake insisted that he'd drawn his sketches weeks ago and accused Cardiman of the same thing. A bystander separated them when it looked like they might come to blows."

"Has she told the police that?"

"She didn't say whether she has or not. But she seems to think he's the one who killed Larry Oake now."

"Where did this go down? Did other people see what happened?"

"Elsa said the actual fight was by the food trailers."

"I should check with Detective Olson, then. He could try to question people who might have witnessed the argument."

TEN

Chase pondered the options on her way to the clinic to see Mike and Quincy. She dawdled, shuffling through the sawdust and crunchy leaves, making a detour to stop at the food vendors. Cardiman was angry with Oake. So was Minsky, Mara's father. So was his own wife, Elsa. She would list all of these to Detective Olson soon.

Chase didn't have to go far to contact Detective Olson. He was in Mike's clinic when she arrived carrying their sub sandwiches.

After she pushed the door to the clinic room open with her hip, Detective Olson asked her to remain in the outer room until he was finished. A sign on Betsy's desk said she was gone for lunch. Chase sat on one of the plastic chairs in the tiny reception area, shivering. The room was cool, but she wasn't shivering from that. The homicide detective's face had held such a serious scowl. Was he going to take Mike away again?

She was relieved when the detective swept out of the room without hauling Mike along with him in handcuffs.

"Detective Olson, wait." Chase jumped up, still clutching the sandwiches. "I found out something you should know."

He stopped and closed those gorgeous dark blue eyes for three seconds. "Chase, are you trying to investigate again?"

"No, no, nothing like that. It's just that Elsa Oake was talking to Anna. You know, Anna Larson?"

"Your business partner. Yes, I remember her."

"Elsa told her that Winn Cardiman had a terrible fight with Larry Oake, in front of a lot of people. He was still very angry when I ques—when I talked to him, too."

"Believe it or not, we have interviewed Mr. Cardiman." He looked irritated.

"But did you know about their fight?"

"You mean a physical altercation? Blows were exchanged?"

"No, only an argument, as far as I know. But you could find others, by the food trailers, who saw it." She gestured with one of the sandwiches in that direction.

"Maybe we could. But I don't see what good that would do us." He crossed his arms across his chest. It was a nice view, but she wasn't in the mood to appreciate it.

"Cardiman," she continued, "seems desperate to win the competition and he thought Oake was copying his own idea."

Olson's look softened and he uncrossed his arms. "He's not that desperate, Chase. He's dropped out of the competition."

"Dropped out? After all that angst?"

"He said he didn't need the money, or the hassle. He's packed up and gone back home to Waterloo, Iowa."

"Well, I'll be darned." Chase plopped back down on the chair.

A man rushed in cradling a howling dachshund in his arms as Olson exited. The man disappeared into the clinic room and Chase waited while the howling gradually subsided, becoming pitiful little whimpers, then a happy yip. The man came out smiling a few minutes later. The small dog looked contented, too, wagging its tail so fast it blurred.

That's where Mike found her when he came looking for her. "Did I hear you talking to the detective before that emergency?"

"Yes. As usual, it got me nowhere. What was wrong with that poor puppy?"

"Just a tiny splinter. She's a big drama queen. Well, a little drama queen, but a good one."

Mike led the way into the examining room. The clinical smell, while not overpowering, didn't provide the best luncheon ambience. Chase thought eating at the reception desk might have been better. Mike took one of the sandwiches and sat at the small desk to unwrap it. "Where did you hope to get with Detective Olson?" he said with a grin. He unfolded a metal chair for Chase.

"I hoped to get *you* off the hook. What did he say to you?"

Mike frowned. "I'm afraid he's going after someone else now, too."

Why was he frowning? "Isn't that good news?"

"No." His brown eyes held hers. They were sad. "He's going after my cousin Patrice."

Chase scraped her chair closer to the desk to set her sandwich on it, too. "What's going on, Mike?"

Their elbows nearly touched. She could feel the warmth of his body. Flushing slightly, she scooted over a bit.

He had just bitten off a mouthful. Chase waited patiently for him to finish. He took a swig from his water bottle before he answered. He was obviously playing for time, getting his reply ready.

"There's a lot going on," he said. "Have you heard that a diamond cat collar is missing from the display in the main building?"

"Yes. I saw the case myself and the empty cushion. It says it was donated by the Picky Puss Cat Food Company. Patrice's grandfather seems pretty upset with her."

"Victor Youngren? What do you mean, he's upset?"

"I overheard that Patrice filched the collar."

"Where did you hear that?"

"I . . . I happened to overhear her talking to someone."

"Yes, she did take it."

"From the display? I'm trying to picture that."

"Patrice does rash things sometimes."

"That's one word for it."

"She told me she wanted to try it on her cat to see if it would fit. Her cat is—well, she makes Quincy look thin.

This is so hard on Viktor. He's scheduled to start radiation in two weeks. Chemo will come after that."

"He has cancer?"

"It's a small growth and we hope it will be taken care of with the treatments. But I can tell it's weighing on him. And now this business with Patrice. Again. He had to retire earlier than he wanted to. He worked full-time until six months ago, when he started feeling tired all the time."

The poor man. "So she wanted to take it home that night?"

"Yep."

"Why didn't she just ask Daisy for permission to try it on her cat?"

"She likes to get away with things. I think that's part of the thrill for her. Not so much having the stolen items as the excitement act of swiping them."

"If that's the case, maybe she wouldn't mind giving me back my ring."

"She stole your ring?" Mike's mouth dropped open.

Chase nodded. "It was pretty slick. She took it right off my finger when she shook hands with me."

Mike rubbed a hand over his mouth. "I'm so sorry. I'll talk to her about it." He pressed his lips into an angry line. "About the collar . . . She said she was going to put it back early the next day."

"Why didn't she?"

"She told me that a man came into her fortune-telling tent and saw it."

"She left it out for everyone to see?" This was sounding nuttier and nuttier.

Mike gave a weary sigh. "I told you, Patrice is—"

"Rash. You didn't say she's crazy."

"I don't think she's crazy, exactly. She's a . . . borrower. Once she borrowed her mother's ruby earrings and wore them to high school. The problem with that was that she forgot to take them off for softball practice and lost one of them jumping to catch a ball. She was an outfielder."

Chase shook her head at the behavior. The woman wasn't a borrower. She was a thief.

"Another time, she borrowed her grandfather's truck and destroyed his next-door neighbor's prize roses. He had to pay the neighbor a ton of money to replace them."

"So she's also a bad driver."

"Not now. She's a pretty good one. But she was fourteen when she did that."

"Oh. I think I'm seeing a pattern here."

"Yes, if she wants something, she takes it. She always intends to give it back."

"So she was going to take the cat collar home, then put it back into the exhibit?"

"Yes, but that man scared her and she decided, instead of putting it back right then, to hide it next door."

"In the butter building."

"In a butter sculpture."

"Yuck! It would get all oily."

"Diamonds are pretty hardy. I'm sure it would wash. It would have been okay, if only . . ."

Chase waited for Mike to continue filling in the last of the blanks of the story as she finished her sandwich in the interval.

Mike put down the rest of his sub beside a pile of folders. "Patrice asked me to retrieve it. I didn't think it would be that hard."

"Did Quincy sneak in there with you?" She saw Quincy's ears perk up at the mention of his name. He stood up and paced a bit. The glossy black cat in a cage next to his gave him a look of boredom, then ignored him.

"He might have. As soon as I got into the building, I saw the body on the floor."

"Did you call the police?" Chase asked.

"I was about to. Before I got my phone out, Quincy jumped up onto the table and started licking Babe the Blue Ox."

"He does like butter." Her sub was a little dry. It could probably use some butter. At least more mayo.

"The cavity in the leg was obvious," Mike continued. "Patrice had tried to smooth it over, but she's not a professional sculptor by a long shot. I punched through and reached into the cavity, but it wasn't there anymore. Before I could try to get my phone out again, Elsa opened the door and started screaming. I was still groping around inside the Blue Ox."

"And you told her you went there to retrieve Quincy."

"It's all I could think of." His deep brown eyes were troubled. "And now the detective has decided to focus on Patrice."

"Did you tell him that story?"

"No, but her mother did—part of it. She didn't tell them that I was there to get the collar, just that Patrice had put it there. Betsy has never gotten along well with her daughter. Betsy is a . . . She's an orderly person. She likes everything kept neat and tidy."

"And I take it Patrice is more . . . disorderly?"

"She's the creative type, I've always thought. I think the world of my cousin, but she is different."

"Are you going to finish that sandwich?"

Mike handed her the last little bit of his sub.

"I thought Quincy might like a bite."

"That is *not* what he should be eating."

"Just the meat?"

"It's pepperoni! No, not even the meat."

Mike seemed awfully grouchy today, Chase thought, walking back to the Bar None booth after a brief Quincy cuddle.

Mike should come clean and tell the police why he was really there. He could get himself into all kinds of trouble if he didn't. He probably didn't want to put suspicion on Patrice. However, her mother had done it for him. What a mess!

She peeked into the butter building and, sure enough, Winn Cardiman's station was empty. Even his sculpture was gone.

Was he innocent of Larry Oake's death, or was he cleverly trying to throw everyone off?

ELEVEN

The last time the man stuck a treat into the cat's cage, the latch hadn't seated properly. The doctor had been in a hurry to treat a dog who had been yelping. The dog had howled forever, hurting the cat's ears. The cat hadn't dared leave the cage while the dog was there. He lay down for a nap and was eventually awakened by voices in the outer room. One was his own human, the other the pet doctor who was watching him lately. It was simple to lift the lever and walk out when his human left. He didn't get as many treats here as he did at home. He went searching for some more.

Dr. Ramos came running after Chase. "Your cat is loose," he called. He caught up with her as she walked out of the butter building.

"You let him out?"

"I didn't let him out any more than you ever let him out when he runs away."

She was glad he recognized that Quincy's escapades were out of her control. "Where are the treats I left with you this morning?"

Mike held up the plastic bag.

"Oh, good, you have them. Give me one, then," Chase said. She started calling his name and waving the treat close to the ground, hoping Quincy would smell it or hear her and would then respond. Those first two wouldn't necessarily lead to the third. After all, he was a cat.

She went up and down the midway twice, sticking to one side while Mike patrolled the other. Her first time past the Bar None booth, she stopped in to tell Anna what was happening. Anna had a steady flow of customers, so she had to stay where she was, but she wished Chase luck with the hunt.

In a tiresome repeat of Quincy's previous escapade, Chase encountered several vendors who had either admired or fed him—or both—but none who had thought to pick him up and capture him until his owner arrived.

Out by the rides, the ring toss barker had seen Quincy this time.

"That cat jumped into my booth and started batting at my rings." He pointed to where they swung on the large nail hammered into the wooden frame.

"Was anything damaged?" Chase asked.

When he said it was not, Chase apologized for her cat and moved on. Quincy had also chased the balls a customer was throwing at the milk bottles and had pounced on the plastic ducks in the kiddie duck pond.

She trudged back to the midway where the Bar None booth sat and walked the length of that again.

The man who sold handmade glass mobiles was adamant that he hadn't let the cat near his booth. Smart move, thought Chase. His wares were fragile. The cupcake sellers had given him a few bites. They stressed that they hadn't let him have any frosting. Chase groaned inwardly. The game vendor said Quincy had jumped up and walked across all the boards, spread out for demonstration. He had fed him a bit of cheese. Some small children thought he was part of the advertising and convinced their parents to buy three games. She thought he might be hiding among the children's clothing. Hand-smocked dresses hung on a line at the side of the booth. He wasn't there, though he had been earlier. The older couple running the booth thought it was adorable the way he had played peekaboo with the clothes. They had slipped him cookies.

Chase wondered if all the other vendors thought he was a cat that lived at the fair. They couldn't, could they, when she and her friends worried and searched for him constantly?

When she passed Harper's Toys, she didn't intend to talk to him, but he asked her what she was doing, waving that bag around.

"I'm trying to find my cat, who ran away," she said.

"Looking for a feral cat?"

"He's not feral," she snapped. "He just got away." She

glanced over his collection and spotted some large, old-fashioned toys made up of a cup on a short wooden stick and a ball attached to it with a string. The object of the game was to toss the ball into the cup. A crude drawing showed how to play.

"Say," she said, picking one up. "Could I borrow this?" She thought she might trail it along after her and lure Quincy from wherever he was. The string was long.

"Gimme that." The horrid man snatched it from her hands. "You can have it if you pay for it." One of his bluish tattoos looked like a cat, but not a nice one. It bared sharp, snarling teeth and had the eyes of a devil-cat.

Chase tried to give him a stern look, but it had no effect. She left and returned to the Bar None booth.

"Hello, dearie."

Chase turned at the familiar voice. "Ms. Bjorn, how good to see you here."

The tiny, gray-haired woman leaned on the arm of her neighbor Professor Anderson Fear. They both lived a short distance from the Bar None on Fourteenth Avenue Southeast. They both peered at Chase through their glasses. Hilda Bjorn's lenses were shiny and wire-rimmed, while Professor Fear's were thick and smudged.

"I came for some more of those Raspberry Chiffon Bars. The girl at your shop said you were out of them there."

"And you came all the way here for them?" Anna said. "I'm afraid we didn't make any this week."

"We didn't think they would hold up here, without refrigeration," Chase added.

Anna held up a small box of Harvest Bars and opened them for inspection. "These are brand-new. Maybe you'll like these."

Professor Fear peered at the box and sniffed. "Pumpkin. I'll take a box, too."

While Anna wrapped their purchases, Hilda Bjorn pulled Chase close to whisper to her. "I know this is nonsense," she said, "but I just saw a cat who looks exactly like Quincy."

"Where?"

"He was napping in that big building."

"On a glass case," Professor Fear said. "In the room with the cat food things."

"We thought the cat might be part of their display."

Chase thanked them, left Anna to finish collecting their money, and ran to the main building.

She cautiously peeked into the cat food company's exhibit room and there Quincy was, curled up on top of the glass case that displayed the cat food bags and photos of cute kitties eating Picky Puss from fancy bowls. His tail covered his nose and he looked so comfy she hated to disturb him.

Oh so carefully, she tiptoed to him and gathered him into her arms. The lights for the display made the top of the case nice and warm. She thought that might be what had attracted him to it. There didn't seem to be food nearby.

"That cat likes the corn chips."

She whirled to face the man she knew only as Papa—Peter's father, the man with the accent. She looked back at the case. It was sprinkled with a few teensy crumbs, next to where Quincy's head had been.

"You fed him corn chips?" Mike wasn't going to like this one little bit.

"He seem like he is hungry." His accent was heavy.

The younger man, the one she'd seen with him the day before in this room, came rushing up. "There you are," he said, relief in his tone. "Where have you been?"

"I want to look where collar was."

"Sorry if my father was bothering you." The man shook hands with Chase. "I'm Peter Aronoff, Ivan's son."

"My good, brave only son," Ivan said.

Peter took his father's upper arm and tried to pull him away.

Ivan shook him off. "I not ready to go yet. Look, see what they wrote?" He pointed to the sign beside the empty cushion and laboriously read the whole thing. "DIA-MOND CAT COLLAR" was in large letters. Beneath, in smaller print, it said "Designed and donated to the Bun-yan County Fair by Picky Puss Cat Food. Pick the only food for your picky cat: Picky Puss." He turned to Chase. "It says it was donated by the company."

"I see that," Chase said. The sign hadn't changed, but she hadn't noticed the parts in smaller print before.

"They are rich company. Too much money. They glory in donating such a thing."

Chase squinted at the card in the glass case. "The print is very small. It doesn't look like they glory in it to me."

"Who are you, anyway?" Ivan said. He took a menac-ing step toward her.

Peter put his hand on his father's arm and shook his head.

"It not right, Peter, and you know it," Ivan snarled.

Peter mouthed the word *sorry* behind Ivan's back. "Papa, let's go. What the company does has nothing to do with me now. It's perfectly fine. These people don't want to hear about this."

He was finally able to lead Ivan away. The older man was still muttering about diamond collars and fairness and glory.

A lot of people were concerned about that cat collar.

"**Here he is,** the rascal," Chase said, settling Quincy back into the roomy cage in the vet clinic. "Now I guess I'm not the only one he's escaped from."

Mike gave a sheepish grin. "No, you're not. I don't think I've ever seen a cat that clever. Somehow, he was able to get that latch open."

"Maybe you didn't shut it all the way."

"Maybe." Mike rattled the latch and the door, testing it and pondering with a frown.

The black cat in the neighboring cage flinched at the rattling, then settled down. She wondered if it was the same one she'd seen here before.

"That's what happens at home and in the shop," Chase said. "We leave a door the least little bit cracked, or the latch not quite seated, and away he goes. It's too bad they're not having an escape contest for cats. Quincy would win that one for sure."

"Are you showing him in the Fancy Cat? Patrice is entering her butterball."

"I thought the cat was Princess Puffball."

Mike laughed. "That's her name, but she *is* a butterball. Wait till you see her."

"I hope to. If I can think of how to fancy up Quincy, we'll be at the competition."

Mike scratched his chin. "How about dressing him up as Quincy Jones?"

"The musician? He's one of Anna's favorites."

Mike started to look excited. "He'll need a mustache and a little suit. At least a shirt and a jacket."

"A mustache? Really?"

"Well, maybe not that. But a little suit coat would be doable, don't you think?"

Chase did not think so. "Let's try some more ideas. A Cat-wich?"

"Like a sandwich or a witch-witch?"

"Not a witch, he's a boy. That would be a warlock. Cat-lock?"

They both groaned.

"I got nothing else." Mike turned up his palms in surrender.

"We'll keep thinking about it. I'd better get back to the booth." Since Halloween was coming soon, that might be a good theme to keep in mind. Bat, goblin, ghost, devil—maybe even a superhero, like so many of the little trick-or-treaters.

When she slid behind the table to help take money

from the horde of customers, Anna gave her a grateful grin. "This just doesn't stop."

"We thought we had baked enough for the whole fair, but we hadn't. Good thing you've been doing so much baking this week. Maybe it's my turn tonight."

During the next lull, Anna perched on the chair. "I don't mind doing all the baking. Bill came over and kept me company after I got back from seeing Elsa at the hotel."

"I think you're seeing about as little of Bill as I'm seeing of Mike." Chase grabbed a Lemon Bar and took a nibble.

"Quite a bit less. You're seeing Dr. Ramos every day here."

"I know, but that doesn't count as *seeing* seeing. You had a late night, didn't you?" Chase was still feeling guilty for leaving all the baking to Anna.

"No problem. Elsa said she would come over tonight and help out."

"Elsa? The wife of the dead man?"

"Yes, that Elsa. The *widow* of the dead man. She's in a terrible state. There's nothing she can do until the killer is caught. She can't even have a service for Larry until his body is released."

"Is she that upset about his funeral?"

"Maybe not. She keeps saying it's so terrible Larry is dead. But then she goes right ahead and starts cursing him for being a sneak and planning to leave her penniless."

Chase took a seat on the other folding chair. It creaked

as she plopped down. "Anna, she's his widow, but she's also a suspect for his murder."

"She couldn't possibly have done it, Charity."

"Why not?"

"She walked in after he was dead."

"Maybe she did that after she killed him. You just said he was planning on leaving her high and dry."

Anna nodded. "More than just thinking. He rented a studio in Costa Rica."

"Yikes! I thought she said Madison."

"That's what he told her, but he was lying. A bill for the rent came to their house. Her sister is taking in the mail and called her, so she just found that out. She wasn't sad that he was leaving, since they hadn't been getting along. But she was so mad she was seeing red that he hadn't told her any of his plans. Elsa says she would have willingly given him a divorce."

"You know that a lot of murders happen on the spur of the moment."

"Yes, I know. Crimes of passion. But Elsa doesn't seem like a person who would fly off the handle."

"How long have you known her? Three days?"

"Four, I think."

"Do you think you should hang out with her?"

A half-dozen customers wandered in. Chase quickly finished her Lemon Bar, dusted the powdered sugar off her fingers, and got busy working alongside Anna.

That evening, while Anna and Elsa were chatting and baking in the kitchen below Chase's apartment, she tried to brainstorm some costumes for Quincy. She wasn't coming up with much, so she went down to the kitchen. Three heads would be better than one. And if Anna could fraternize with a murder suspect, so could she. Besides, if Elsa *was* a murderer, it wasn't good for Anna to be alone with her.

As the three women assembled dough and layered the sweet treats together, putting baking pans into the oven and pulling them out like an assembly line, Chase tried to learn more about the woman. Elsa wore cowgirl boots again—red ones tonight—and a long, black skirt. Her arms were flecked with flour and powdered sugar.

"Do you know when you're going back to Wisconsin?" Chase asked.

Elsa knitted her brows in distress. "No, I'm not allowed to leave right now. My sister is on her way tomorrow to keep me company."

"That's good," Anna said, sticking a bowl of sugar and butter under the mixer to cream. "Are you close to her?"

"We're twins, only sixteen minutes apart. She's bringing my birdie. I miss her so much."

"What kind of bird?" Anna asked.

"She's a parrot, an African grey. I'll be so happy to see her. I'm just not sure the hotel will be pleased about it."

"Would you like to stay at my place? I wouldn't mind having her. What's her name?"

Chase stared, wide-eyed. Anna was offering her home to a murder suspect, and her family, plus her pet. She shook her head behind Elsa's back, but Anna pointedly ignored her.

"You and your sister are both welcome. It's costing a fortune for the hotel, isn't it?"

"That won't be a problem. Larry left me well provided for. He had a huge insurance policy. I'll be more than fine when that comes through."

Another motive, thought Chase. She never did get around to mentioning cat costumes.

TWELVE

The kitchen was cleaned up and the two older women had left. Chase stood in the middle of the room, deep in thought.

Elsa could very well have killed her husband. Her motive was good, since he had a large life insurance policy. Chase assumed that he would have indeed left her high and dry if he had succeeded in divorcing her and moving to Costa Rica, cleaning out bank accounts on his way out of town. No need to spend the money on a divorce when you could leave the country and disappear.

She started pacing the floor as her thoughts warmed up.

Winn Cardiman, the butter sculptor whose design was, he said, stolen by Larry Oake, had made such a good suspect. It was a pity he had dropped out of the competition and gone home. He was angry enough to have killed the man in a fit of passion when Chase had been talking to him. Wait, maybe he did kill him, then, realizing what he'd done, left in a hurry. He could still be a suspect. Even if he didn't need the prize money, he was angry that his design had, he perceived, been stolen.

She paced faster, suspicions tumbling over one another in her mind.

The other sculptor, Karl Minsky, was desperate for the money. He was fiercely proud of his daughter's artistic talents and wanted the best for her. The only problem was, he couldn't afford the expensive art school she wanted to attend. If he eliminated some competition, he believed he would win, using Mara's design. To Chase's eye, it was a little too abstract to appeal to a general population, but maybe the judges were more modern, artistically, than she was.

All three—Elsa, Winn, and Karl—had engaged in loud arguments with Larry shortly before his death. Or had they? Elsa said Winn argued with the victim, but no one else had mentioned it. Had she lied about that? Detective Olson didn't seem to know about it. Karl's daughter talked to Chase about his shouting match, so that one probably happened. And Elsa's argument? She told Anna about it, so it probably had happened, too. There was no advantage, Chase reasoned, in telling Anna about these altercations, because they could incriminate Elsa.

Neither Mike nor Patrice had ever argued with the man. Had never even met him—she would bet money on that. Why would they be acquainted with a butter sculptor?

Mike was merely trying to retrieve the bauble—okay, the valuable jeweled bauble—for his cousin. And she was just being her thieving self. Their timing was very, very bad. And so they were the preferred suspects.

Chase stopped pacing. Say that Elsa had killed her husband. Wouldn't it be an excellent tactic to wait for the next person to enter the building, then to "find" that person—Mike—with the body?

The butter sculpture tool, the pointed dowel, was most assuredly a weapon of convenience, so the crime had to be one of passion. If someone had planned to kill him, he or she would have arrived with a weapon. Who would be more passionate than Oake's spouse?

That was another factor in Mike's favor. How could he kill the man in a fit of passion when he didn't even know him? The same held true for Patrice, surely.

Her phone rattled in her pocket and she saw Tanner's number. She hadn't gotten anything for him yet. She opened the phone and ran into the office.

"Hi, Tanner. I'm working on the product list right now." Not really a lie. She was opening a document file this very minute to begin typing the descriptions.

"Can I have part of the payment, if this is going to, like, take a long time to finish up?"

That was fair. But she didn't want to use the shop bank account. "Can you come by to pick up a check?" She would have to use her own account until this was revealed to Anna. At this stage, she probably wouldn't appreciate the potential.

"This isn't too late for you?"

It was a little past ten o'clock. Not all that late. Usually she would be lounging in her PJs by now. At least she was still dressed, but only because she hadn't had time yet to get ready for bed. "Oh no. Not too late at all."

"Cool. I'll be right there. I can look at what you've done so far."

Chase groaned after she ended the call. She furiously began typing very bad, short descriptions. Strawberry Cheesecake: cheesecake bar with strawberries. Hula Bars: pineapple, coconut, walnuts. Lemon Bars: lemon-flavored. This wouldn't do.

The back doorbell rang. She closed the file and hit "Don't Save" as she exited the screen.

"Hey, Ms. Oliver. Thanks for letting me come by. So, you got my check?"

"Just a sec. I have to run upstairs for my checkbook."

"I'll look at your product description file while you do that."

"Oh. You know what? I was working on it and something happened. I lost everything. Don't worry, I can redo it."

He gave her a look that unmistakably let her know he thought she was a moron.

He no sooner left than her cell chirped again. She was delighted to see Mike's number. "Hey, my favorite doctor," she said.

"I hope I'm your favorite animal doctor and you have a people doctor you like." She heard the smile in his voice.

"You're right. You're Quincy's favorite doctor."

Maybe her saying his name set her cat off. Just after she said it, she heard loud, insistent meowing from her apartment above. She mounted the stairs while she talked. "What's up?"

"I called to see how you're holding up. It seems that you and Anna are working awfully hard this week."

"Ha!" She opened the door to her apartment, sticking a leg in to keep her cat from bolting. "This week is no different. We always work hard. I will say that the hours are longer, though."

"Did you just get home?"

"No, but we finished baking for tomorrow a few minutes ago. I'll admit that we do have a better rhythm during normal workweeks. Have you heard anything new about the murder?"

"They're hardly likely to tell me what they've found."

"So you're still suspect numero uno?" She stuck a Kitty Patty in the microwave to heat for a few seconds.

"As far as I know, unless Patrice has replaced me. Your Detective Olson questioned her for a long time this afternoon. I've just talked with her. She's not sure whether he's trying to pin the murder on her or whether he's trying to get her to say I did it."

"How could she be a suspect?"

"She's admitted being in the building. I think anyone who was ever there is on that guy's list. I heard your microwave ding. Are you about to have dinner?"

"No, that was Quince's treat." She set it in his dish and he *mrow*ed as he chomped on the Kitty Patty. She gave him only half of one, since he'd had so much to eat at the fair. She just couldn't deny him his treat completely.

"Is it too late for me to bring something over?"

"Depends on what it is."

"Pizza. And something else."

As soon as he came in the door, he reached his fist out to her, turned it over, and opened his fingers.

"My ring!" Chase cried with a huge grin.

"She knew right away what I was talking about and gave it to me. She says to tell you she's sorry."

"Is she?"

Mike shrugged. "That's hard to tell with my cousin. At any rate, I've warned her off taking anything else from you or Anna."

"She shouldn't steal anything from anyone!"

He slipped it onto the ring finger on her right hand. His fingers were warm and firm. Chase resisted the urge to reach out and stroke them. She pulled her hand back and dashed to the kitchen to get plates and paper towels so he wouldn't see her blushing furiously red.

A half hour later, she and Mike had devoured a medium pepperoni with olives and extra cheese and she was curled up on the soft leather couch beside him, wanting to rest her head on his sturdy chest. Quincy sprawled across both their laps, his eyes nearly closed while Mike stroked his head. Mike and Chase had discussed, round and round, who could have killed Larry Oake and why—and when. The "when" was the only thing they'd gotten very far with. It had to have been shortly before Mike entered the building. Unfortunately, he couldn't recall seeing anyone else there. In fact, he had made sure no one saw him go in, or so he thought. He knew he shouldn't be inside messing with that sculpture. Elsa Oake either opened the door at exactly the wrong time by coincidence, or she saw him go in and screamed to get attention and frame him.

"You know, Anna has been getting palsy-walsy with Elsa Oake. She refuses to see that she could very well have killed her husband."

Mike stiffened. "That doesn't sound like a good idea."

"That's what I told her. She's asked Elsa to move in with her until she can leave town."

Now Mike sat straight up. Quincy gave a huff of annoyance and jumped off the couch. "That's a terrible idea! Her house is becoming a hotel. Maybe I should loan her a large dog for protection if she's going to invite everyone to stay with her. She doesn't have any pets, does she?"

"No, she says Quincy is enough for her."

"Since you say she's the one who sneaks treats to him, it might be better that she doesn't have any pets."

"She will have one for a few days. Elsa's sister is driving here from Wisconsin and bringing Elsa's pet parrot. Apparently she misses it so much. They can't very well stay in a regular hotel with it. She's very attached to that bird, Anna says."

Mike shook his head. "And Anna's putting all of them up at her place?"

Chase nodded.

"She doesn't know Elsa at all, does she?"

"Not really. I tried to tell her that. She's never even seen the sister yet."

A few minutes after Mike walked out the door, still grumbling about Anna, Julie called. Chase glanced at her clock as she answered it. She needed to get to bed soon. But she would always make time for her best bud.

"Did I wake you up?" Julie asked, almost in a whisper.

"It's almost midnight. But no, I'm still up."

"Jay just left. We had the most dreamy evening."

Chase was about to say that Mike had just left, too, but Julie continued. "We talked and talked about what I should do. I liked real estate in law school. Jay thinks I should give that a try."

"Do you know anyone with a practice in that field?" Chase wiggled out of her jeans and sat on the edge of her bed.

"Sure. My school buddies all went into different areas. I think our own class covers the gamut of law practice. I'm going to call up a couple of them tomorrow."

"Sounds good. Have you talked to Anna today?"

"Briefly. I didn't quite understand, though. She's having a parrot stay at her house?"

"She is. The parrot's owner is staying there, too. And the sister."

"Why on earth?"

"The parrot's owner is Elsa Oake, who has been staying at the Crowne Plaza. Anna thinks it's perfectly fine to put them up. Elsa misses her pet, and since she can't leave town, her sister wants to come keep her company. She's driving here tomorrow with the bird. I think. Anyway—"

"Anyway, my grandmother is off her rocker! That woman probably killed her husband."

"Well, I think that, but Anna doesn't." Quincy seemed to have forgiven Chase for interrupting the earlier session with the two cozy laps. He climbed onto Chase's legs, now stretched out on the bed and clad in flannel.

"The television reporters seem to agree with you. They're starting to mention both her and Mike. Maybe I'll see if I can stay there while the suspect is bunking in."

"Anna doesn't have room enough for all those people and you, too, does she?"

"She doesn't have room for them without me, so what's the difference?"

"Do you know if Jay has gotten anyone to represent Mike yet?" Chase asked.

"No, but I have. We went to school with a little power-house of a guy named Gerrold Gustafson. I called him today, and he should be getting in touch with Mike soon. Gerry said there's nothing for him to do at the moment, though. As soon as they charge Mike, he'll go into action."

" 'As soon as they charge' him?"

"Oh. Yes. I mean *if* they charge him." There was a moment of silence on both ends of the conversation.

Chase contemplated what Julie had said and it gave her a chill inside. "You know, they only questioned him and released him."

"Let's face it, Chase. If you listen to the local news reports, it sounds like the cops think either Elsa Oake or Dr. Ramos did it."

"I'm not listening to the local news right now."

"Good idea."

They must not know about Patrice Youngren yet, Chase thought.

Chase had a restless night, worrying about Anna and her insistence on consorting with a murder suspect. She would try to talk her out of it tomorrow at the fair. For all the good that would do. Anna's stubbornness was almost a force of nature.

When Chase arrived at the Bar None booth, Elsa and her sister were there with Anna. The parrot didn't seem to be around. Chase saw the two women from the back and couldn't tell them apart. One wore a russet broomstick skirt, the other a bright blue one. As she came closer, they turned around and she still couldn't tell which one was which.

"Hi . . . Elsa," she said, looking from one to the other.

They both laughed. The one in the rust-colored broom skirt stepped forward. "Chase, this is my sister, Eleanor."

"Your identical twin sister?" Chase asked, shaking Eleanor's hand.

They both shook their heads. Eleanor spoke. "They say we're not identical, but many people disagree with that."

Chase moved behind the counter to stow her purse. She studied the two women. "I'll have to agree with the many people. I don't think I could tell you apart."

"We have different allergies," said Elsa.

"I don't really have allergies, Elsie," said the one in the blue skirt.

"Oh, you don't have allergies. You just sneeze at every other thing, Ellie."

Elsie and Ellie! This is going to be confusing, thought Chase. She decided she would call them Elsa and Eleanor. Maybe she wouldn't have to call them anything if she never saw them again.

"Bye, Anna," said Elsa. "We're going to go see Grey."

Both women swished away, their skirts swirling around their cowgirl boots.

Chase gave Anna a blank look. "Who's Grey?"

"That's the parrot. She's a sweetheart. Her name is Lady Jane Grey, but Elsa and Eleanor call her Grey."

"She's alone in your house? Is she in a cage?"

"No, she's with Dr. Ramos. She was at the house last night."

"He's going to have to start charging boarding fees, poor guy. Everyone is dumping their pets on him."

"Only you and Elsa, right?"

"And a black cat that is usually there."

The weather was much colder and there didn't seem to be nearly as many people at the fair today. Maybe Wednesday was Hump Day here, just like in an office—and at the Bar None store. The plug-in heater made the booth toasty, but even that didn't draw people in as it had before. The people simply weren't there to be drawn in.

After an hour of meager sales, Chase's cell rang. It was in her purse under the table. She dove for it and fished it out as it quit ringing.

"Who was it?" asked Anna.

"Inger. I'll call her back." But Chase didn't get an answer when she tried and Inger hadn't left a message. She worried about her friend for the rest of the morning.

At lunchtime, Bill Shandy, Anna's recent fiancé, strolled up the aisle and turned in to the Bar None.

"How's my favorite baker?"

Anna answered with a brilliant smile and a hug. Bill was a few inches taller than Anna, which, given Anna's small stature, put him only at medium height. His curly gray hair was a match in color for Anna's, but a patch was missing at his crown. His bushy mustache made up for the baldness on top. Chase liked Bill. It occurred to her that she should appeal to him for help getting Anna away from Elsa and her coterie.

"Do you want to see the parrot?" Anna asked Bill. She said to Chase, "I told him about Lady Jane Grey, and he said he'd like to see her."

Bill owned a pet store near their Dinktytown treat shop. His family had gone through an ordeal recently, and Chase thought Bill had handled his wacky relatives with infinite patience and grace. He and Anna had become closer during that time, and Chase was glad they had each other. Anna hadn't shown any interest in a man since her beloved husband had passed away several years ago. Chase loved to see the romance blossoming between them.

"Go ahead," Chase said. "I'll be fine here if you both want to head over to the vet clinic."

"I think I want to meet the parrot's owner as much as I want to meet the parrot," Bill said.

If Anna hadn't been there, that would have been the perfect entrance for Chase to bring up the subject of Elsa. She put out a feeler, which was all she could do.

"Do you know that they're all staying at Anna's? Elsa, the parrot, and Elsa's twin sister?"

"Yes, she told me, but I haven't had a chance to meet any of them."

"Elsa is the one whose husband was murdered here," Chase added.

"Poor woman." Bill shook his head in sympathy.

When Chase frowned slightly at that, he raised his eyebrows in question.

"I don't know how poor she is. The insurance settlement should be hefty."

"Charity!" Anna finally joined in. "That's no way to talk. Bill, Charity thinks Elsa might have been the one who killed Larry Oake." She took off her Bar None smock, crammed it under the table, donned her parka, and headed for the midway.

"I'm not the only one who thinks that way," Chase said. "The police have told Elsa not to leave town."

Anna kept going. Bill looked back at Chase long enough for her to mouth the words "call me" and then followed Anna.

THIRTEEN

After Bill and Anna got back from seeing Eleanor's parrot, Bill took his leave with a quick kiss on the lips while Chase looked the other direction, smiling.

"Did you ever get hold of Inger?" Anna asked, coming around the table and tying on her smock.

"No, and I'm worried. Maybe her parents changed their minds and kicked her out again."

"Already?" Anna said. "It's only been a day."

"I know. Do you get the feeling that it's more her mother or her father having the problem with her being pregnant?"

"I don't really know. I haven't met either one of them. Come to think of it, don't you think it's a little strange that they have never come to the shop to see where their daughter works?"

"Now that you mention it, yes. You didn't meet them, did you, when you took Inger home from your place?"

"No, I just dropped her off." Anna frowned, thinking. "I don't remember the exact address, but we have it on file in the office. Maybe you could stop by their place and try to see what's going on."

"Good idea. I can meet the parents, if they're there."

"Are you going to call first?"

"No, I think I'll drop by. If all three are there, maybe I can get a feel for the family dynamics. If not, I'll talk to whoever is home."

"I don't suppose you can convince the Uhlgrens to go easy on their daughter." At that point, the first of a steady stream of customers interrupted the conversation.

Chase thought it would be a miracle if she could sway the minds of two people she had never before met concerning a family matter that was probably none of her business. But she knew she should try.

When she was working in Chicago, one of her fellow waitresses got pregnant. The young woman's mother was very hard on her but didn't kick her out of the family home. After the baby was born, the mother fell in love with her precious granddaughter. Chase felt that's the way it ought to work when there was no father to share the burden with the new mother, like with Inger's intended getting killed in war and not coming back. Families should support each other. What would she do without hers? If her own parents hadn't made a will naming Anna as her guardian, she would surely have been made a ward of the state when they died. She shuddered to think of what some of those poor kids went through, being sent to homes where they weren't really wanted and weren't understood. There were some excellent foster parents, she was sure. You only ever heard about the ones who were . . . not excellent. But what if she had ended up with, well, anyone but Anna?

Overcome with the gratitude welling up inside her, Chase reached over and gave Anna a quick hug. Anna smiled in surprise and they both kept working.

When Chase went to get Quincy at the end of the day, Mike, in the small outer room, was deep in conversation on his cell phone, his face expressionless. It sounded serious, so she gave him a finger wave and went to the examining room. Quincy rose, stretched his front legs, curling his pink tongue as far out of his mouth as he could, then straightened each back leg.

"You've been a lazybones today, haven't you?" Chase said. "Sleeping your life away. I can hardly blame you. It's pretty boring in here." She unlatched the cage and lifted Quincy into his carrier.

"Boring in here," said a raspy voice behind her.

She whirled around. No one was there. Ah, but Elsa's parrot was in a cage on a shelf.

"Hi there," Chase said, walking over to the shelf.

"Hi there," mimicked the bird.

"Are you Lady Jane Grey?"

"Lady Jane Grey, Lady Jane Grey, Lady Jane Grey." The parrot flapped her soft gray wings, ducking her head and wiggling her red tail feathers.

"I guess you'll be going home with Anna." Chase

caught herself and froze for a moment, then laughed. Was she having a conversation with a bird? She told the animal, "Bye bye."

"Bye bye," Grey replied.

Chase giggled at herself and left the room.

Mike was still talking, frowning and shaking his head slightly. She didn't think he noticed her leaving. She would find out what was going on eventually, she hoped.

As she drove, she decided to call Bill Shandy first, as soon as she got home, then go to Inger's family's place and see what she could find out there. She was sure of one thing. Inger should not move back in with Anna. Anna was full up.

Bill answered on the first ring. "I thought you'd call about now, when the fair let out."

Chase settled into her cinnamon-hued stuffed chair with a cup of steaming-hot tea.

"What was that all about at the fair?" he asked. "You were obviously trying to tell me something."

"Bill, I'm worried about Anna." She sipped, savoring the hint of jasmine in her drink.

"You think she's overdoing it, letting Elsa and her sister stay with her? She's doing fine, really."

Chase laughed. "No, not worried about that. I don't think that woman will ever run out of energy." She grew serious. "I'm worried that she's consorting with a murder suspect." Quincy leapt softly into Chase's lap.

"Hm. I guess you could be right."

"What if Elsa is the one who killed Larry Oake? The spouse is always the most likely culprit, according to the mysteries I read." Quincy butted the hand that held her mug, but Chase managed to keep the tea from spilling into her lap.

"Frankly, I don't see her as a murderess. You think she killed him?"

"I have no clue, but if she did, I hate the idea of Anna hanging around with her. Why don't you think she's guilty?"

"Her own parrot. Anyone who's nice to pets is a good person in my book. Lady Jane Grey is well taken care of and in very good health."

Chase had to laugh. "I guess that makes sense, coming from a pet shop owner."

"Besides," Bill added, "even if she did kill her husband, she's probably not a danger to anyone else. Anna's not involved in their family matters. There had to have been a trigger, something the killer was passionate about. Otherwise Oake wouldn't have been killed right there. It was a risky thing. The killer could easily have been caught if someone walked in at the wrong time." Maybe Bill read mysteries, too.

"I sure hope you're right."

Chase didn't feel that much better about what Anna was doing after she hung up. Bill hadn't convinced her that Elsa didn't kill her husband. Just that the killer was a daring person, able to take risks. Distracted, she plopped her cup on the side table and stood up. Quincy, who had been curled into a ball and comfy in her lap, protested the loss of his resting place with an annoyed *mrow*. He then stalked to his bowl and licked the remnants of his din din.

"Sorry, Quince. I forgot you were there." She rubbed his head as she passed, on her way downstairs to look up Inger's address.

When she got to the address in Hopkins, she found a white clapboard ranch house with a driveway and a neat front yard. One large maple tree stood sentinel smack-dab in the middle, and trimmed bushes nestled close to the house. Chase left her car at the curb and climbed the three steps to the small front porch.

A red-faced man answered her second ring. He frowned at Chase.

"I'm here to speak to Inger," she said. "I'm Chase Oli—"

"Inger isn't here." His voice was gruff and his frown menacing.

A small woman with wispy, graying hair appeared behind him. "Roger, let her in. She might know something."

He gave Chase an annoyed look but opened the door wide.

Chase stepped into a wood-floored living room heated by a large brick fireplace. The space was furnished with matching yellow-and-orange chairs and a couch, and softened with brown area rugs. The woman motioned Chase to the couch, and the couple sat facing her in the chairs. The room smelled of lemony furniture polish.

"What do you know about Inger?" demanded the man.

"Roger, let me." The woman's voice was soft, but

commanding. "How do you know our daughter? You said your name is Chase?"

"Yes, Chase Oliver. I'm her employer?" Had Inger never told her parents the name of her boss? "You do know she works for me, don't you?"

They both gave her blank looks.

"At the Bar None."

"You own the Bar None?" Roger sounded incredulous. "You look too young to be a business owner."

Chase was going to ignore his rudeness. "Inger called me earlier today and now I can't get in touch with her. She doesn't answer her phone and I'm worried about her." *Knowing that you people kicked her out once*, she added mentally. Chase had tried to call Inger again before she set out, but it rang to her voice mail. She didn't leave a message, not having any idea what to say.

"We're worried, too," the woman said, twisting the edge of her cardigan into a knot. "She's disappeared. We have no idea where she is."

"Have you tried her friends?"

The couple exchanged looks. The woman answered. Apparently, Roger was going to let her handle this, as she had requested. "We don't know any of her friends. Inger is a very private person."

"She's shy," added her father. "Doesn't run around much."

"She spent all her time with Zack, until . . ."

"Until he was killed overseas." Roger finished her sentence as his wife became too choked up to speak.

"No friends? None at all?" Chase wondered what that would be like. Poor Inger.

"Maybe." The woman looked doubtful. "But we don't know any of them."

"How long ago did she leave?"

They both shrugged. They apparently didn't keep track of their daughter any better than they communicated with her.

On her drive back to Dinkytown, she dialed Inger's number twice more but got no answer either time. Chase shed a few tears for poor, lonely Inger.

FOURTEEN

Distracted by worries about Inger, and wondering how on earth to go about finding her, Chase trudged up the stairs to her apartment. It was getting late. She hoped Inger had found shelter somewhere, in her condition.

The door opened wide and no one stuck a foot in it so that the cat wouldn't get out. He scampered through the opening and down the stairs, ignoring his name being called behind him. The tabby reached the bottom of the stairs, zipped through the door to the Bar None kitchen, and made a bee-line for the front salesroom. When he got there, he slowed. He padded silently to the figure huddled in the corner, behind the sales counter, sobbing. He rubbed against her legs, which

were bent against her body. She was clutching her shins tightly but let go and reached one hand out to stroke the cat's soft back.

"There you are!" Chase flicked on the light switch when she heard Quincy's loud purr. Then she saw Inger. "There you *both* are." Her voice quavered with her sudden relief.

Chase dropped to the floor beside Inger. The young woman raised her head, and Chase saw that her gray eyes were red-rimmed, her face awash in tears. Chase couldn't help letting some slide down her own cheeks. She stroked Inger's curly, tangled hair and Inger leaned against her.

They sat on the floor behind the counter like that for at least fifteen minutes.

Someone rapped on the front window. Chase jumped up but couldn't see outside. The lights inside threw her own reflection back at her and obscured whoever was knocking against the glass. She flicked off the light, gave herself a few seconds to adjust, then walked to the front.

The person outside was lit from behind, but Chase could tell it was Julie. She unlocked the door and let her in, being careful to keep Quincy, who had followed her, corralled.

"I saw the light and thought I'd better check to make sure everything is okay. You're not supposed to be open now." Julie bent to rub Quincy's head. "Jay and I had dinner, then talked and talked. Do you mind if I come up?"

Chase hesitated and threw a glance behind her. Inger was still on the floor, out of sight.

"Is something wrong?" Julie started to look alarmed.

"No, no, nothing's wrong with me. Our employee, Inger, is having some problems."

"I'll be all right, Ms. Oliver." Inger rose, sniffing daintily, and appeared behind the counter. She clutched the edge of it with white knuckles.

"Let's all go upstairs and get something warm to drink," Chase said, rushing to stand beside Inger in case she fell. She looked so wobbly on her feet.

"Oh dear." Julie, who had no idea what was happening, came to the counter and pushed Inger's blonde curls out of her wan face. A few strands stuck to her damp cheeks and Julie swiped at those, too.

When they reached the apartment, Inger staggered to a stool in the kitchen. "You'll need something to eat, I suspect," Chase said. "Have you had anything since breakfast?"

"I didn't really have anything then."

Chase whipped up a peanut butter and jelly sandwich and put it on a plate with some carrot sticks. From the way Inger wolfed everything down, Chase wondered if she had eaten yesterday. She put another sandwich together.

Julie had been heating up some cider while Chase made the sandwiches. She nudged Chase in the side. "Inger, you don't look too steady on the stool," she said, nodding toward the living room. Chase took the hint and helped Inger off her precarious seat.

After they were all three seated in the living room with mugs of hot apple cider, Quincy stood on the floor, looking from lap to lap. His tail twitched twice, then he jumped into Inger's. It heartened Chase to see her smile down on the little guy.

"Inger is having some family problems," Chase told Julie, not knowing if she should air them in front of Julie. She looked at Inger, who nodded.

"It's okay. You can tell her," Inger mumbled, taking quick sips of the cider, and keeping her eyes on Quincy.

"I . . . I'm not sure what's going on myself, Inger. When I couldn't call you today, I went to your house. Your parents said you were missing."

"Why should I tell them where I go and what I do? They don't care."

Chase had a feeling she was right. It still made her heart ache to hear Inger say it. "Did you have a quarrel?"

"Kind of. I'm trying to pick names for my baby. So, over the last few days, I've been looking at names online and collected a few that I like. At breakfast today I tried to ask my parents which ones they like. They don't even care. Not one little bit."

Inger snuffled and Chase ran to the kitchen to get her a tissue. Inger swiped at her nose and looked Chase in the eyes. "They just ate their stupid oatmeal and went off to work. They always have oatmeal. I hate oatmeal. I can't live with them. I hate them." Chase saw the deep, raw emotion in her eyes. How could her parents treat her that way?

"They're still mad at me for getting pregnant. They don't say it in so many words. But they do other hateful things."

Quincy, who wasn't getting petted at the moment, looked up at Inger. She smiled down and resumed stroking. "You're so cute, Quincy. I wish I had a cat."

"Chase, can I talk to you for a moment?" Julie motioned Chase into the kitchen. She pulled her to the corner and whispered, "She can't stay with those horrible people. Can you keep her here?"

"Until her baby comes? That's a long time."

"I know, but I think she needs some therapy, and Quincy is giving it to her."

Chase looked into her living room. Inger's head was bent over the cat again, and she could hear his purr from where she stood. "I suppose I could give it a try. I do agree that the atmosphere in her house is terrible."

"Did they seem worried about her?"

"Well, yes, they did. But they don't know any of her friends and didn't even know my name. I think they barely know where she's working."

Julie rubbed her chin. "I'll tell you what. I'm staying at Anna's while those murder suspects are there—"

"Only one is a suspect."

"True. But that's one too many. Anyway, my condo is empty. She could stay there if this doesn't work out."

"This is all temporary. You're not moving in with Anna, are you?"

"No, not forever. Let's do this for now. Let her stay here for a bit. I think the poor girl could use Quincy's pet therapy."

Chase nodded. Who knew what would happen over the next few days? She could leave Quincy in the apartment and not have to keep him in the cage at the fair. This would work very well until after Sunday, when the fair ended.

Then Inger could stay at Julie's, or maybe they would

find another place for her. She might even find her own place. Inger was so depressed, and Chase thought that if she roused from that, she would be able to function better.

That night, Chase gave Inger her own bed and slept on the couch. She loved her leather couch, but in the morning decided she loved it for sitting and for lounging only, not for sleeping. The blankets kept slipping around on the slick leather. She woke up once with her face plastered against the cushion. Her hair was sweaty and sticky and she had drooled on the seat. Maybe she should have gotten a suede couch. The covers might have stayed in place then.

In the morning, she stumbled through making coffee. Inger emerged from the bedroom as it finished brewing. She looked sick.

"Oh dear, is that coffee?" She ran into the bathroom to throw up.

When Inger returned to the kitchen, Chase asked her what she'd like for breakfast.

"Do you have tea and toast?"

"Yes, indeed." Chase stuck two pieces of bread into the toaster. I have Earl Grey and Irish Breakfast." She rummaged in the cupboard for more jasmine tea, but she must have finished it up last night.

"No green tea?"

Chase held down her irritation and her thoughts: *Don't you think I would have mentioned it if I had it?* "I have Earl Grey and Irish Breakfast tea," she repeated. "Do you eat whole wheat toast?"

"Not usually. But it's okay. I can eat it today. I'll take the Irish Breakfast."

Chase put the breakfast together hastily and left as soon as she could. Before she could discover that Inger didn't like the brand of margarine she used. The last thing she had expected was that Inger would be a difficult houseguest. She had to admit, she herself was extra crabby from sleeping on the uncomfortable couch.

This was Thursday. The fair would be over Sunday. She could put up with Inger for four days. After that, other arrangements would have to be made. She hoped the Wisconsin women with their bird would be gone from Anna's and that Julie would be back in her own place by then.

FIFTEEN

As Chase walked toward her booth with two cups of steaming coffee for her and Anna, just before opening time, she passed the travel agency booth and heard sobbing from inside. She paused for a moment.

"Do you need any help?" she asked, taking one tentative step inside.

The cute short redhead blinked at Chase, tears streaming down her freckled cheeks. "My mother called just as I was leaving. Couldn't get her calmed down." She looked between her partner and Chase. "She's prone to fake heart attacks. All I can do is talk to her until she thinks she's over it."

"Another visit to the emergency room?" asked the blonde, who had just arrived.

"No, I convinced her to see her regular doctor later

today." The redhead dashed a hand at her tears and leaned down to retrieve some pamphlets from a box. "But, somehow, it always makes me feel guilty when she does this and I don't rush to be with her."

"She's manipulating you," the tall blonde said, patting her partner's shoulder. She wore a ring on each finger again.

"What if she does go to the hospital? I don't want to leave you alone here."

The blonde shrugged. "You do what you have to do, Holly. If you think you have to go to her, then . . ."

The redhead smiled and the storm seemed over.

"Will you be all right?" Chase asked. She felt like a fifth wheel, standing at their booth, learning secrets she had no business knowing.

"Thanks for being concerned." The redhead seemed recovered. "She's right." She nodded at her partner. "I'll just do what I have to do."

"I hope your day goes well," Chase called as she went toward her own booth with the coffee. The blonde, as usual, was wearing a lot of bling. Did that mean she really, really liked diamonds? Would she be tempted to steal a diamond collar?

Chase and Anna got a chance to gulp down most of the strong coffee before the customers started coming.

When there was a break at the Bar None booth shortly before lunchtime, Chase ran down to talk with Mike. Luckily, he had no patients in the clinic.

"I know you're not a people doctor," Chase began.

"I am definitely not a people doctor." He continued putting stainless steel gizmos into the sterilizer.

"But people are mammals."

He turned to face her. "It's a question of licensing and legalities."

"Like in losing your license, right?"

"Among other things." He went back to preparing the machine, twisting dials and pushing buttons.

"But you could never lose your license from anything you told me."

"Come on. Sit down and tell me what your problem is." He waved her to a chair in the corner and pulled one up facing her as the autoclave began to hiss.

The glossy black cat hissed, too.

Mike chuckled. "He does that every time I run it. It annoys him, I think. Okay, what do you need?"

"It's my houseguest, Inger."

"Yes? Isn't she seeing a doctor? An ob-gyn?"

"She saw someone at a clinic. I don't know if she'll go back—I hope so. But she needs another kind. I'm not sure exactly which kind."

"Because?"

"She's depressed. At least that's what I think."

"How is she behaving?"

"Weepy, sad, and she's hard to get along with." Chase gritted her teeth as she said the last part.

Mike reached over and took Chase's hand. "Try to imagine what she's going through. She's alone in the world, about to have a child. She probably has no idea what to do with it once it's born. Her parents aren't any help at all. In fact, they're piling on top of her problem stack, from what little you've told me. Wouldn't you be a little cranky?"

"Yes, of course. But I think she's having trouble coping and could need some professional help."

"You might be right about that. Let me call around tonight and see if I can find someone for her to see."

"Someone who doesn't cost much."

"Yes, I agree."

As she strolled back to the booth, munching on a taco from the food court, it occurred to her that she didn't have a good excuse anymore to see Dr. Ramos during the day, since Quincy wasn't there. She wasn't exactly glad that Inger was having problems, but it at least gave her a reason to visit him.

As she approached the booth, she saw Detective Olson walk inside it. She waited outside, quietly, behind the opening flap, to see what he wanted. She could see his back as he looked over the displayed wares. Anna jumped up from the chair when she spotted him.

"What's the best?" he asked Anna.

He was there to buy dessert bars?

Anna suggested Hula Bars, of course, and pointed out the Pink Lemonade Bars and the Margarita Cheesecake. He asked for two Hula Bars and one each of the other two. He was buying treats, all right, but Chase didn't think that's why he was there.

"Is Ms. Oliver around?" he asked.

"She's out for a few minutes. She'll be right back."

Chase moved back a step to be sure Anna couldn't see her.

"Good," he said. "I want to talk to you."

Chase almost dropped her taco. Why on earth did he

want to question Anna? He couldn't believe she had anything to do with Larry Oake's death.

"It's come to my attention that you're housing one of our . . . a person of interest in the Oake murder case."

Was he about to say Elsa was a suspect?

Anna must have nodded because Chase didn't hear an answer.

"I want to make sure," he continued, his voice so low Chase had to strain to hear the words, "that you know to be very careful."

"Careful about what?" Anna sounded alarmed.

"Careful in case she's dangerous."

"To me? Why would she be dangerous to me?"

"Let's say that I don't think it's a good idea for her to be staying with you."

"But she can't find a hotel that will take a parrot."

"Huh?"

Chase almost giggled. She could picture the puzzlement on his normally composed, self-assured, clean-cut face.

"Her sister brought Elsa's parrot, Lady Jane Grey, when she came from Wisconsin."

"Lady Jane Grey?" He seemed to drawl and sneer a bit when he repeated the name.

"I think it's a fine name." Anna was bristling, Chase could tell. "She's an African Grey."

"Uh-huh. But that's quite an imposition on you, isn't it?"

"Not really. I'm not there most of the day."

"What do I owe you?" Chase heard the rustle of a paper bag.

"Oh, for the dessert bars? They're on the house."

It sounded like he was leaving, so Chase sauntered into the booth. Maybe she could find out if he knew about the Minskys. Detective Olson handed Anna a few bills. She tried to wave them away, but he put them on the table.

"Hi, Detective Olson. It's good to see you. You like those Hula Bars?"

"I don't know. I haven't tried them yet. They look good. I'm glad you're back." He motioned to a uniformed policewoman standing in the midway. "Since you're both here at the same time, it makes this easier. I'm very sorry, but we have to do this."

Before Chase could even open her mouth to protest, the policewoman had thoroughly patted her down. Detective Olson and another policeman who had materialized out of nowhere proceeded to open and go through every box in the booth. After the woman patted Anna down, she left and the other uniform left shortly afterward. They were extremely efficient in their search. It had taken only a few minutes.

Chase caught her breath and got her mind into gear before Detective Olson could follow them out to the midway. "Wait just a minute. Am I a suspect now? Why are you searching me and Anna now?"

He paused. "We got a new anonymous tip on the valuable article that's missing. It might still be on the fairgrounds. We're not just searching you, we're searching everyone. Keep your eyes open and you'll see that." He started to walk away again.

Chase was getting annoyed. "Wait. I want to talk to you about Karl Minsky. And his daughter."

"Mara."

"Yes."

"Did you know that he quarreled with Larry Oake the morning of the murder?"

"Why do you think that?" Those dark blue eyes narrowed at her. Did he not believe her?

It was Chase's turn to bristle. "I'm not just trying to get Dr. Ramos off the hook. I talked to Minsky and his daughter the other day. She was very upset because it happened outside the exhibition hall. She's afraid a lot of people might have seen them, and I'll bet she's right."

He looked upward for a second, considering. "I think we'll look into that. Thanks for the information."

After he left, Chase let her breath out. Maybe something would come of questioning the Minskys that could clear Mike. She sure hoped so.

SIXTEEN

C hase picked up the money Detective Olson had left on the table and added it to their cash box.

"That was nice of him to pay, wasn't it, Charity, after I said I would give them to him?" Anna must have gotten over the parrot insults and the pat-down and search quickly. "So what are you thinking?"

"I think that it's very possible Karl Minsky is the one who killed Larry Oake."

A shadow fell across the table. The bulky form of Karl Minsky inched into the booth.

"You'd better watch your mouth, young lady," he snarled at Chase.

Her initial reaction was to cower, but she squashed the

impulse and stood as tall as her five-foot-five frame would let her.

He came closer and loomed over her, at least a foot taller. His menacing scowl hit her in her clenched stomach, but she wouldn't let him know that.

"You were eavesdropping on me and Mara?"

"No. But you were eavesdropping just now. Does the detective know you were there?"

"He never saw me."

Chase wondered about that. The man was hard to miss. "If you didn't harm Mr. Oake, then you have nothing to worry about."

"Except busybodies like you poking their noses into my affairs and stirring things up." He shook his meaty fist inches from her nose. "I'm warning you." Then he stomped off down the midway toward the butter sculpture building.

"I think you'd better tell Detective Olson about this, too," Anna said. "That man is threatening you."

"I think I will. But Karl Minsky has to get far, far away first."

Chase waited until an influx of dessert bar buyers had bought their fill, then she poked her head out of the booth and looked up and down the midway to make sure Karl Minsky wasn't anywhere in sight. It would be hard to miss him if he were there. His daughter, though, would be easier to overlook. Chase looked carefully. No, Mara wasn't around. She stepped to the back of the booth and called Detective Olson. He didn't answer. All that preparation for nothing! She left a message that she had new information for him and went back to working the booth.

As the end of the day approached, Anna started fidgeting.

"Everything okay, Anna?" Chase asked.

"Sure. Hunky-dory."

As she said it, though, the worry lines didn't leave her brow.

"Say, if you don't mind, I'll do the baking tonight," Anna said.

"I don't mind, but I'll be happy to help out."

"No, don't bother. I can do it."

Chase knew she could, but why didn't she want help?

After they closed up and got everything packed to go, Anna took the leftovers and the cash box and rushed out. Chase was chatting with the travel agents next door when Anna left. The short one's mother hadn't had another crisis, and she was in a cheerful mood. Chase wondered what her relationship with her own mother would be like today if she hadn't died so young. A lot of time had gone by and the pain of losing her parents had faded. In fact, some days she didn't think about them at all. But when grown children didn't get along with their own parents, it made her sad, made her wish hers were still alive.

Chase stepped back into the booth to check that everything was wrapped up. There was Anna's cell phone on the table. Chase reached to pick it up just as it rang, nearly sending her through the roof of the tent. Her nerves were on edge all the time here, knowing a murderer might be lurking anywhere.

"Yes?" The light was too dim for her to check the number.

"Anna?" said the voice on the phone.

She was almost certain it was Bill Shandy. "No. Is this Bill?" He said it was. "Anna left her phone in our booth. I'll take it to her, since she's baking tonight."

"That's what I'm calling about. Tell her I'll be a little late. Not too bad, maybe a half an hour."

Late for what? Chase wondered. Was the pet shop owner helping her bake? Maybe the man had hidden talents. Bill had given Anna an engagement ring in September, thrilling Anna, Chase, and Julie. Chase thought he was a catch and a good match for Anna. Every time her eye caught the sparkle of Anna's diamond, it cheered her heart.

As Chase walked to her car, she pulled her jacket close. A colder front must be coming through, she thought. Fall was progressing toward winter in Minnesota.

The temperature kept dropping perceptibly from the time she left the tent to the time she reached her car, and the wind whipped her hair into her face. She spat out a strand, scooted into the driver's seat of her Ford Fusion, started the engine, and cranked up the heat.

Halfway to the dessert bar shop, Chase realized that she didn't know if Anna was going home first or to the shop. She called the shop, but there was no answer. Maybe Anna was going past her own house first. Chase would swing by there to make sure she had her phone. It wasn't that far out of her way. She took the next left and circled the block to turn around.

A few miles later, Anna's phone rang again. This time it was Julie.

"Jules? This is Chase. Anna forgot her phone. Is she home yet?"

"I don't think she's coming here. She told me she would go straight to the kitchen." Julie's voice sounded strained.

"Are you cold?"

"Yes. I'm in the backyard so those women won't hear me."

"Elsa and her sister?"

"Yes, Elsie and Ellie. Stupid, confusing nicknames. I can't ever remember which is which. Chase, I'm not sure I want to be alone with them. Can you come over and keep me company?"

"Well, Inger is at my place right now."

"Oh, right. I forgot. Why don't you bring her? Pick up Chinese or something."

"Why don't you want to be alone with them?"

"I don't know. It's a feeling I get. For one thing, they're expecting me to cook for them."

"Really? They should be taking Anna out to dinner."

This time Chase slowed, let traffic pass her by, then swung out and made a U-turn, heading back to her place.

Anna wasn't in the kitchen downstairs, but Inger was pacing the living room floor in the apartment upstairs. Quincy crouched at the edge of the seat on the stuffed chair, swiveling his head to keep track of Inger's movements, looking uneasy about this unsettled person in his space.

"Where have you been?" Inger demanded when she saw Chase.

"I've been at the fair, you know that. I'm not that much later than usual. I had to . . . make a few turns on my way home."

"Turns?"

"We're going to Anna's house for dinner. You need to get your coat on."

"I'm awfully hungry." The woman was whining. Chase wondered if her parents had been looking for a reason to kick her out. No, that was extremely uncharitable. The poor gal was probably beside herself with worry about her future. And was probably also pretty darn hungry.

Chase put a cheese sandwich together and slipped some carrot sticks in a plastic bag.

"Here, eat this on the way. It'll tide you over."

Inger regarded the offering in Chase's outstretched hand with suspicion, or maybe distaste, pursing her small mouth like a pouting child.

"Do you like cheese? Carrots?"

"I guess so."

Chase swallowed a retort that had to do with thanking people and being gracious. Her situation must be getting to her, Chase thought. Or maybe there's a bit of her parents in her? Did pregnancy give women mood swings? This wasn't like her, at all, but Chase didn't know how much more of the bad behavior she wanted to take. After giving Quincy his din dins, they trundled down the stairs and headed for Chase's car to drive to Anna's house. She still hadn't shown up at the Bar None.

SEVENTEEN

Chase sat back in the kitchen chair and wondered why the two sisters didn't dry up and blow away. They had hardly touched the Chinese food she had picked up . . . and paid for. The parrot, however, should soon be waddling like a penguin. They fed tidbits, almost nonstop, to Lady Jane Grey, who perched on a corner of the table, chattering with Elsa.

"Who's your baby?" rasped the bird. "Hello. Hello. Grey hungry. Grey hungry."

Elsa laughed every time the parrot opened her beak, then she pushed another morsel across the table to her.

Chase eyed the trails of sauce and grease this was leaving on Anna's table. At least it was the rustic, scarred kitchen table and not her nice maple dining room one.

And the parrot did make her smile, she had to admit. Such a silly bird!

Julie said the twin sisters had told her they hadn't eaten all day. Then they asked her to cook for them, and after Julie had come from a long day at work.

Inger made up for the sparse appetites of Elsa and Eleanor and cleaned out two cartons by herself.

"Eating for two." Julie smiled at Inger and held out the egg rolls to her.

"Eating for two, eating for two," echoed Grey.

Chase laughed out loud. That bird was cute.

"No, I think that's it," Inger said. "I'm stuffed." She turned to Chase. "Thanks for getting this. Sorry I was snippy before. I was so hungry."

"Hungry, hungry," cawed the bird, who flew to the kitchen counter.

"You can feel free to help yourself to anything in my kitchen during the day," Chase said.

Inger got a pained look on her face. "There's not much there that I like."

Chase decided to help clean up so she wouldn't say something to Inger she would regret. She jumped up to carry the plates to Anna's sink.

"I wonder if Anna ever made it to the shop," Julie said.

Chase winced. "I should have left her phone there. I wish I had thought of that." She got out her own phone and called the office at the Bar None.

Bill Shandy answered on the fifth ring. "Bar None. Best little shop in Minneapolis, bar none."

Chase chuckled. "I wanted to check that Anna made it okay. I still have her phone."

"I'll put her on," he said.

"Hi there." Anna sounded much more relaxed than she had been when she'd left the fair.

"Everything okay? I have your cell. I guess Bill told you?"

"Yes, he did. Where are you and Inger?"

"We're at your place. We had dinner with Julie and your houseguests."

"I'm glad you came over. I think those women are driving Julie nuts. Just leave my phone at the house. I'll get it tonight. We'll talk later. I have some news."

The three retired to Anna's pastel living room while Julie and Chase finished cleaning up. When the two younger women joined the sisters and Inger, Elsa asked if there was any coffee.

Chase thought she could see steam rising from the top of Julie's head. "That's a great idea," she said. "Would you like to go out and get some?"

"It's late," Eleanor said. "You'd better stay in, Elsie."

"I suppose so." She had the nerve to look put-upon because Chase and Julie weren't acting as her minions. "Oh, Chase. I almost forgot to ask you if you saw that other sculptor today."

"Which one? Most of them are still there, working on their pieces for the contest on Sunday."

"That Cardiman person. I couldn't help but wonder if he had the nerve to show up."

"I don't think he's still around. I heard he quit the competition and left town."

Elsa straightened in her chair. "I knew it. He's fled, running from the police."

"Not exactly." But was he? Did they know where he was? "He decided not to compete."

"And why would he decide that? No, he has run away because he murdered my husband. And now I suppose the police won't be able to track him down."

Driving home with Inger, Chase pondered Elsa's accusation. It seemed to come out of the blue. As if she was trying to incriminate him. And why would she do that? To throw suspicion off herself?

The sound of Inger softly snoring in the passenger seat came to her. Was there a bit of a bump under the seat belt? Maybe not. It should be too early to show. Chase tried to put herself in Inger's position.

It wasn't a crime to fall in love. It wasn't a crime to love the guy without protection, although it wasn't very smart. Everything would have worked out for the best if he hadn't been sent overseas. Even then, things could have turned out well if he hadn't been killed. Chase reflected that the real bad actors here were Inger's hard-hearted parents. How could they abandon their daughter at a time like this? Chase felt a swelling of protectiveness. She glanced over at Inger's pretty face, slack in her sleep, her small mouth slightly parted, her gray eyes hidden behind her pale eyelids. She determined to find out what Inger's favorite foods were and make sure the apartment was stocked with them. It was the least she could do.

Inger awoke when the car stopped behind the shop. She stretched and yawned.

"That was a good idea. The food was great. Thanks so much, Ms. Oliver."

"You can call me Chase."

They walked toward the back door, and Chase noticed that the light was on in the kitchen. She saw that both Anna's blue Volvo and Bill's SUV were parked near the door.

Inger went straight up the stairs, pleading exhaustion. It was after eleven, heading toward midnight, and she would open the shop alone tomorrow morning. Chase knocked on the door to the kitchen, unsure of what the newly engaged couple would be doing.

Bill's hearty voice told her to come in. He was perched on a stool at the granite counter, and Anna was up to her elbows in soap suds at the sink.

"Come here and help me dry these and put them away," Anna said. "Bill, you'd better go. It's late."

Bill tried to hide his yawn behind his fist but failed.

"Go, Bill," Chase said. "I'll help Anna finish up here."

He gave Anna a peck on the cheek as he passed. She answered him with a radiant smile that crinkled the corners of her eyes.

"What's up?" Chase asked, grabbing a towel. "Why were you so antsy all day?"

"I was nervous because, well, yesterday I saw this great deal for a space for the wedding and reception. So last night I went ahead and booked it without consulting Bill. I guess I'm so used to making my own decisions, I completely forgot that he might like to have some input."

"Anna! You've set a date? And you didn't tell me?"

"I haven't told anyone. We had some tentative dates, but they depended on what we could book and when."

"And when is the date?"

"December. I got the hall for Christmas Eve."

Chase gave Anna a fierce hug. "I'm so happy for you. Does Julie know?"

"I told you. No. All day I've dreaded telling Bill about it. What if he got upset with me?"

"My married guy friends hate that sort of thing," Chase said. "They would rather let their brides deal with it."

"That's Bill. He's fine with whatever I want, he said." Anna gave the ceiling a dreamy look. "I love that man."

"You'd better. You're marrying him. I'm relieved nothing is wrong. I was afraid something had happened between you two. Or, worse, something bad happened with Detective Olson."

Anna gave her a blank look. "Why would you think that? I'm not involved in any of the drama at the fair."

"I know, but it made me nervous when he talked to you earlier today. I wonder if he thinks you're consorting with Elsa because, well, because maybe you're helping her conceal her guilt."

"What guilt? She didn't kill her husband."

"How can you be so sure?"

Anna shrugged. "I don't know. I just am."

Chase wasn't sure at all.

EIGHTEEN

It was nearly midnight, but Chase had ignored three more text messages from Tanner during the day. She had to give him something to work with. He wanted to do the project, needed the money, she was sure, and was doing a good job. She should hold up her end of the bargain.

She sat at the computer and typed until she was bleary-eyed, but got good descriptions written for fifteen of their best sellers.

Hula Bars: These coconut-pineapple-walnut bars will transport you to the South Pacific at the first taste.

Lemon Bars: Just the right amount of tang and sweet. You've never tasted better Lemon Bars.

Harvest Bars: Imagine a crisp fall day, just before the

frost is on the pumpkin. That's where you'll be when you taste these pumpkin spice delectables.

She used words like *goodies* and descriptions like "heavenly creations" and even "masterpiece confection" in describing the Peanut Butter Fudge Bars.

Finally, just before two o'clock, she sent the file to Tanner and stumbled up the stairs to fall onto the couch with her clothes on.

The next morning, Inger's good mood of the night before had vanished. The first thing she said was that she wished Chase would get some decent coffee. "I think the smell of this kind makes me sick."

"I don't think you're supposed to drink caffeine when you're pregnant, are you?" Chase asked, continuing to make her usual coffee, French roast from the grocery store. She was too tired to rouse herself to get angry at Inger.

"Where did you hear that?"

"Around. I supposed it was common wisdom. What does your doctor say?" She poured water into the coffeemaker and switched it on.

Inger plopped into a kitchen chair as if she were eight months pregnant. "I didn't really see a doctor. They just gave me a test and told me I'm pregnant."

"Oh dear! You haven't seen anyone?" Now that she was awake, she felt a headache coming on. What was Inger thinking?

"I didn't need to go to the clinic anyway. I got a test from the drugstore. I did it three times. I know I'm pregnant."

"That's not the point." Chase, reaching for two coffee mugs, hesitated, then realized what she was doing and put one on the table. Maybe Inger would have some tea again. "You're supposed to take special vitamins. There are probably all sorts of things that should be looked into."

"They gave me some vitamins at the clinic, but I don't like to take pills."

"You have to take them!"

"Why?"

"To help the baby grow strong, I think. Look, you need to see someone right away."

"I don't even know if I'm keeping it or giving it up for adoption."

"Whether you keep it or not, it's your job to make sure the baby is healthy. And, speaking of keeping him, or her, do you have anyone helping you with that decision?" Chase knew the answer, but wanted to make sure Inger understood she had a momentous choice to make.

Inger shrugged. "I'm not hungry. It's cold in here." She got up and went into the bathroom.

Morning sickness, Chase thought. The apartment *was* chilly. Fall had arrived in earnest, from the looks of the blowing tree leaves outside the window. Chase nudged her thermostat up a notch, even though she would be leaving soon and Inger would be downstairs.

The sounds of retching and of the toilet flushing, plus the smell of the bathroom freshener bolstered Chase's assumption of morning sickness.

After Chase had eaten a piece of toast and a banana and had given Quincy his breakfast, Inger emerged. She looked wan and pale. Chase had no idea how to proceed. She must get Inger to a doctor for both the baby's sake and hers. Before she could say anything, Inger spoke.

"Look, this isn't working out too well. We're getting on each other's nerves. I appreciate what you've done for me, but I need to find someplace else. Maybe I could stay at Anna's again, even if those women and the parrot are there. The parrot is something else." Inger flashed a quick smile.

"I don't think so. There are four people sleeping there now. It's a small house."

"Four?"

"Yes. Julie Larson is staying there."

"Well, where does Julie live? Is her place empty?"

It was, and Chase and Julie had even talked, briefly, of Inger staying there. They had both decided that Quincy was good therapy for her. But maybe that wasn't very important at this point. Chase agreed that she and Inger needed a break from each other.

"Let me call Julie. I'll talk to her about you staying at her place. It's Friday. The fair is over on Sunday. We might close up the shop that day."

"Don't we usually close Monday and Tuesday?"

"Yes, but you've been running the store all by yourself for long enough. Monday and Tuesday, we'll be recovering from the fair, bringing everything back, moving back in. It might be best to close an extra day. I'll see if I can get you an appointment with a doctor for next week. And you can take some extra time off."

"How long?" Inger perked up and looked alarmed. "I need the money."

"Just the three days. Would that be all right? You could stay at Julie's and we wouldn't have to worry about transportation over here for you to work. Maybe we can even find you another place to live. Do you want me to make you tea and toast before I go?"

"Not if it's the same kind you had before." She wrinkled her nose. "Maybe you'd better take the cat with you today."

"You can't look in on him?" The pounding in her head got stronger.

"It's bothering me, climbing these stairs."

Chase clenched her jaw and enticed Quincy into his carrier. He wasn't thrilled about getting into it again.

"It's only for a couple more days, little fella," Chase crooned. "Then you can get back to normal." She turned to Inger. "You'll be okay running the shop today?"

Inger lifted one shoulder. Chase was getting tired of Inger shrugging her off. Her pity of last night seemed remote this morning. As Inger said, they definitely needed a break.

Chase left Inger to open up the Bar None and drove out of Dinkytown and to the vendors' lot at the Bunyan County Fairgrounds. Before she got out of her Ford Fusion, Julie called.

"You got a minute?" she asked.

"I just got to the fair, still in my car. Sure. What's on your mind? Have you decided anything about your job yet?"

"Not definitely. But I talked to a guy in real estate and he's going to get together with me over dinner tonight."

"Oh, *oh*. Does Jay know about this?" she teased. She got Quincy out and started walking toward the fair.

Julie tittered. "I invited Jay. He's still too busy on his case. He wants to hear what Bud says, though, so I might even take notes."

"I want to see your notes, too. Unless you write them in lawyerese."

Julie laughed again. "How do you think Anna is doing with those two women and their parrot?"

"I'm not sure. I'm glad you'll be there, but they're not ideal houseguests. Anna doesn't suspect her at all, but I wonder if Elsa killed her husband. I hope they leave very soon. Speaking of—"

"Gotta go. I'll call you after the dinner tonight."

The weather had made up its mind. It was blustery when she got out of her car in the parking lot. She held tight to Quincy's cage so it wouldn't blow away. Would this affect the fairgoers? At least it would keep her awake.

The door to Dr. Ramos's clinic was standing open, so Chase walked in with Quincy in his carrier. "I hope it's all right if I leave him here today."

"What happened to your employee? Quincy too tough for her to handle during the day?"

"She's not feeling well. In fact, if Julie okays it, I think she should move to her place tonight. If that doesn't work out, I don't know what to do next. You wouldn't happen to know of a cheap place she could rent, do you?"

"No, but I'll keep my eyes open."

"That's so nice of you, getting a therapist *and* a room. You barely know her."

"I haven't done anything yet."

"And I don't know if she would take your suggestion either."

"If I find a place."

"She doesn't even want to see an ob-gyn."

At Mike's questioning look, she explained that Inger had gotten her pregnancy confirmed and had received vitamins but wasn't taking them.

"They probably booked her to see a doctor at the clinic, didn't they?" Mike said.

"If they did, she didn't tell me. I doubt she'll follow up on anything without supervision."

"She's probably used to being looked after. She's been living at home, right?"

It didn't seem like the right time to dump on Mike about Inger being such a persnickety houseguest.

Dr. Ramos scooped Quincy out of the carrier and into one of the large cages, giving him a head rub on the way. Quincy didn't seem to mind being back in the cage. He curled up in the corner and started to purr. He was probably glad to be out of the wind. The other cat who was usually there, the black short hair with a white star on his chest, hadn't arrived yet.

Mike hit the latch on the cage. "I got a great idea last night."

"You know who committed the murder?" asked Chase, hoping he had information that would free him from suspicion.

"No, not about that. About Quincy and the contest."

Chase hadn't done a bit of thinking on that subject.

She had nearly decided she wouldn't enter him, since she hadn't had any costume inspirations. "What's your idea?"

"Puss in Boots! You like it?"

Chase didn't want to hurt his feelings, but it didn't sound too original. "Not sure. Let me see what Anna and Julie have come up with." Probably nothing, since she hadn't asked them to.

"A little hat with a feather," he said, "and leather-looking wraps on his front paws. I think it would go over great."

"It's not very glitzy."

A knock sounded on the door to the inner room. It wasn't closed, so the knocker pushed it open.

"Elsa," Chase said, looking somewhere between them, since she didn't know who was who. "And Eleanor."

"And Lady Jane Grey," added one of them, holding up a large cage with a white cloth thrown over it.

Chase wondered what they thought she thought was in the cage. Of course it was Lady Jane Grey. Could those two be any more annoying?

"Is she doing all right today?" he asked, looking at the cage. "Are you leaving her again?"

Elsa reached over and whipped off the covering. "If that's all right."

"*L'amour est un oiseau rebelle, que nul ne peut apprivoiser,*" the bird warbled in a screechy falsetto.

Chase covered her ears and Mike looked horrified.

"What's she doing?" Chase asked. She had been cute the night before, mimicking and doing parrot noises. This morning, the screech was sending her headache into her eyeballs.

"Oh, you naughty birdie," crooned Elsa, down two or three octaves from Grey's pitch. "She just adores *Carmen*, doesn't she, Ellie?"

The bird answered by swinging into, *"Toreador, en guard! Toreador, Toreador!"*

Chase groaned inwardly at the thought of an opera-singing parrot. She wasn't even crazy about opera when it was sung by humans with excellent voices.

"Could you please replace the cover?" Mike kept his tone even.

Elsa redraped the cage and set it on the examining table. "Can we leave her for the day?"

"She might get lonesome if we leave her by herself," Eleanor added.

"She hasn't sung opera in here before. I can't have her disturbing the other animals," Mike said.

Elsa looked around. "I don't see many here."

"They're in and out all day," Chase said, getting tired of their attitude. They took over every place they entered, like the world belonged to them. Besides, she had just about run out of patience. "He has to treat animals who have a problem while they're here, being shown, or in competition."

Mike surprised Chase by telling them that, starting today, he had to charge for boarding animals.

"Is she paying?" Eleanor pointed at Chase.

"Absolutely," Mike said, lifting the cage to a shelf next to Quincy.

Chase managed to keep from laughing. Elsa handed Mike the money and they swept out.

The cacophony had ceased, but the cat eyed the cage warily nonetheless. He didn't take his eyes off it. When the man set it next to his cage, he sniffed. He smelled bird. A claw snaked out under the cloth, between the bars. The parrot found the latch to the cat's cage and jiggled it. The cat watched, purring.

When she got back to the booth, Anna had opened up and it was full of buyers. The wind had died down and it didn't feel nearly so cold. The heater Anna had brought still felt wonderful.

She would talk to Anna about the cat costume during their first slow period.

Before that happened, the two Aronoffs walked by the booth, both in fur-collared coats and those Russian-looking fur hats. Chase wasn't sure it was quite *that* cold. The nutty father, Ivan, was waving his arms at his son, Peter. "What do you know about it? Have you ever seen one?"

Peter's voice sounded so reasonable after Ivan's slightly hysterical words. "I haven't, but I still think Puss in Boots isn't the best idea." Peter held a small pet carrier.

Chase called to them. "Are you putting a cat in the contest?"

Peter smiled and held up the carrier. A black cat was in it. It looked like the cat she'd seen being boarded in the vet clinic. "Yes, this is our cat. His name is Shadow. I want him to be Batcat. A Batman costume, but with his own ears and tail."

"Puss in Boots." Ivan sounded cranky. But it was hard to tell if he was or not. He always sounded that way.

Should Chase speak up and alienate the crabby man? "I think Batcat would be perfect for a black cat."

Ivan stuck his face in hers. "What is wrong with Puss in Boots?"

Chase took a step back. "Nothing's wrong with it. It's just not . . . original."

"No one else will do it," Ivan said.

"I heard someone else talking about Puss in Boots." That wasn't a lie. Mike Ramos had talked about it. But she wasn't going to use his idea.

Peter grinned and Ivan scowled and they went on their way to drop the cat off at the vet's. She wondered if Shadow liked opera.

The customers had thinned out at their booth, although the toy booth next to them was going full speed ahead. Chase cocked an ear in that direction. She was surprised that Harper had softened his voice today somewhat for the little ones. He was still gruff as could be when he gave the prices to the parents.

Sally, the tall blonde travel agent, came by and ordered four Almond Cherry Bars for herself and her partner. Chase waited on her while Anna helped a family group stocking up on Peanut Butter Fudge Bars.

"How's your jailbird doing?" Sally asked.

Chase was confused. "I don't have a bird."

The blonde leaned over the table and lowered her voice, pointing to Harper's booth. "*That* jailbird. The ex-convict toymaker."

"How do you know he's an ex—"

"Shh!"

Chase had inadvertently raised her voice.

"Don't let him hear you," she said.

"How do you know he's been prison?" Chase continued softly.

"Those tattoos. That's the kind you get there."

"How do you know?"

She waved a bejeweled hand. "One of my cousins, the black sheep of the family, was locked up for drug charges a few years ago."

"Say," Chase said. "You're not missing any jewelry, are you?"

She peered at her hands. "No, it doesn't look like it. Is Harper a jewel thief? Is that why he was in prison?"

"No, no, nothing like that. I mean, I don't know."

"Well, why do you ask, then?"

She didn't want to spread Patrice's name and her weakness all over the fair. "I had a ring taken. It's nothing to do with Harper. I'm not even sure it was here." She cringed a little at the lie. She should never have brought it up.

"See you," Sally said, leaving with her package.

Chase got Anna's attention as she finished up a sale. "Can you think of a costume for Quincy for the Fancy Cat Contest?"

Anna held her chin in her fist, thinking. "I did think of Puss in Boots, but, as you say, that's probably too easy.

I also thought of Supercat, but if that one is going to be Batman—"

"Batcat."

"—Batcat, then another caped crusader wouldn't be good."

"Patrice wanted to try that jeweled collar on her cat. I imagine there would be more to her getup than that. Maybe a frilly princess dress."

"You're right, Charity. After all, what was that cat's name? Something frilly."

"Princess Puffball."

"Are you talking about my cat?" Patrice, decked out in her purple caftan and gold turban, came into the booth, trailing her gauzy robe behind her. She held up a tiny pink ballerina tutu. "I wanted to show you what Princess will be wearing. Isn't it adorable?"

Anna nodded. "Very fitting for a princess."

Chase thought it looked ridiculous, but she smiled and nodded.

"Wouldn't it be fun if Quincy came as Puss in Boots?" Patrice said. "He's the same color as the cat in the movie."

Maybe, thought Chase, that's what was giving everyone the idea. She would have to rack her brain to come up with something. Quick. The contest was day after tomorrow.

NINETEEN

At lunchtime, Chase volunteered to get sandwiches for both of them. She was getting a second wind. Her headache had receded, and she felt so much better than when she had gotten up. Anna wanted turkey and Swiss, and Chase was hungry for a meatball sub.

"I'll stop in and see Quincy first," she said to Anna as she was slipping on her coat and leaving the booth.

Anna gave her a smile that meant she knew Chase was also going to see Dr. Ramos.

On her way, Chase pondered the costume situation. Yes, Quincy was the color of the Puss in Boots cat, but Chase definitely didn't want to do that. It was way too obvious. What *did* she want to do? Something brilliant, something that would wow the judges. If they were going to enter, she wanted them to win. Quincy was also the color of marmalade. Could she coax him to curl up on a huge piece of fake toast and BE marmalade? Not likely.

She hummed "Put on a Happy Face" from *Bye Bye Birdie* as she walked past Patrice's booth. Yes, she was in a much better mood. Maybe it was because she was away from Inger and Elsa and Eleanor.

Sometimes, when an old show tune popped up on her lips or in her mind, unbidden, she was taken straight back to her childhood, after her parents' deaths, when she began living with Anna. Her surrogate parent and grandparent, all rolled into one, was an aficionado of musicals. Anna and Chase, and sometimes Julie, would pile into Anna's gold Pontiac. It was the pride and joy of both the Larsons. Anna's husband didn't care for musicals, so it was always a girls' night out. Anna would do it up right, with dinner before the show at a nearby restaurant, a leisurely walk—if it wasn't raining—to one of the theaters in Minneapolis that showed musicals in the summertime, and usually good seats that Anna had purchased well ahead of time. Chase loved sitting in the plush seats, imagining she was one of the characters, usually the female lead, and that she could sing like they did. She couldn't, and wasn't very musical then or now, but, somehow, a lot of those old tunes had stuck with her. She still liked to go to musicals and sometimes, when their busy schedules allowed it, she and Anna and Julie would all do a rerun of those long-ago days, minus the Pontiac.

Patrice's fortune-telling booth seemed to be doing well. The purple gauze cloth drape that served as a door was closed, which meant she had a customer. The usual lavender scent hung outside the booth, drifting to the midway and dissipating with the competing aromas from the food court.

Madame Divine kept her booth so dark, she could have hidden the cat collar there after she stole it from the display and before she stuffed it into the sculpture and most people would never have seen it. She was, as Mike said, flaky. What had possessed her to cram it into a butter sculpture? The collar hadn't been there when Mike tried to retrieve it. Stolen, no doubt, by the person who murdered Larry Oake. The same person who threatened Patrice. Did it make sense that Patrice might have the collar now? That she had murdered Oake? That she had set her cousin up as the number one suspect? Chase shuddered. She hoped not.

The jewelry booth was next. Could one of them have taken it? Chase hadn't spoken to them much, but they were a little old couple, rather dowdy and ordinary-looking. Just the type to get away with things because they looked so innocent. They knew jewelry, Chase presumed. Would they be tempted by such a dazzling item?

Passing the butter building, she detected extra bustle there. More people than usual were dashing in and out. Maybe they were all getting lunch. It was almost noon. Mara Minsky rushed out and ran into Chase.

"Oh, sorry," she said. "We're in such a hurry to finish up. Everyone in there"—she jerked a thumb at the doorway behind her—"is crazy right now."

She was ready to hurry past, then recognized Chase.

"Oh, you're the one Daddy insulted the other day. I'm so sorry about that."

Karl Minsky hadn't insulted her. He had threatened her. There was a big difference. Had she seen that? Or maybe he'd told her? Chase thanked the young woman and started to go on.

"He didn't really mean it. He's so awfully upset that the policeman thinks he murdered that poor man," Mara said. "He's beside himself. He gets, well, mean when he's upset."

"Your father needs to learn not to threaten people. That could get him into a lot of trouble."

"He's been so desperate to win that prize money. It would make such a difference to us."

Chase took a step closer to her and spoke softly. "Maybe you shouldn't go around saying that."

She frowned. "Why not? I think everybody knows it."

"Think about it, Mara. That attitude gives him a perfect motive for eliminating his chief competition."

Mara sucked her breath in through rounded lips. "Oh. Oh. Okay. I won't go around saying it anymore. But that can't make people think he murdered the poor man. Daddy was with me when that man died. I told the detective that. My father couldn't have done it."

Chase could see that Detective Olson might call Minsky's alibi weak. If all it depended on was the word of his very loyal daughter, it was shaky indeed. She still hadn't told Detective Olson about her most recent encounter with the awful Karl Minsky and his threatening behavior.

Behind Mara, one of the sculptors opened the door and hurried out. Chase did a double take, peering inside the building.

Mara was starting to walk away, so Chase touched her sleeve. "Mara, did I just see Winn Cardiman inside there?" She had glimpsed that distinctive monkey-like face and those prominent ears.

She turned back to Chase. "You could have. He's here."

"I thought he took himself out of the competition and went home."

"He did. Maybe he forgot some tools or something."

Maybe he was returning to the scene of the crime, like murderers often did.

She ducked into the largest building on the fairgrounds and walked toward the back, where the vet clinic was. Before she rounded the corner, she heard two men's voices.

"No, she couldn't wear the collar, Papa."

It was Peter Aronoff again, talking to Ivan, his wacky father. She stopped to listen.

"Yes, she can. It should be ours. Shadow should wear it. That company should not have cut you. It was wrong. They don't know good people when they have them. They owe you for making us homeless."

"I got a severance package, Papa. Picky Puss doesn't owe me anything. I've told you a million times. Your talking is getting me into a lot of trouble."

Chase didn't catch Ivan's grumbling response. Did this conversation mean that they actually had the collar and were arguing about using it in the competition?

"Anyway," Peter said, "even if I'd gotten a better

severance, we would have run through it by now. That fancy collar has nothing to do with me. Nothing to do with us. But it's all you're talking about. And now, because of your big mouth, that detective thinks I killed the guy. I don't exactly have an alibi."

Ivan grumbled again. The two men appeared from around the corner, and Chase started walking so they would think she had arrived a second ago. Ivan still wore his fur hat, but Peter's was stuffed into his pocket, a bit of fur poking out.

"Hi there," she said with a smile. "How's it going?"

"Hi," said Peter. "We were discussing the costume for Shadow."

"Weren't you doing Puss in Boots?" Chase said, with a glint of devilment in her eye.

"That is what I keep telling him," Ivan said. "Puss in Boots. Perfect." He flung his right arm out for punctuation.

"Thanks," Peter said with an ironic twist to his mouth. It turned into a smile, though, so Chase knew he'd gotten her little joke. Ivan must not have remembered discussing it in front of her previously.

"But I'll bet he'd look better as Batcat," she said, not willing to side with Ivan against his son.

Now Peter gave her a full grin. Chase thought she might like Peter, in a little-brother sort of way, if she got to know him better.

"We go now," Ivan said gruffly. The Aronoffs took off quickly. The son didn't have an alibi? Did Detective Olson really think he was the killer? Or maybe the detective was good at giving all the people he questioned the impression that they were the prime suspects.

Elsa came hurrying up behind Chase after the two men left and before Chase could continue to the vet clinic. The older woman looked worried.

"My purse is gone," she blurted when she was still fifteen feet away.

"Where did you lose it?"

"I have no idea! I would know where it was if I knew where I lost it, wouldn't I?"

"What does it look like?" Chase vaguely remembered that she carried a red purse.

"It's very expensive. Red tooled leather with my monogram in gold." Elsa panted, but Chase thought it wasn't from exertion. She was very worried about losing her purse. Chase would be, too, if she had lost hers. What a horror it would be, canceling credit cards and worrying about identity theft.

There was a metal bench in the hallway. Chase guided the distraught woman to it and sat beside her, trying to calm her down.

"We need to think of every place you've been today and when you noticed it missing."

"Every place." Elsa squinted and frowned. "We got here and dropped Grey off."

"Yes, I was there for that. Ellie was with you."

"And then we had something at the food court. I had it then because I paid. Ellie is very cheap that way. Always wants me to pay when we eat together."

"What time was that?"

"Not too long ago. We looked at some exhibits first."

"But you had it at the food court. And Ellie was with you. Where is she now?"

"She's trying to retrace our steps."

Chase wondered why they had split up but didn't ask about it. "Then where did you go after you ate?"

"We came here"—she gestured toward Mike's office—"to say hi to Grey."

That couldn't have been more than two hours after they had dropped off the parrot. "Then where did you go?"

"I went to the jewelry booth. When I wanted to buy a pair of earrings, I noticed my purse was gone."

Thieves at the jewelry booth? "How big is it?"

"It's very small." She indicated six inches square or so with her hands. "Do you think the jewelry seller lifted it? Pickpockets are sometimes very clever."

"You were at the vet's right before you missed it. Have you looked there?"

"That was going to be my next stop."

TWENTY

M ike's aunt Betsy was on receptionist duty when Chase and the distraught Elsa entered Dr. Ramos's clinic.

"He's tending a sick sheep," she told them.

Chase had never been here when Betsy was on duty, since she was usually dropping Quincy off early, picking him up late, or visiting during lunchtime. Betsy smiled at them.

"He should be almost finished," she said. "Is he expecting you?" She looked at a mostly blank appointment book open on the desk.

Dr. Ramos opened the door to the examining room. He ushered a young man through the door, leading a sheep on a leash.

"Thanks, Doc," the sheep owner said. "I was afraid I'd done something terrible, letting her have that gum."

"You're welcome," Mike said. He leaned down to pat the sheep's back and gave the boy a reassuring smile. The boy took off whistling, his sheep trotting behind him.

"Chase, come on back." He said to his aunt, "She's here to see her cat."

And to see you, thought Chase, in case you haven't noticed.

"Elsa wants to take a look for her purse, too," Chase said.

Mike laughed. The deep, rich sound resonated somewhere deep inside Chase. "I was going to try to track you down." He walked to the parrot's cage and pointed. "Here's your culprit. I think she grabbed it when you were here. I saw it after you left."

He picked up the red purse and handed it to Elsa.

"It's damaged," she said. She pointed out two indentations in the soft leather.

"I think those are Grey's bill marks. I found it in her cage and rescued it."

Elsa's worried expression finally left. She approached Grey's cage with a little smile. "You naughty birdie. What are we going to do with you?" She stuck a finger through the bars, which were certainly wide enough to admit the slim purse. The bird was fast asleep and ignored her owner. "Thank you, Dr. Ramos."

"No problem. I'm sorry you were concerned. I couldn't get away and don't have your phone number."

She thanked him again and left without giving him her phone number.

Chase had been thinking Patrice might have stolen the purse, had even suspected the jewelry sales couple, so she was glad that neither of those had been the culprit.

"Do the police still suspect Patrice for Oake's murder?" Chase asked.

"I think not. Vik finally told them that he and Patrice were having pizza at a picnic table at the food court during the critical time."

"Why did it take so long for her grandfather to tell the police? To clear his granddaughter?"

"For some reason, they never questioned him. Patrice hadn't told him she was a suspect. Didn't want him to have one more thing to worry about. She slipped up and let him know, then he went right to the police station and told them."

"I'm glad she's off the hook."

"She's only off the hook for the murder because she stole the collar. After she admitted stealing it, he was bawling her out for that and kept her there for an hour." Mike gave an ironic smile.

"Whew. She knows how to get into trouble. What was that about, with the sheep?" Chase asked, unlocking Quincy's cage and picking him up.

"The young lad left a package of gum where the sheep could get it. She ate it, package and all, and he thought he might have injured her."

She was glad he'd gotten over the patient confidentiality thing with her. "They're here for the sheep jumping contest?" When Chase had walked past the exhibition room, low jumps were being set up. The idea was to make it look like the standard cartoon pictures of counting sheep to get to sleep, except in this case, the judges would count how many jumps each sheep made successfully before losing interest, according to the description that had been in the brochure about the contests. "Did you fix up his sheep?"

"No need. Sheep can eat almost anything. They don't even chew their food until it's been swallowed, broken down, and digested."

"Like cows chewing their cud?"

"Exactly like that. Gum is not an ideal diet, but it won't hurt the sheep at all."

Mike busied himself with updating his notes and Chase stroked Quincy, enjoying his enthusiastic purr. It was still bothering Chase that she hadn't told Detective Olson about her latest encounter with Karl Minsky. Mike's examining room was so nice and private, it gave her an idea.

"Do you mind if I make a phone call here? It's not something I want to do in our booth on the midway."

"Sure. Do you need me to leave the room?"

Mike was so sweet. "No, but I need to speak with the policeman. If I can get him."

She set Quincy down on the floor and dialed the detective, expecting to leave a message but hoping to talk to him. She was pleased when he answered.

"Olson here."

"This is Chase. I have something to tell you that may help your case." Quincy prowled the area beneath the bird cage, looking up with his ears pricked forward.

She glanced at Mike. He was trailing a string for Quincy. Sometimes Quincy decided to play along and chase a string. Other times, he made it clear, by following the string with his eyes up to the human's hand, that he knew exactly what was going on and that this wasn't a huge mouse tail. Today, he was pouncing with delight.

Chase continued. "Karl Minsky threatened me on Thursday."

"How did he do that? What did he say?"

"He said, um, that I'd better watch my mouth and that . . ." What else had he said? "He was warning me."

"Okay. First of all, what did you say that prompted him to tell you to watch your mouth?"

"I was talking to Anna and I said I thought he may have killed Mr. Oake."

"If I were an innocent suspect—not saying he is or isn't—I wouldn't appreciate that. Second, did he threaten to do anything?"

"It was the way he said it. He was acting like a bully."

"I'll note that in my file, Ms. Oliver. Thanks for the information."

He ended the call. That hadn't gone at all like she thought it would. She almost wished Karl Minsky had threatened her with something specific. Vague, intimidating warnings weren't much good, it seemed.

Following the string was fun for the cat for a while. But humans never got the movement quite right, never exactly like a mouse, or a wounded bird. The cat sat on his haunches

while the man hoisted himself onto the stainless steel table,
waiting for his mistress to finish her phone call. As she put
the phone away and the man started to speak, the door
opened. Maybe there was something more interesting than
a piece of string out there. He had to look.

Once again, Chase was at it, running after her cat, who
had not only gotten out of the clinic when Betsy opened
the door, but had managed to scoot all the way out of the
building and was scampering down the midway.

He headed straight for the butter sculpture building.
Horrified that he might get inside again and ruin one of
the masterpieces, Chase picked up her pace. Mike, who
had been pounding along behind her, seemed to sense
the same fear and bolted past her on his much longer legs.

As Quincy reached the door, it swung open and he
slipped through. Mike dashed inside. Chase, thirty feet
behind, gave it all she had in a final burst. And ran full
tilt into Winn Cardiman.

They both crashed to the ground and landed on their
bottoms. To her amazement, the man started laughing.
The tote bag he had been carrying had spilled most of its
contents.

"I'm so sorry." Chase jumped up. "Let me help you."
She started gathering his things. "Ouch!" Something
stuck her finger, and she drew her hand back.

"Leave it. I'll get the stuff." He started laughing again.
His wrinkly, freckled face scrunched up in his glee.

"Am I funny?"

"No, it's just that your cat got into the building again. He's a crazy animal. I hope he eats Minsky's mess. Not that anyone could tell if he did." He got to his feet and dusted off his jeans.

Chase had to agree that the abstract the man was working on wouldn't suffer from a few chunks missing. "Yes, Quincy is a handful."

"Good at getting away, is he?"

Chase sighed. "That's a huge understatement. That cat is an escape artist."

Cardiman scooped his tools into his bag.

"Those are your sculpting tools?" she asked.

"They are. I got so mad at everyone that I stormed out and left them here. Then I got to thinking, some of these are my favorites. They're not expensive, but I've had them for years. I work well with this wooden spatula and this metal dowel." He reached into his bag and held them up. "So I came back to get them."

The metal dowel looked almost like a surgical scalpel. It was probably what had pricked Chase's finger.

"You've been in there a long time."

"Yes, I got to chatting with some of the other sculptors. The exhibit will be good. There's some good work in there."

"Besides Minsky's, you mean."

"Yeah, that son of a gun. Why he let his idiot daughter design their piece, I'll never know." His pale face flushed bright red with anger for a brief moment. He looked at the finger Chase was unconsciously rubbing. "Is your finger okay?"

Chase looked at the place where Cardiman's sculpting

tool had poked her. A small drop of blood oozed from the tip of her finger. "It'll be fine." That tool was so sharp that the hole was small. The murder weapon was also a pointed dowel. Did the fact that Cardiman still had a pointed dowel mean he wasn't the killer? Or did sculptors normally have more than one of those? If he only had one, he wasn't the culprit.

"Did I hurt your tool?"

Cardiman shook his bag. "I'm sure you didn't. Those dowels are sturdy. Anyway, I have half a dozen."

That theory was shot. He could still be the killer. Unlikely but possible.

She hurried into the butter building. If the weather got any colder, they would be able to leave the door open.

Mike, holding Quincy, stood talking to the man who had been sculpting a gopher. Chase looked around. It seemed to her that all of the sculptures had been finished. The artists who were there were cleaning up and putting their things away. Chase moved to approach the two men.

On her way, she saw one woman smoothing a flat piece of her sculpture with a finger she was dipping into a bowl of cold water. Chase stopped to admire it.

"Your North Star is so intricate. I don't know how you do that."

The woman beamed. "Years of practice."

She wiped her buttery finger on a paper towel. "I have to quit now. It's so hard to leave it be."

Chase reached the man Mike was chatting with. "I love your gopher," she said. "It looks like he actually has fur."

"Yellow fur." The man chuckled.

"Yes, but it does look like fur," Mike said. He held Quincy up next to the statue to compare their fur coats.

"Did Quincy get into anything?" she asked.

"I caught him right inside the door. Decided I wanted to see these. Where have you been?"

"I've been outside knocking down people." I wish I were knocking down killers and revealing their guilt, she thought, but how would I even do that?

"Is your cat competing in the Fancy Cat Contest?" the sculptor asked.

"I think so." If she could come up with a costume very soon, he would be.

TWENTY-ONE

Anna came over to Chase's apartment that evening to help get Inger moved to Julie's place. She insisted on lifting Inger's suitcase onto Chase's unmade bed.

"It's no problem for me, Mrs. Larson," Inger said, taking her clothing from Chase's dresser drawers, where she had crammed her things in on top of Chase's.

"You shouldn't be lifting in your condition," Anna insisted.

"Everyone keeps telling me what I should and shouldn't do." Inger threw her hands out in frustration. "How do I know what I can do?"

"Inger, I'll get you a book about being pregnant," Chase said, "but really, you need to make an appointment."

"I don't know any baby doctors."

Chase remembered what Mike had said. "Don't you have an appointment with a doctor at the clinic?"

"I guess. But I can't go to someone I don't know anything about."

"You help her pack," said Anna to Chase. "I'll get a doctor's name."

She left the room and came back as they were stuffing Inger's underwear into the corners of the suitcase.

"Here." Anna thrust a piece of paper, torn from the pad in Chase's kitchen, into Inger's hand. "This is the number of the doctor my friend's granddaughter is using. She's due in three months and likes Dr. Ingersoll very much."

"Inger and Ingersoll," mused Chase. "You should be able to remember his name."

Inger smiled for the first time that evening, a small smile. "If it's someone you know, that's different. I promise I'll call him Monday."

"Give him my friend's name. It's there on the paper."

Chase wondered who was going to pay for the doctor, but she wasn't going to start worrying about that yet. Chase hoisted the suitcase off the bed and wheeled it behind her. They made their way into the kitchen, where Anna put the kettle on for herbal tea.

"Next project." Anna dusted off her hands symbolically. "Quincy's costume."

"Oh, can I help?" Inger sparked to life. She gave a wide grin. "I've been thinking and I have some ideas."

Chase cocked her head toward Inger in surprise.

"He should be Babe the Blue Ox," Inger said, clapping her hands.

Quincy lifted his head at the noise.

"It's better than Puss in Boots," Chase said. "But how are we going to do it?"

"It shouldn't be too hard." Inger turned the piece of paper over on the counter and started drawing. In two minutes she held up a sketch of a cat with horns and ears on a headdress, and a little bodysuit with a cow's tail at the back.

Chase looked skeptical, but Anna grabbed the paper and said, "Yes! This will be great. I have a bolt of blue felt that I bought for half price. I thought we might be able to use it in the shop somehow."

"Do you have white felt for the horns?" Inger looked better than she had in days. Her blue eyes twinkled and her smile brought sunshine into the apartment.

"I have something, I'm sure."

"So," said Chase to Anna, "we need to go to your place." Anna had the sewing supplies.

"Everyone else is there," Anna agreed. "Might as well."

Chase had a sudden thought. "Should we bring Quincy, with the parrot there? We'll have to. He has to be there in order to be fitted, doesn't he?"

"Lady Jane Grey does have a cage," Anna said. "She'll have to use it tonight."

The three of them, four counting Quincy, drove to Anna's. Anna and Inger went in Anna's blue Volvo, and Chase followed with Quincy in his carrier.

"You're going to look great," she cooed to him on the way. "The other cats will all be dull next to you." She hoped she was right.

At Anna's, bedlam broke lose.

As soon as the carrier was set on the floor of the strange living room, the cat sensed something very different was in this place tonight. When the huge parrot walked up to his crate and started pecking, he swatted, claws out. The people ran to them and they all started making a lot of noise. A pair of hands picked the parrot up while the cat's owner snatched his crate. But, before the bird could be caged, the clever cat hooked his claw in the latch, nudged it open, and jumped out. The cat stopped, mesmerized by the biggest bird he had ever been this close to. The parrot hopped to the floor.

"Control that filthy animal," shrieked Elsa, stooping to grab her parrot's feet and pick her up. The bird squawked and flapped her wings, scattering feathers onto the floor. "He's going to kill Lady Grey."

Chase cradled Quincy in her arms and looked at the animals. They were about the same size. "How much does your bird weigh?"

"Fifteen point eight ounces."

"Ounces?"

"She was a pound when I weighed her at my place," said Eleanor. "Here, let me have her."

Quincy hadn't taken his wide, staring eyes off Grey

since he'd escaped. Chase made sure she had a good grip on him. He wasn't struggling to get at the parrot. Maybe he was intimidated.

Eleanor deftly got the parrot into her cage. Quincy didn't relax one bit.

Eleanor eyed the cat. "I'll take Grey into the bedroom."

"You'd better put her in the bathroom," Anna said, picking the feathers off the floor. "My sewing machine is in the bedroom."

"That doesn't seem very convenient." Elsa stood watching as Anna cleaned up after her bird.

"It's convenient for me," Anna said evenly. "I live here."

The sooner these women left Anna's place, the better, thought Chase. If Elsa isn't a murderer now, she might become one. Or Anna might.

Anna got a tape measure and wrapped it around Quincy in a few places, then handed the cat to Inger, but before she and Inger made it to the bedroom, a knock sounded on the front door. Bill Shandy didn't wait but came right in.

He greeted Anna with a tight hug.

"How are you doing?" she asked him quietly so Elsa and Eleanor couldn't hear. Chase was close enough to, though. "You still okay with my decision?"

Bill ran a hand over his face. "I'm fine now that I'm here. The sight of you cures everything."

"Oh, you sweet-talker, you." Anna patted his shoulder.

"I can't stay long, but I wanted to see you for a few minutes."

Chase gave them some space and they talked together on the couch for fifteen minutes or so about flowers and music and wedding details.

After Bill left, Anna and Inger finally retreated to the bedroom to do some work on the costume. They took Quincy with them. That left Chase with the twin sisters. Julie had called to say she'd be very late. It had sounded like Jay Wright was involved. Chase couldn't very well blame her for finishing her evening up with Jay. She probably wanted to discuss her findings with him from the dinner with Bud, the real estate lawyer. Chase hadn't mentioned that she wanted to move Inger to her house tonight. Chase inwardly kicked herself and felt a stab of pain behind her left ear. If Inger stayed with Chase again, it would be her own fault.

Chase envied the speed at which Julie's romance was progressing. For that matter, Anna and Bill Shandy were moving quickly, too. They were all further along than she was with Mike Ramos. Everyone was leaving her in the dust! Then she considered the woman in the same room who had just lost her husband and gave herself a mental slap.

Elsie and Ellie, as they called each other, sat side by side on the couch, both of them staring at Chase with the same hard brown eyes. Grey, brought in from the bathroom, chattered away in her cage on the table at the end of the sofa.

"Who wants to play? How *are* you? Nothing is forever. Everyone's a critic."

Chase burst out laughing.

"What's so funny?" asked Elsa.

"Your parrot! She's a regular little philosopher. Did you teach her all her phrases?"

Eleanor leaned forward like she was going to spill a secret. "She watches TV."

To illustrate that point, Grey started shrieking like a police siren. Chase's head almost split open.

Anna ran out of the bedroom, looked around, glared at the cage, and went back to the bedroom muttering, "That bird again."

"She's . . . something," Chase said, rubbing her temples.

Elsa and Eleanor smiled identical smiles.

The cat had been turned loose in the bedroom when the two women brought him there to work on a noisy machine with some cloth. The animal that so intrigued him was on the other side of the bedroom door, so he stayed close to it. The animal smelled like something delicious, but it was much too big to bring down. Besides, it had almost acted friendly. He was intrigued. When the animal shrieked and the older woman ran out of the bedroom, he slipped out. He slunk around the edges of the room, nearing the big bird cautiously. Nothing was going to keep him from investigating this strange creature.

Everyone had eaten, so, besides talking about the parrot, there wasn't much else to do.

"It's too bad I can't let her out." Elsa gave Chase a baleful look. "She could show you her tricks."

"It's too bad there isn't a parrot competition at the fair," Chase said.

"It *is* too bad," said Eleanor. She spoke to Elsa. "Maybe you could suggest it for next year."

Elsa drew back in horror. "I'll never be at that fair again! I'm never coming to this town again! As soon as I get my husband's poor body, we're leaving. We may never—I mean, *I* may never come back to Minnesota again."

That was understandable, thought Chase. If Elsa hadn't killed him and didn't get locked up in Minnesota for a good long time, why would she ever return? Maybe, thought Chase, she could do some digging while they were here together.

"I suppose," Chase said to Eleanor, "your sister told you about how she found her husband after he had been killed?"

"Oh my, yes. She did. She said she screamed her head off."

Elsa leaned her head on the back of the couch and closed her eyes. "It's something I hope to never see again. I close my eyes and it's right there, every night. I wonder when that will stop. He was lying there in the straw. There wasn't very much blood. That metal dowel handle was sticking out of his ear." A tremor went through her.

"You must have gotten pretty close to see all that," Chase said.

"Oh no," both sisters chorused.

"I might have taken two steps," said Elsa, "but I backed right out. It was full of straw."

"She couldn't go inside the building," Eleanor said.

"No way," Elsa added. "I couldn't get close to him. I wanted to run over and check to see if he might be alive."

"Why didn't you?" Chase was missing something here. "You saw Dr. Ramos and my cat there, too, right?"

"Yes, I saw everything."

"But you weren't inside the building?"

"Oh no. I couldn't. I saw everything from the doorway."

"Why couldn't you go inside?"

"We're both deathly allergic," Eleanor said. "That straw on the floor might kill her."

Elsa nodded. "As it was, just getting a whiff and screaming like that set me off. I had to use my inhaler four times that night."

"When Elsie called me, she was wheezing so hard I thought she might have to admit herself to the emergency room." She turned to Elsa. "Good thing you had an extra inhaler with you."

"Yes, I'm glad you told me to bring it. I sure needed it. The first one ran out on me."

She hadn't even entered the building? Allergic to straw? Maybe she hadn't killed him after all. Chase remembered how awful her face had looked. It had been red and splotchy. Was that from her hay allergy? If so, did that mean she *had* been inside? Or would she react that way from the exposure from the doorway?

Could she have stabbed him and he staggered into the building after that? Probably not. There had been no indications that he didn't die where he was found.

"You know, they've let that man loose," Elsa said. "The one who was there when I found my dead husband."

"Who are you talking about?" Chase asked. "Dr. Ramos?" Chase was indignant. "He didn't kill your husband!"

"He was right there. But I think now he didn't do it; he's so good to Grey. Do you know why he was beside his body?"

"He went in there to get my cat!" And Patrice's cat collar. "Your husband was dead when he went in." Chase heard her voice getting strident. Pain spiked behind her eyes.

Elsa huffed. "That Winn Cardiman. Nasty man. I'm pretty sure he did it. And they've let him go free, too." She acted like the argument was over and she had won.

"I wonder what's on TV tonight," Elsa said, sounding bored.

And now we change the subject, thought Chase.

Elsa looked around for the remote and found it on the side table, where Anna always kept it, next to Grey's cage. As she picked it up, Chase noticed a paw reaching up over the edge of the table. Before she could react, Quincy had jumped onto the table and swatted at the lock on the cage door. Grey nosed the door open and flew out.

All three women held their breath. Grey perched on top of her cage and peered down at the cat. Quincy crouched, his tail twitching slightly. Then he stretched his nose up. Grey put her beak down and they touched.

As Quincy purred and licked Grey's beak, the bird started squawking, "Everything's coming up roses." She sounded exactly like Ethel Merman.

TWENTY-TWO

Since Julie hadn't shown up yet when Chase needed to get to bed, she abandoned the plan to move Inger that night and brought her employee back home with her, lugging the suitcase up the stairs to the apartment. She also brought home a crashing headache. Lady Jane Grey had shrieked through three sitcoms and part of a singing competition show. She especially liked to mimic laugh tracks and high sopranos, as Chase remembered. No wonder Anna was getting tired of having the bird around. By the time Chase left, she didn't think the parrot was cute at all, even if Quincy was quite taken with her.

However, she was very pleased with Quincy's costume. Anna and Inger had done a bang-up job. A band around his head secured the lightweight horns and ears of Babe the Blue Ox. A simple blue felt cape, buckled around his body, completed the transformation. Quincy didn't even seem to mind it too much. Anna had managed to fasten a tufted bit of cloth onto the rear of the cover-up for a bovine tail. The cat's extra girth gave more credibility to the thought that he might possibly be a miniature of the giant ox.

Chase took the costume out of the carryall to admire it. "Inger, you're a genius. This is wonderful. You'll be a whiz at making baby clothes."

That must have been the wrong thing to say, because Inger's face crumpled and she burst into sobs.

"I'm sorry," Inger wailed between blubbers.

Chase ran to get a tissue. "Oh no, don't *you* be sorry. I'm sorry I brought up the baby."

"It's not that." She wiped her face and blew her nose, the storm past as rapidly as it had sprung up. "I don't know what's wrong with me. All of a sudden, for no reason at all, I'll burst out crying. I've even done it in the shop with customers there."

"I guess your hormones are wacky, aren't they? Doesn't pregnancy do that?"

"How would I know?" She looked on the verge of crying again.

"Look, we'll get you to a doctor and find a book that will tell you what's normal and what's not. There's no need to worry about something that's normal for mommies-to-be."

"I guess." Inger looked doubtful. New sobs shook her small shoulders.

"If this continues, I think you should see someone about depression, too. You're under a lot of stress."

Chase put her arms around Inger's delicate frame and they sat on the couch together until Inger's occasional quaking sobs had stopped. Even though Inger had said, "It's not that," about the baby, Chase knew she should be thinking about what she was going to do to take care of it. This, however, wasn't the right time to bring that up.

Quincy jumped up beside them and butted Inger's side, purring through her remaining sniffles.

"Oh, Quincy," Inger said, gathering him onto her lap. She gave Chase a shy look. "Can I give him something?"

Chase hesitated. He didn't need more treats. "I'm not sure. What do you want to give him?"

Inger set Quincy in Chase's lap and jumped up. "I'll show you. I've been working on it in the kitchen this week when the shop was closed, before and after hours."

She ran out the door and down the stairs. Quincy raced after her and Chase decided she'd better go, too.

Inger was reaching into the refrigerator. She brought out a plastic bag full of small round balls.

"I've been experimenting. I think he'll like these."

"What are they?" To Chase, they looked like tiny meatballs.

"I don't know what to call them. I mashed together some tuna fish and cream cheese, then added some catnip."

Chase relented, confronted with Inger's eager, happy face. "Sounds like he'll like them. Give it a go."

"Here, Quincy." Inger put one of the balls on the floor and Quincy approached it cautiously. He sniffed it, then batted the sphere a few inches. A couple more bats, then he pounced and devoured it.

Both women were laughing at his antics.

"One more?" Inger asked Chase.

"Sure. I think you have a hit. Go, Quincy, go!"

He rolled on the floor where the treat had been.

"I don't have a name for them."

As Quincy chased the next one around, Chase said, "I know. Those are Go-Go Balls."

"Yes! I like that. I'm so glad he likes them." Inger slid Chase a sideways glance. "Thank you, Ms. Oliver, for turning the heat up in the apartment."

"You're welcome. You can call me Chase, you know."

After Inger had gone to bed, Chase and Quincy curled up together on the couch. Quincy was tired from chasing his Go-Go Balls around the kitchen downstairs. He purred with his eyes tightly closed. Chase felt the pain in her head ease up just a tad. The tension melted out of her neck and shoulders. The headache receded further. Cats were such good therapists.

The ox costume was on the arm of the couch, where she had dropped it to comfort Inger. Chase fingered it and spoke to her little guy. "You'll win the contest, won't you, Quincy Wincy? We'll come home victorious. Without an extra houseguest, I hope. Maybe by Sunday night we'll be in our own bed. Wouldn't that be nice?"

The Fancy Cat Contest was going to be held in the

afternoon on Sunday. She and Anna had decided to close the booth for it so Anna could watch. They had heard other merchants saying they would close up, too. It would be the last day of the fair. Chase panicked a bit at that. She wouldn't have a chance to observe all the suspects together in one place again after the fair closed. It would be a relief not to be on the lookout for a killer, though.

Her mind wanted to dwell on possible suspects a bit longer. Reluctantly, she decided to cross Elsa off the list. It was a shame. She had such an obvious motive, with her husband about to leave her high and dry, taking all their cash to open a butter-carving studio in Costa Rica. But she claimed to have that straw allergy. It occurred to her that it would probably be easy enough to check.

Who else was still on her list?

Karl Minsky. That was a given. Should she consider his daughter Mara? True, they alibied each other. But if they were both in on it, or even if one knew the other had done the deed, they would surely provide alibis for each other. Had their excuses been verified? Detective Olson was being closemouthed about all this.

Maybe she would have to return Winn Cardiman to her list. He had left, so everyone said, but he wasn't gone. She rubbed her finger, still sore from being pricked by his carving tool. He wasn't any less angry at Oake now than he had been.

There were other butter sculptors, too. Was it too late to check out all of them? She kicked herself for concentrating only on those two. She should have considered all of them.

Patrice Youngren was Mike's cousin. Did that mean she was a good person? Mike said she was flaky. That didn't mean crazy or sinister, but it could. Since the collar seemed to be involved with the murder, she should be kept on the list, even if she had an alibi. She was definitely wrapped up in this mess somehow.

Then there were the two Aronoff men. The father, Ivan, who was sort of bonkers. He went on and on about that diamond cat collar. Where could it be? Peter, Ivan's very sane son, as far as Chase could tell, was worried that he didn't have an alibi. Maybe the fact that he was worried about that meant he was guilty. Maybe not.

Chase would have to do her best to get to the truth. Somehow. "Use What You Got" from *The Life* popped into her head.

Saturday dawned as an almost exact twin of Friday, cold and blustery. Almost done, she told herself. Tomorrow would be over before she knew it and life would return to normal. Then she kicked herself for thinking that. Life would never be normal again for anyone associated with the dead man. Or for his killer.

Before she got out of the car at the fair, Chase pulled on her wool gloves and looped her scarf around her neck several times, watching leaves and papers leap into the air and dance, whipped by the same wind that whistled through the door gaskets. She took a deep breath and hauled Quincy's carrier out of the car. A gust immediately sent it sideways and up several inches. Quincy howled.

"I know, little guy. This isn't pleasant, is it? Wouldn't a person have to be crazy to want to stroll around a fair on a day like this?" However, it was Saturday, the penultimate day, and she knew hordes of people would flock to the venue. "One good thing," she told Quincy, "we've done good business this week. Julie was right in telling us we needed to be here." Quincy didn't seem to care about the income. "We would never have made this money in the shop this week. And Inger says business isn't bad back there either." Neither she nor Anna had reconciled the books since the fair had started. The books would be there when it was over.

The walk through the parking lot was short, and soon she was inside the large building. It was so well heated today, she had to set the crate down and unwind her scarf. "They don't have to overcompensate for the cold outside by making it like a sauna in here," she mumbled, picking Quincy up and trudging down the hallway. The place bustled with exhibitors and fairgoers alike who had arrived extra early to get in a full day.

She turned the knob on the door to the vet clinic. Nothing happened. Mike wasn't here yet? That wasn't like him. No sooner had she stuck her fist on her hip, wondering what to do next, than Mike's aunt Betsy Youngren hurried up behind her. She looked so worried, Chase had to ask her if everything was all right.

"No, it's not." Her words quavered and the hand holding the key shook.

"What's the matter?"

"They've arrested Michael." Betsy bit her bottom lip.

"For what?"

"The murder of Larry Oake."

If a chair had been behind Chase, she would have plopped into it. The wall was there, though, so she fell back against it. "But they questioned him and let him go."

"I called to see what I could find out, and all they would tell me is that there's new evidence."

"Who did you speak to?"

"That detective. Olson."

"But he wouldn't tell you what the evidence is?"

Betsy shook her head. "Michael asked me to call a colleague of his in Edina to get a replacement in here for today."

"You spoke with Mike?"

"No. I tried to, but they wouldn't let me." *They*, Chase assumed, being Niles Olson. "A lawyer named Gerrold something called me. Michael had asked him to."

"Gerrold Gustafson?" Chase asked.

"That's it."

Gustafson was the man Julie had mentioned, a "little powerhouse," she'd called him. Chase didn't care how big or little the guy was, just that he be able to defend Mike. Mike hadn't killed Oake!

Betsy unlocked the door and flipped the light switch on. "You might as well take your cat back to the cages. Dr. Drood should be here soon." She busied herself taking off her outer garments and hanging them over the back of her chair.

Chase hesitated a moment, wanting to know more about Mike. Before she could ask, the outer door was flung open and a gaunt, stooped man shuffled into the room. He peered at the two women through thick, round glasses that magnified his eyes and gave Chase the impression of a staring owl. His expression wasn't friendly. He seemed indifferent to Betsy and Chase.

"What have we here?" he said in a high, quavering voice, starting toward Quincy's crate, which stood on the floor at Chase's feet.

"Who are you?" Chase stepped in front of her cat, shielding him from this man.

"Are you Dr. Drood?" Betsy smiled at him as best she could, beneath her worried brow.

"I am," he said, straightening slightly but remaining stooped.

Betsy came from behind the desk and opened the inner door. "Here's the clinic. Please go in and make yourself at home."

Dr. Drood stared at Quincy.

"I'll send Ms. Oliver back in a moment." Betsy was firm, clipping her words. Chase got the feeling Betsy disliked the man as much as she did, on first sight.

The man stared at them a moment longer, then opened the clinic door. "I'm ready anytime," he said. He slammed the door behind him. Chase heard *skritch*ing noises from Quincy's crate. The man had scared her cat slamming the door like that. What kind of an animal doctor was he?

"Where did you say he came from?" Chase whispered to Betsy.

"Mike said this colleague of his could get him someone at the last minute."

"He didn't say he could get anyone good, I guess." Chase picked up the crate. "We might as well go in. I do have to drop Quincy off and get to the booth."

She reopened the door, closing it quietly. She set the crate on the counter and started to unlatch it.

The doctor bumped her aside. "Wait just a minute." The doctor's breath smelled like fish and sweat socks. "I have to know something about this animal."

Chase wondered what he needed to know. "His name is Quincy. He's very clever. He's on a diet, so I have his food and a treat here." She drew the plastic bags from her tote and handed them to him.

He set them on the small desk. "What kind of animal is it?"

It? *It?* "This is a cat, and he's a boy, not an it."

"Breed?"

"I don't really know. Plain old shorthair, I guess. I got him from the pound. His litter was rescued from the beach in Chicago."

He stuck his face close to the case, peering into the slits.

"He stays in that cage during the day." Chase pointed to the large enclosure. "I'm dropping him off, and I'll pick him up tonight, though I'll probably come see him during the day."

"You can go." He gave her an imperious look.

"I'll put him in the cage first." Chase bumped the doctor aside, just as he had done to her, quickly unlatched the carrier, and put Quincy into the cage. He didn't curl up as he usually did. Instead, he crouched and kept his eyes on the doctor. Chase spoke to her cat. "You'll be okay, babykins. I'll be back soon."

Elsa and Eleanor were coming in with Lady Jane Grey as she left. She had misgivings about Dr. Drood, but what could she do?

TWENTY-THREE

Q uincy and Mike were both on Chase's mind all morning as she made herself smile at a steady stream of cold customers coming into the heated booth to warm up and to satisfy the sweet tooth so many people at the fair had. She hoped her cat was in the cage and not wandering around loose. She should have warned Dr. Drood about how easily Quincy escaped from wherever he was. She should have mentioned, even more so, that Quincy and Grey were a lethal combination, probably able to unlatch each other's cages.

Chase had told Anna what little she knew of Mike's arrest. Anna said Julie and Jay were coming to the fair today, so Chase held off on calling Julie.

She felt her cell phone buzzing in her pocket every

half hour. After checking the first two calls and seeing Tanner's number, she ignored the rest. He had called early, before she left, asking for more data and another payment. She had grabbed her good camera and, during the morning, had succeeded in photographing all the dessert bar varieties she and Anna were selling at the fair. This was by no means their entire list, but it would be a start. Maybe they wouldn't have to picture every single one, just the prettiest, and could list the rest.

Chase had definitely decided not to sell on the Internet, so the website would just be to entice people to the store. Bar None was not set up for remote merchandising or shipping, and it would take a lot of work to get to that point, if they ever did.

After the first two pictures Chase snapped, Anna asked her what she was doing.

"They're so pretty, aren't they? I just want to get pictures of all of them." Chase stepped to the next batch on the table and took another shot. They weren't nicely displayed in a glass case, like in the shop, but Chase was taking close-ups of the samples that were set out on paper plates to give the customers an idea of what they were selling. On reviewing her photographs, she thought they looked pretty good.

Julie and Jay showed up midmorning.

"Need a hand?" Julie asked.

"We sure do," Anna said. "Can you give out samples like you did the last time? I think that helps business."

Jay looked around at the booth, which was packed with people waiting to buy. "Looks like business doesn't need that much help. Maybe we can take over and give you two a break."

Anna's eyes twinkled with her bright smile. Chase hadn't seen her smile up to her eyes all morning. "That would be wonderful. You'd better hang on to this young man, Julie."

"Do you know anything about Mike?" Chase asked, breaking into the conversation.

"Did something happen?" Julie said.

"They've arrested him."

"Oh no. No, I didn't know." Julie turned to Jay. "Have you heard from Gerrold?"

"I'll text him right now." Jay punched a message into his phone. "I'll let you know as soon as I hear something back."

Jay declined Anna's offer of a smock, but Julie donned one, and Chase and Anna left them in charge. Julie had worked the store often, so the booth was in good hands.

"Chase, why on earth did you take pictures of every single dessert bar?"

"Not every single one, just one picture of each kind."

Anna puffed with exasperation. "All right. Why did you take pictures of every single kind? There's something you're not telling me."

"So, 'just because they're so pretty' isn't good enough?"

"No, it's not."

They had headed toward the food court, which was also the direction of the vet clinic. As they reached the coffee vendor, Chase said, "Why don't you relax here with some coffee, and I'll go check on Quincy?"

Anna grabbed Chase's arm. "Why don't you stand still and answer my question?"

Chase was reminded of being twelve years old and being raked over the coals for not having cleaned up her room when she had told Anna it was fine. She always knew she was going to have to tell Anna about the web-page eventually. It seemed that "eventually" might be here. Unless she could stall a little more.

"Yes, there is something I'm not telling you. When the time is right, you'll know everything, I promise. It's a surprise and it's not ready yet."

Anna frowned. "Am I going to like this surprise?"

"You'll love it." Chase crossed her fingers behind her back. If Tanner did a good enough job, she would. Chase hoped all of Anna's objections would vanish and she would be wowed by the site. She couldn't let her see the current, mostly empty, one with placeholders and no substance. If they hadn't been at the fair this week, getting the pictures to Tanner and using her evenings to type up cute, clever product descriptions would have been easier to work in.

"I'd better go see if Quincy is surviving that awful man."

Anna gave her a doubtful look and got in line at the Coffee Caravan trailer. "Should I get something for you?"

She usually got a plain, strong cup of coffee, but she felt like having a cup of comfort today. "How about a white chocolate mocha? With whipped cream."

Chase hurried away toward the big building. However, before she got there, she met Patrice, on her way to the food court.

"Chase, did you hear about Mike?" She looked very much like Betsy, her mother, when worry creased her face like that.

"I don't know much, just that he was arrested."

"It's my fault." She was in her Madame Divine outfit, and she twisted the folds of her robe with restless fingers. "I'm the one who told them."

"Your fault he was arrested? Who did you tell what?"

"I told that detective why he was in the butter building. I thought it would help."

"What exactly did you say?"

"I said that I took the diamond collar and that I hid it in the butter and that I asked my cousin to get it back for me so I could return it to the display and that he said he would. And that's what got him hauled in in the first place." Her whole body shook almost imperceptibly.

Chase wasn't sure why that information would get him arrested for murder. She would have to talk to "that detective" and see what was going on. Or maybe Jay could find out from Gerrold Gustafson, the lawyer friend who was working for Mike.

"Maybe it's not your fault," Chase said, trying to calm Patrice.

"It is! It's my fault, and now Mike will hate me forever."

Chase fished a tissue out of her pocket and handed it to the poor fortune-teller. Too bad she couldn't really tell fortunes, or at least predict the consequences of her own actions.

"You know Jay and Julie got him a good lawyer. I'm sure he'll be released soon." Chase patted Patrice's trembling shoulder and hoped she was right.

"You think he will?"

Chase nodded. "I'll bet he'll be out today." She crossed

her fingers behind her back again, looking down to make sure her nose wasn't growing a foot.

Patrice went on her way and Chase continued to the vet clinic.

As she entered the outer office, she heard pandemonium coming from the clinic.

"Wild cat here! Everyone watch out, I've got a wild cat here!" It was Dr. Drood's querulous voice.

Chase dashed into the clinic, making sure nothing got through the door. "What's going on?"

Dr. Drood held Quincy one-handed, under his belly, just outside the cage. Quincy's tail was puffed up like a squirrel's, his ears were back, and all his claws were out. In one more second, he would claw Dr. Drood's arm.

"What on earth are you doing?" Chase ran to them and snatched Quincy away, supporting his back feet, holding him the way one is supposed to hold a cat. The way a veterinarian should know how to.

"Careful, that's a wild cat," Dr. Drood snapped. "There are other people in here."

"He is *my* cat. You're scaring him out of his wits. Do *not* yell like that around someone's pet." Who had he been yelling to, anyway?

Chase looked around and saw that the twins were in the room, opening the door to Lady Jane Grey's cage. The bird hopped onto Elsa's shoulder, shrieking, "Wild cat, wild cat, wild cat," in perfect imitation of Dr. Drood's elderly, shaky voice.

"Why did you call Quincy a 'wild cat'?" she asked. "He's a pet."

"You said he was a rescued feral."

"Rescued. Not wild." Chase shook her head. She looked around for the plastic bag she had left with his treats. "Please give me the bag I left with you."

The rude man pointed to a paper bag with a grunt.

It wasn't the plastic baggie she had left. "What's that?" She opened it. It was full of birdseed.

"There it is," Elsa said. "We were looking for Grey's food."

"What's this mess at the bottom of her cage?" Eleanor asked, poking a finger into something that resembled roadkill, Chase thought.

An empty plastic bag lay next to the bird's cage. Some smears of grease remained, but the Kitty Patty was gone. It was now, Chase was horrified to see, the mess at the bottom of Grey's cage. From the looks of the claw marks, she had trod on it.

"What in the world?" Chase looked inside Quincy's large cage and saw a pile of birdseed in the corner. "You gave them the wrong treats?"

"What's the problem?" A deep voice sounded at the door. Chase looked to see Dr. Michael Ramos striding toward them, frowning. She grinned.

"Look what he did," Elsa shrieked, pointing to Grey's cage. "He gave Lady Jane Grey the cat's treat."

"Look what he did," the parrot repeated a few times.

Chase pointed to the birdseed in Quincy's cage.

Mike stared at Dr. Drood, his mouth partway open. "You gave birdseed to a cat?" He shook his head. "And meat to a parrot?"

"Those are the treats their owners left for them." Dr.

Drood's voice was even shakier. At least he wasn't yelling anymore.

Chase could see Mike composing himself. He must have counted to ten, because he spoke ten seconds later. "Dr. Drood, you may leave now."

"When do I get paid?"

"Leave your address with Betsy. We'll mail you a check."

"I want to get paid for the whole day. I was contracted for the whole day."

Mike stepped forward and put his face in the old man's. "You may leave. Now."

Dr. Drood gave angry looks to all the women and stalked out the door, slamming it, of course.

Quincy flinched in Chase's arms, but as soon as Dr. Drood disappeared, he started purring.

"I'm glad he's gone, too," Chase said, nuzzling her face in his fur. "But, hey, I'm glad you're here, Dr. Ramos!" She thought she should be formal and use his title, since the twins were present.

Mike chuckled. "Not nearly as glad as I am. I have to hand it to the lawyer your friends sent. He got me out as soon as humanly possible."

Mike busied himself scraping the squashed meat patty from the bottom of the birdcage. Chase took his cue and scooped the birdseed out of Quincy's place. She scattered it on the metal counter and Grey hopped to it and gobbled it up. Quincy's Kitty Patty didn't look edible, but Mike put it on a paper towel and Quincy licked it up as if it were a fresh steak.

"No harm done, I guess," Elsa said, watching the two animals eat their correct, respective snacks.

"But what if you hadn't gotten here today, Dr. Ramos?" Eleanor said. "That man was a menace."

"Where did you say you got his name?" Chase asked, knowing full well he hadn't said anything like that to them.

"I'll talk to my friend tonight and see if we can get his credentials pulled. He's too old and confused to be practicing animal medicine."

"If he weren't so cranky, I'd feel sorry for him," Chase said.

"I'll make sure someone talks to him," Mike said.

The twins secured Grey in her cage and left, thanking Dr. Ramos for showing up when he did.

"Did you have to pay bail?" Chase asked. She hadn't wanted to say too much about the murder in front of the widow.

"That's the best part. They brought me in for lying about why I went into the building. But Gerrold convinced them they couldn't hold me because of that—too flimsy. So no bail. They have a print from the weapon, but it's taking time to process it. They took my prints before I left."

Chase would like to have heard that all charges were dropped. That was too much to hope for.

All four of them—Chase, Anna, Julie, and Jay—were working the crowded booth. Since the fair ended tomorrow, people seemed desperate to get the sweet treats today. Tomorrow, after all, the final big contests would be held.

Daisy came by the booth midafternoon to say hi to her nephew Jay. She picked up two Toffee Bars for herself. While

Julie was wrapping her purchase and putting it in a Bar None bag, Anna asked her if she had been fingerprinted.

"Oh yes. They did a thorough job." She nodded her approval.

"Did they do the other sculptors?" Chase asked.

"Definitely. I think they did them first." She bobbed her head again. "Thanks for these delights." She waved her bag in the air as she left.

Tanner sent three more texts that afternoon.

Chase and Anna, helped by Inger, baked some more bars that night.

"How did we ever think we had enough stockpiled before the fair started?" Anna asked, taking out the last batch of Pink Lemonade Bars.

They had underestimated how many they would sell by several dozen, but they weren't complaining.

The cat was back home after another long day at the fair. His owner fed him but skipped her own dinner to sit at the computer in the office. She also skipped a petting session. He tried to jump into her lap twice but was shooed off. He snaked between her legs, but it had no effect. They were both unhappy with each other.

When Chase got to the office, she was determined to finish up the data for Tanner. She pored over the screen, coming up with dessert bar descriptions for the rest of the products that surprised her. For some reason, she was in the groove. Glowing imagery rolled from her fingertips.

Pink Lemonade Bars: Bring yourself a taste of a lazy summer day, lolling in a hammock.

Much better than "You've never tasted better Lemon Bars."

Oatmeal Raspberry Jam Bars: Gooey goodness that will bring back warm memories on winter days.

Peanut Butter Fudge Bars: Go ahead, be a kid again.

That was better than the one she'd sent him.

She liked the Harvest Bar description she had done before: Imagine a crisp fall day, just before the frost is on the pumpkin.

She kept that one and several others. She sat back and admired her work. The descriptions were good. At least, she liked them.

She finally sent the file to Tanner shortly before one AM, telling him she would have the rest of the pictures by midweek, when the shop was back to normal. Since they would be closed Sunday, Monday, and Tuesday, he would get them on Wednesday, but she didn't say that. He replied immediately that he would look at her file.

As she was brushing her teeth, her cell phone chirped. Quickly rinsing her mouth, she saw it was a text from Mike. At this hour! No doubt he hadn't called because he didn't think she would be up. It seemed no one was sleeping that night. The gist of the text was that Jay had checked Dr. Drood's credentials and phoned Mike just now to say there were none. The poor old vet had let everything lapse. Mike had let his vet friend know.

Chase wondered if Mike would pay the doctor anything. Knowing him, she thought he might.

Just before turning out her bedside lamp, Tanner texted again asking for payment. They didn't have a formal agreement, and the amount seemed steep. Granted, he had put in a lot of time and was doing excellent work. Her checking account might not stretch that far, though, and she didn't want to sneak a payment past Anna. She would have to spill it all to Anna very soon. Maybe tomorrow night, after the fair, when she could show her the home-page screen. If Tanner had added some of her new data, that would help.

She had to put him off one more day.

Sunday morning, Inger rode to the fair with Chase. She wanted to see the Fancy Cat Contest. She chattered nonstop on the way, clearly in a good mood, and told Chase she would hang out until then, watching other competitions and seeing the booths. Chase made sure she had money to buy lunch and some snacks.

"Be sure you're drinking enough," Chase said, vaguely remembering that pregnant women needed to drink a lot of liquids. She had no idea why that should be so, but Inger wasn't doing much else to actively benefit the baby. True, she wasn't drinking alcohol or smoking, but pregnant women did all sorts of special, weird things. At least Inger had a heavy, lined, woolen coat.

Tanner sent three more texts on the way in. She muted her phone.

The two women parted ways at the midway, and Chase hurried to the big building to drop Quincy off. Patrice, already in her Madame Divine getup, was leaving the vet's place in tears. The fortune-teller shoved past Chase and rushed down the hallway, so Chase didn't even get a chance to offer any sympathy.

Once inside the back room, she asked Mike if his cousin was okay.

"She's still being chewed out by Viktor."

"Her grandfather?" She had been so impressed by his imperious demeanor. An elegant gentleman. But maybe one who held on to his anger?

"Yes, Viktor can be a harsh man sometimes. He's still upset she didn't tell him she was a suspect. He's also incredibly angry that she's stealing again after she went for such a long period without doing it. It's bad for his health."

"Why is he so angry about that? Is he overly upset about things because of his cancer treatment?"

"No, that's not it at all. He's spent a lot of money on counseling for Patrice, to cure her of her addiction to stealing things. He even sent her to San Francisco to see a renowned hypnotherapist. The man claimed he could cure anyone of anything. It cost a lot of money. And, until now, we all thought it had worked."

Oh yes, that made sense. He loved his granddaughter and had put a lot of effort into helping her. "How much is the cat collar worth?"

"I don't know, but it's a lot."

If Patrice had it, Chase would think she would give it

back to get her poor grandfather off her back. "It's too bad no one has found it."

"The police have searched almost every inch of this fairground. If it were here, I think it wouldn't still be missing."

"Do you think someone has sold it?"

Mike shrugged. "Doesn't matter what I think. I sure wish someone could find it, though, to keep peace in my family."

Chase wished someone would find it—or turn it in—to get Mike off the hook for murder. She was still sure the two crimes were connected.

She noticed that several cages had cats in them today, besides the black one that was usually there. "Are all these cats being held here for the contest?"

Mike nodded. There was a gigantic Maine Coon, a pair of Siamese in the same cage, and another glossy black cat, this one with a white-tipped tail and four white boots.

"Are their costumes here?"

Mike grinned. "You want a peek at the competition, don't you? No, they didn't leave them here."

Oh well, she had tried. "I'll be back around one to get Quincy into his costume."

"You finally decided on a costume? What's he going to be? Puss in Boots?"

Chase gave him what she hoped was a sly grin. "It's a good one, but I'm not telling. You'll have to wait and see."

She stepped inside the exhibit hall on her way out of the building. A Fancy Dog Contest was about to start. She looked around for Inger, but didn't see her there. Nervous dog owners clustered about with their charges. Some were adorable, others bizarre. A bulldog wore an eyepatch and a tricornered hat with a tiny parrot perched on the brim, a darling pirate. A dachshund wore a brown sweater with bristling triangles on his back—some sort of dinosaur, Chase thought. The poodle ballerina and the Scottie peacock were awfully cute. How would a judge decide who to give the prizes to? They were all so well done.

She hoped the cat competition wouldn't be this fierce.

On her way back to the Bar None booth, she stopped at one of the food trailers for a cup of strong coffee. The large heat lamps felt good on her head and shoulders as she waited in line there. She had slept poorly, worrying about Inger and her baby and about Michael Ramos and the evidence against him. Now she was beginning to feel that a nap would be nice. Too bad she couldn't take one today. Maybe strong coffee would keep her awake. She still had the remnants of her intermittent headache, and the caffeine might help with that, too.

The door to the butter building was, as always, closed to keep the refrigerated air inside. She opened it and went inside to see if she could get any last-minute info from the artists. Right away, she noticed the smell of the straw that covered the floor. She hadn't been especially aware of it before, but since Elsa had declared herself allergic to it, she couldn't help but notice. The straw may have also harbored an aroma of all the stale butter that had been dropped into it.

She strolled past the completed sculptures. The judging would be at eleven, in a little over two hours.

The one carved by the Minskys hadn't improved, in Chase's opinion. It was still an abstract mess. She did notice one on the other side of the room that was also an abstract, but much more attractive. There were no recognizable objects in the Minsky sculpture, but the other one, as Chase neared, proved to contain a number of Minnesota symbols. A stylized gopher held a North Star, and ripples, here and there, probably represented the lakes. There might have been a pair of ox horns and an axe to indicate Paul Bunyan and his companion.

The woman who had done the North Star had done a spectacular job, and the gopher Chase had noticed on the first day was almost lifelike. Other pieces represented the state's teams, the Vikings and the Twins. The only artist present was the woman who had done the huge star.

Chase approached her and complimented her work. "I would never think a five-pointed star could look so good," she said. It held a map of the Mississippi, beginning with Lake Itasca at the top left, tumbling past St. Paul and Minneapolis in the center, and flowing on to form the Iowa-Wisconsin border near the bottom right. The river was carved deep into the butter, making a path through the star that was edged with figures of birds, ducks, and geese. Little clusters of buildings jutted up, indicating some of the towns.

"Thank you," the woman said. She was short and plump, with curly brown hair and twinkling eyes. "I've been working on this design for nearly a year."

"It shows. What do you think your chances of winning are, now that Larry Oake isn't competing?"

Chase watched her reaction closely. She looked genuinely distressed.

"Oh, isn't that horrible? I still can't believe what happened. Right here in this room. I don't know who will win, but Larry should have. I wouldn't mind if they awarded the prize money to his family."

She didn't seem a likely suspect. She had so hoped to find a really good one here. Someone who was obviously the killer. How disappointing.

TWENTY-FOUR

C hase left the butter building. Her side trip had been a bust as far as finding a great suspect. Carefully sipping her coffee, which had no cover and was cooling rapidly, she headed toward the Bar None. The coffee vendor had only two sizes of cups left and no lids. She feared she and Anna might run out of paper bags for the individual sales. They made a lot more of those here than in the Dinkytown shop.

Madame Divine was standing in front of her own booth. Fewer people than usual were strolling the midway right then. She was probably trying to attract customers.

Patrice said hello to Chase. "I hope business picks up," she said, adjusting her gold turban. Her earlier tears were gone and she looked serene.

"Who knows? It's the last day. Shouldn't we be swamped?"

"I don't know. They have all the contests and the butter sculpture judging today. People might not be that interested in the booths."

"Have you done this fair before?"

"Oh yes, plenty of times. The last day is sometimes good, sometimes not. It's a toss-up. I have a feeling today won't be that good." She poked at her turban again.

It struck Chase that a small diamond-studded cat collar could easily be concealed in that headdress.

Two giggling teenage girls walked past, zigzagging their way down the midway. One of them jostled Chase's arm, and her coffee sloshed onto the hem of Patrice's purple caftan.

"Hey!" Patrice snatched her robe and stepped back, giving Chase an alarmed look. "Look what you did."

The two teens were long gone. "I'm sorry, Patrice. One of them jiggled my arm." She nodded her head in the girls' direction.

Patrice bent over to inspect her garment. Her gold turban tumbled off her head, onto the dirty walkway. "And *now* look what you've done!" She grabbed the turban and swished into her booth.

There had been no jeweled collar inside the turban. But there was plenty of room for one.

The coffee was mostly gone, so Chase pitched it in a barrel and continued past the travel agency booth. The short redhead was arranging pamphlets on the table at the front of her booth. She kept glancing anxiously up and down the midway.

"Are you looking for someone?" Chase asked.

"Oh yes, my partner isn't here yet."

"Sally, right? I've met her."

"Yes, I can't imagine what's happened to her."

"My name is Chase. I'm in the booth next door."

"Oh yes, sorry. I haven't ever introduced myself. Holly Molden." She took Chase's hand. "I'm terribly worried about Sally. I can't get her on the phone, and she's not answering my texts. I hope nothing's happened to her. She said she would be in extra early this morning." She stuck her forefinger between her teeth and Chase saw that her hand was trembling.

"Has she been here at all?"

"It doesn't look like it." She lifted a new box of pamphlets, slammed it onto the table, and dug some out. "It's not like her at all to be late and not call." Her hands continued to shake, and she was blinking back tears. Some fell past her lashes and spilled down among the freckles on her cheeks.

"I hope so, too. Let us know when she turns up," Chase said as she went toward her own booth, wishing she had some more hot coffee.

Holly seemed overly dramatic, going to pieces because her booth mate was a little late. Still, the blonde wore a lot of bling. Maybe all of it wasn't fake. Maybe she'd been mugged for her jewelry. Chase had the idea in the back of her mind that, if the woman loved diamonds, she might have been tempted to steal a diamond collar. At any rate, Chase hoped nothing terrible had happened to Sally.

She peeked in at Harper's Toys. The curmudgeon was putting his finger puppets into a box.

"Leaving early?" she asked.

He squinted at her and screwed up his mouth. She backed up a step, afraid he was about to spit. He refrained, however, and shook his head. "What business is it of yours?"

"None. Sorry. Just wondering." She fled to her own booth next door.

The day did start slow. Patrice may have been right, Chase reflected.

Soon, a crowd began to gather in front of the butter building. Eventually, some fair security personnel came along and organized them into a line. Chase watched the proceedings, wondering if she and Anna should take time off to see the judging.

"I'm not interested," Anna said when Chase asked her. "You go ahead if you want to see it. You could look in at the exhibit hall, too. That's where Inger said she'd be, right?"

"Right, but I didn't see her there when I peeked in just now."

"We ought to try to keep track of her."

Chase considered that. "Inger's a big girl. She might object if she knows we're trying to babysit her. I guess I don't need to see the actual butter judging. It will all be on display for the rest of the day."

She heard a familiar voice next door, at Harper's toy booth. Detective Olson was there. He kept his tone low, and she couldn't make out his words.

Soon, though, he walked into the Bar None booth. He was followed by two uniformed policemen. "We're doing one last search for the missing artifact," he said, sounding strict and official.

"I need to tell you a couple of things," Chase said softly, coming up beside him.

He gave her a doubtful look but stood still to listen.

"I was thinking that Madame Divine's turban could be a good hiding place for the collar."

"We had the same thought a few days ago. She was quite upset we made her unwind it."

"Oh." They had been more thorough that she would have been.

"Any more ideas?"

She leaned even closer. "The travel agents next door? The blonde one, the tall one, loves jewelry, and she's missing."

"What do you mean? Has anyone made a police report?"

"No, her partner said she hasn't shown up yet. They have a jumble of boxes at the back of their booth. Those would make good hiding places."

"Believe me, we've been through every box and searched all the exhibitors."

She remembered the quick search of their own boxes and the pat-downs. "I know. It's just . . . We need to find that collar."

"I would like to. But I would like to nail the murderer even more. Do you have thoughts on that? Any new ones?"

She wished she did.

The crowd disappeared from the midway as the queue was gradually let into the butter building. After half an hour or so, she heard clapping.

"They've awarded the prizes," Anna said. "Maybe one of us should have gone. I wonder who won."

Had Detective Olson gone to the judging? Would knowing who the winner was provide any leads?

There were three browsers in the booth, eyeing the Harvest Bars. Anna could handle those. "I'll go see," Chase said. She ran toward the door of the building. People were streaming out, so she had to wait to the side for them to clear. She could have asked who'd won, but she wanted to see with her own eyes.

She wandered back toward the booth beside the butter building, the jewelry booth, intending to browse their wares. Instead, as she reached the opening between the two, Detective Olson brushed past her with two uniformed policemen and a fair security guard, into the opening. They disappeared behind the jewelry booth. They had all been so intent, in such a hurry, she wasn't sure Olson had even seen her.

No one else seemed curious, but she had to see what was going on back there, behind the booths. The opening was barely wide enough for an average-size person. Someone hefty would find it difficult to squeeze through. Every other booth was set up with a similar passage. The Bar None booth was up against the travel agency booth, with an opening between Bar None and Harper's Toys.

When she reached the back of the jeweler's, she stopped. An official-sounding murmur came to her. She stuck her head around the corner. Detective Olson was kneeling on the ground beside someone. He looked up at one of the policemen.

"What do you think?" he asked. "Strangulation?"

The policeman nodded.

Then Olson saw her. He was at her side in two seconds. "Chase, get out of here."

"Is someone dead? Murdered?"

"Get out of here. This doesn't concern you."

She left, but not before peeking around him and catching a glimpse of blonde hair fanned out on the grass and a gleam from the rings on the travel agent's outstretched hand.

Then she ran, blindly, until she was at the food court. She stumbled to the window of the nearest vendor.

"Are you all right?" the avuncular man asked, concern on his face.

She realized that tears were streaming down her face. "Something to drink, please." Her words came out in a strangled tone. With shaking hands, she paid for a cola, then sat and sipped it until her breathing and heart rate returned to normal. Poor Sally.

There was another murder! And this time the victim had been strangled. Her mind worked furiously. Were the two related? Who would murder both Larry Oake *and* Sally Ritten? Had they even known each other? She didn't think so. It was a stretch to believe that there were two murderers at the Paul Bunyan Fair, though. It had to be the same killer. Didn't it?

Slowly, she tossed her half-empty cup into the trash and started walking.

She got back to the midway and saw that the crowd exiting the butter building was thinning. Paralyzed by indecision, she didn't know whether to hurry back to tell Anna what she'd seen or to go ahead and find out what had gone on in the sculpture contest. One thing she definitely did not want to do was to let Holly know what had happened before the authorities did. She couldn't bear to be the one to tell her. She would zip into the contest, then get back to the Bar None booth. Maybe, by then, Holly would have been told what had happened to Sally.

Another consideration was whether or not she and Anna were in even more danger now. She would have to be very careful for the rest of the day. She felt an overwhelming sense of relief that today was the last day of the fair. There would be safety in the crowd at the butter contest, so she moved toward that building quickly.

She squeezed inside between two people who were coming out the door. For the first time, the door was propped open. A small cluster of spectators remained, taking pictures, around the woman with the beautiful North Star. Chase smiled. She was glad the woman had won and that she'd come to the butter building after all. She would get back to the booth as soon as she could to warn Anna, but first she wanted to stick around to see if she could find out anything else. It shouldn't take long.

Chase slipped past some other contestants on her way to congratulate the winner.

However, she found she had to pause at the Minskys' table on the way. Mara stood quietly weeping and trembling as her father gouged chunks out of their sculpture and flung them into a trash barrel.

"Daddy, don't. Please don't," she whispered.

Chase watched, horrified, as the man seemed to grow more and more angry, hurling bigger and bigger pieces of their creation into the garbage. She looked around to see if any other sculptors were destroying theirs. The man who had carved the lifelike gopher was taking pictures of his. The man who had carved the Vikings football team was walking away. She caught him.

"What happens to the sculptures?" she asked.

"The maintenance people will clean up," he said. He frowned at Karl Minsky. "At least that's what most of us do: leave them here to be disposed of."

Chase steered around the Minskys on her way to the North Star woman. The anger radiating off the man was almost palpable. It was frightening his daughter, and it frightened Chase almost as much.

On an impulse, she stooped and picked up a bit of the straw with a tissue, then stuck it into her pocket.

Once again, she admired the detailed work on the woman's sculpture. A blue ribbon had been pinned into the butter. She wondered what it would be like to create something like this, to work so hard, and to have it turn out so well, then to see it destroyed. Or to know, from the beginning, that it would be. Butter sculptures couldn't last long, she was sure. She snapped a cell phone picture of it, just because everyone else was photographing it.

Several people had gone around to the back of it and were taking pictures there, too, so she followed suit and took a few of the back side. She was sure Anna would like to see it.

The detail there was equally as exquisite. While the front captured the route of the Mississippi through the state, the back depicted the Twin Cities with the most prominent buildings in relief. The IDS Tower shot up next to the Capella Tower, with its distinctive round top. The Wells Fargo Center nestled between them. The waterway between the two burgs was sketched in, and the state capitol building stood by itself near the big river bend.

Chase's cell beeped for an incoming text message. She glanced at it. The message, from Mike Ramos, read, "So s." He must have started to send something and gotten interrupted. She turned her attention back to the contest winner.

The sculptor, whose name tag said she was Astrid, beamed and posed beside her creation. She didn't look like she would tire of this any time soon. Chase couldn't blame her. That amount of prize money would have made her glow for a few hours, too.

A man came in pushing a cushioned cart and wheeled it up to the North Star.

"It's time," he said. He pulled on a pair of gloves and reached for the statue.

"Where's it going?" Chase asked him.

"Big building," he said, jerking his head in that

direction. "So everyone can see it and take pictures. We'll display it there on a tray table to catch the drips until it starts to melt too much, then we'll cart it away."

So this was the beginning of the end for the prize-winner.

Elsa and Eleanor were standing outside when she left the building. Chase couldn't believe her luck. She said hello to them and walked closer.

"Who won?" asked Elsa. "We don't dare go in to find out."

Chase would see if that was true. She fished the tissue out of her pocket and waved it near her nose, taking a tiny swipe at a nonexistent itch. A couple of straws of hay fell out of her pocket with the tissue.

The twins sneezed in unison.

Elsa started sniffling and Eleanor's eyes began to water. "Do you have another tissue?" Elsa asked, her voice choked.

"No, sorry. This one is used." She stuck the tissue back into her pocket with the straw. Yes, the sisters were definitely allergic to it. "Astrid, the woman who carved the North Star, won."

"Thank you," Eleanor said, choking. They both hurried away.

That answered Chase's question about the allergies once and for all. She didn't think Elsa could have entered the room long enough to kill her husband.

Chase hurried back to the Bar None booth. Anna was waiting on a few stragglers. Chase turned back to where Holly Molden, the redheaded travel agent, was standing in the back of her booth, chewing her fingernails. Holly raised her eyebrows to ask Chase what she wanted. Chase opened her mouth but couldn't tell her about Sally. Someone official should do that.

She returned to the Bar None booth. Anna was the only one there now.

"Where is everybody?" Chase asked.

"I think they're all watching the judging of the contests today. We had a handful right after you left, but no one to speak of for the last fifteen minutes."

"Anna," she whispered, so the travel agent wouldn't hear her. "I just saw the most horrible thing. Our neighbor is dead."

"The toymaker?"

"No, Sally, the tall travel agent. I saw her body behind the booths. Detective Olson and some other official people are there. He told me to leave, but I heard him say he thinks she was strangled."

"Strangled?"

"Shh." Chase tilted her head toward the next-door booth. "She doesn't know yet. Anna, if she was murdered, we'll have to be very careful. I have no idea what's going on around here."

Anna glanced around at their empty booth. "Do you want to close up now and watch some of the contests, then? There will be more people there."

"Have you noticed the time? I think we'd better do it and get Quincy ready for his big moment."

Her cell beeped again. It was the same puzzling message from Mike except without any spacing between the letters this time: "Sos."

Why wouldn't he just call? Or text something more intelligible? She was going there soon to pick up Quincy. She'd ask him when she got there.

"Anna, do you know what this means?" She held the screen out.

The older woman took the phone and frowned. "It doesn't mean anything."

Holly came into the booth as Anna set down the cell phone and started scooping up the few dessert bars that remained unsold.

"Wait, I want to take some of those home," Holly said, pointing her stubby fingernails at the Almond Cherry Bars. Her nails looked raw and ragged. Almond Cherry was the flavor Sally had bought.

"Do you know anything about your partner yet?" Chase asked. Somebody should tell this woman soon.

"No." She pursed her lips and a tear rolled down her cheek. "I don't know what to do."

Anna came around the table, gave her the goodies, and hugged her. "I'm so sorry you're going through this."

Holly collapsed into her arms, sobbing, for a few minutes. The she raised her head, took a deep breath, and gave a tentative smile. "Thank you. I'm sure she's just stuck somewhere with a flat tire and a dead cell phone."

Chase almost gasped at how wrong that was. It was upsetting she hadn't been told about her partner's death yet, but Chase didn't want to be the one to tell her. She barely knew the woman. Quick, she thought. Change the subject. "Have you heard anything new about the missing diamond collar?"

She gave a nonanswer. "Maybe." After she paid for the bars, Holly started to leave. She got to the midway and then came back.

"You know the toymaker on the other side of you?" She spoke in a whisper, glancing around to make sure no one overheard.

Chase nodded. She'd noticed that he was still packing up. His booth was nearly empty.

"He says he saw someone run out of the sculpture building right before the veterinarian went in."

"Did he tell the detective that?"

"No. Sally heard him tell his smelly friend. His friend said he should tell the cops, but Harper said he doesn't like the police. Judging from some of his tattoos, I'd say he's had some bad run-ins with the legal system."

That had been mentioned earlier, but Chase had failed to see the significance. Now she did. Sally knew Harper had been in prison and Harper might know who murdered Oake. Harper was a link, a connection between Oake and the dead agent. And a killer? Now there was another suspect!

"Did he say who he saw?"

"Sally didn't hear that part, she said. From what she overheard, she thinks that he does know who it was. But she told me she was going to try to convince Harper to go to the police." Holly sniffed, another tear dropping down her cheek. "And she would if he didn't."

"You don't think he would do anything to Sally, do you?"

"He looks like a rough man. I don't know what he'd be capable of."

247

Could Harper have killed Sally? It was more likely someone would want to kill Harper for what he was saying he'd seen.

Holly went back to her booth holding her head high, trying not to cry.

Chase had to find out who Harper saw. She would be very careful. But she had to know.

TWENTY-FIVE

"Excuse me, Mr. Harper." She smiled to set the toy-maker at ease. It didn't work.

"Whaddya want now? Did you sic the cops on me?" He taped up a box. There were only two left in his booth. He must have started carting his toys to the parking lot much earlier.

"What? No. They're questioning everyone. Please, I need some information you have. But first, you have to understand how important it is. Dr. Michael Ramos has been accused of murdering Larry Oake. He definitely didn't do that."

The man stopped working and scowled at her. "How do you know? Did you kill him?" Venom shot from Harper's narrow eyes. Chase felt a chill inside.

"No, of course not." She forced another smile, kept her voice light. "But I know Dr. Ramos very well. He devotes his life to helping animals. He couldn't hurt anyone."

The horrid man smirked, letting Chase know he thought she was extremely naïve.

"He couldn't," she repeated, more loudly, stepping closer. The man reeked of sweat and cigarettes. She tried to remember if he had worn the same thin flannel shirt every day. Didn't the man have a coat? "But if you know something and don't tell the police, he may go to prison for something he didn't do." She now took a judicious step backward.

"Worse things have happened. And I don't know nothin'." He shrugged and turned his back on her, lifting the two remaining boxes off his table with a grunt. They looked terribly heavy.

Chase shuddered and returned to the Bar None booth. It was so pleasant and cheerful compared to Harper's. Mainly because Anna Larson was there and not that awful Harper. She had to let Detective Olson know that the man had important information. She started out of the booth.

"Chase, where are you going?" Anna was finishing up a transaction with a customer who was buying three boxes of Peanut Butter Fudge Bars. "We have to get Quincy ready."

"Did you hear our conversation just now?"

"What conversation? Come on and help me. We have to get packed up."

"With the toymaker."

"No, but we'd better hurry or we're going to be late."

Chase didn't want to take the time to explain. She snagged a Lemon Bar as Anna was beginning to seal the last box.

"You go get Quincy started," Anna urged. "I'll take this stuff to the car, then come back and help you."

"Okay. Be careful." She gave Anna a quick smooch on her weathered cheek and dashed to the big building. Maybe she'd meet up with Detective Olson somewhere. Maybe he was still with the body. She knew she couldn't go back there without getting scolded. How long would he be there? Would he come to the contest arena when he finished? Surely, if the woman had been murdered, his best suspects would be there. They would need to detain people, question everyone. She had to find him soon.

Hurrying past the open doors to the large exhibition room, she saw that workers were getting ready for the Fancy Cat Contest in one half of the room. The dog agility trials were still going on in the other half. A ring made of metal supports and sturdy canvas was being set up for the cat show, with three-tier risers flanking it on one side for the judges and spectators. The canvas was printed with cats' paws in pastel colors. This was supposed to prevent the cats from escaping, but they hadn't met Quincy yet.

So many people milled about that she couldn't tell if Olson was there or not. Two policemen stood guard near the door, but neither was Olson. She looked for Inger, too, but didn't spot her. She didn't know where else to look for the detective. Surely she'd run into him soon.

Going on, she opened the door to the vet's office. Betsy, the receptionist, was alone in the outer room.

"I came to get my cat for the show."

"Everyone else has already gotten theirs. Go ahead." She waved Chase into the inner room.

Mike wasn't there. Chase stuck her head out and asked where he was.

The woman shrugged. "He went off with some man. Something about a pet collar. Didn't say when he'd be back. I might leave in a couple of minutes."

Chase wondered why he had left. Maybe someone needed help with a pet in the show ring. The dog agility test was finishing up. There may have been some other shows in other corners of the cavernous room, too. Quincy's Babe the Blue Ox costume was in a bag beneath the cage. The black cat, Shadow, was gone, probably being prepared for the show. Maybe even already dressed. It was still early, though. There was over an hour before the contest was due to start. She hoped Quincy would cooperate and make this relatively easy. She could envision taking an hour to get him costumed.

However, he cooperated fully when she did a test run. He seemed to enjoy the blue jacket she slipped onto him. He wouldn't tolerate the horns that strapped around his head, though. She tucked them back into the bag. It would be easy enough to put them on at the last minute.

She lifted him into his carrier and picked up the costume bag. Incredibly, his little jacket stayed on.

Anna burst into the room. "Oh, good. You're ready. Some of the other cats are already beginning to line up." She grabbed the carryall and headed out the door.

"Really?" Chase followed her into the reception room, then stopped.

"A pet collar," she said, slowly. "Mike left with someone who was talking about a pet collar." Betsy had left already. Was there nothing that needed to be locked up here? Surely there were some animal medications. Maybe people didn't steal those. Or maybe Betsy was as flaky as her daughter.

"I'm sure we'll see him there," Anna said. "Come on."

Chase couldn't help but think about the missing cat collar. Maybe Mike was finally finding out what had happened and where it was.

TWENTY-SIX

C hase was lost in thought on the way to the contest. Entirely too much was going on and she hardly understood any of it. She was sure that the Bunyan County Fair had never seen two murders back-to-back like this. More police personnel gathered in the midway.

When she and Anna got there, Mike wasn't in the exhibition room. Chase was starting to get anxious about him. She knew he wanted to see the Fancy Cats.

Anna found the stand with Quincy's name on it and set the bag containing the rest of his costume on the ground next to it while Chase put Quincy, in his carrier, on the top.

Ivan Aronoff, Chase knew, felt that his son had been done a grave injustice and was angry at the Picky Puss company. He had fixated on the diamond collar as a symbol of that injustice, it seemed. The company hadn't done right by his son. He had made that abundantly clear. He also seemed a bit unhinged, in Chase's opinion. Dangerous? She didn't know. But if the man thought Mike had his treasure, and if Mike had left with the man, Mike could be in danger. Where were they?

She saw Peter, Ivan's good-looking son, right away, but there was no sign of his father. Where was he?

Ingrid stood not far from Peter on the other side of the room. Chase waved, and Ingrid waved back. Chase wondered where she'd been all day. Ingrid turned and climbed into the bleachers.

"Earth to Chase." Anna waved her hand up and down in front of Chase's face. She had gotten Quincy out and held him, still wearing his little blue jacket. "Isn't he cute? Take his picture."

"Wait a sec." Chase patted her jeans pocket, feeling for her phone. She wanted a picture of Quincy as well as some of the other cats with their costumes. Her cell was gone. "Where's my phone?"

"Ah. I believe it's in the booth," Anna said. "I laid it down to wait on the travel agent. You were showing me a text, remember?"

Chase ran to the booth, now full of their boxes. Her cell phone sat on the table, the lone item there. At least no one had taken it. She thumbed it to see if she'd gotten any more cryptic messages from Mike. Two more from Tanner. They were dropping off in frequency. But none from Mike. She ran back and looked around the exhibit space.

"Mike still isn't here." She was getting a bad feeling

in her stomach. She twisted a few strands of her hair frantically. She flipped through the pictures she had taken in the butter building.

"Oh dear." Anna's mouth dropped open. "I just realized. That text? He's in trouble."

"What do you mean?"

"He was sending you an SOS."

Of course! That's what it meant. Chase's mouth dropped open, too. "You're right. Mike is in trouble. But I don't know where he is."

Detective Olson entered the exhibition room and headed toward the bleachers. She wondered if he was there to see the contest. Or to take another look at some suspects? She knew she needed to tell him to talk to the toymaker and to do something about Mike. There seemed to be time right now. Cat owners were still trickling in.

Something clicked. Those pictures on her phone. She glanced through them.

"I have to show a picture to Niles," Chase said. She caught him before he reached a seat.

"Detective," she said. "Niles?"

"What?" It sounded like he meant, *Not now*.

"I think Michael Ramos is in trouble."

The detective stopped and listened.

"He texted me 'SOS' a couple of times and he's supposed to be here. I have no idea where he is, but . . ."

"He's not hiding out?"

"Why would he hide out? He didn't kill Oake, you know that." What an exasperating man Detective Olson was.

"I'm beginning to think you're right." He seemed to

be watching Ivan and Peter as they readied their cat, Shadow. Chase hadn't seen Ivan arrive, but there he was. "We got a nine-one-one hang-up call from the doctor's phone, but when we located it, outside the exhibit building, he wasn't with it. Where do you think he might be?"

"He dropped his phone? Take a look at this picture." She showed him the image on her phone.

"It's a butter sculpture."

"Look at the doorway."

He drew the phone close to his face. She reached over and pressed a button to enlarge the photo.

"There are people going past. I didn't realize these shots were in my pictures. I think I took one with Mike in it. This might be a stretch," Chase said, ignoring Olson's disparaging look, "but Mike's aunt Betsy, his receptionist, said he left with someone who mentioned a collar. If this concerns the missing diamond collar, maybe this person has it. I thought Mike might be going with him to learn more, but what if he left with the killer?"

"Or, more likely, the thief."

"But what if he's the same person?"

"There's a good chance of that, but who is he? Or she?"

She tried a different tack. She pointed to the picture. "That looks like Harper the toymaker to me. See the tattoos? The travel agent—Holly Molden, the redheaded one—told me that her partner, Sally Ritten, heard the toymaker say he saw someone run out of the building at about the time of the murder." She didn't mention that she had recognized Sally behind the booths. "Maybe Mike is trying to get that information. The other person here is tall. It looks like Mike to me. Maybe he left with the toymaker. Maybe both murders are tied together."

"*Both* murders?"

"I couldn't help but see . . ."

Olson took another look at the phone picture. "The toymaker." He scratched his chin. "Harper?"

"That's what the sign says on this booth, but a guy visiting him called him Hardin."

"Hardin?" He squinted at her. "I think I'm connecting some dots," Olson said, nodding slowly. "I bet I know why he wouldn't want to talk to us. I should have taken him in when I first got a funny feeling about him. I should have known who he was. He's let his hair grow long in the back and he's gotten bald on the top. He's a little more wrinkled, but I should have recognized him."

"Who is he?"

"Frank Hardin, if I'm right. He's a wanted felon. He murdered two women in Iowa ten years ago. Threw them in the back of a van and drove them to a wooded park to strangle them and bury the bodies in a shallow grave. He was convicted and sentenced to life, but he escaped from prison three years ago."

"He's an escaped murderer? And he has Mike?"

TWENTY-SEVEN

C hase's knees buckled. Detective Olson caught her around the waist with an iron grip and plunked her onto the hard bleacher seat.

"How long ago did you take this picture of Hardin and Ramos?" he asked. "If it *is* them."

"I guess about half an hour, forty-five minutes, maybe a little more or less."

"He might not have left yet. We'll get a dog here, block off the parking lot and start searching. I'll get his license number from Daisy. He had to register it for vendor parking."

Detective Olson was speaking into his cell almost before he quit talking to Chase, requesting an APB on

Hardin's vehicle. Quickly he found Daisy, and they hurried away toward her office.

Chase's heart hammered. She clenched her fists, almost jumping out of her skin. Hardin was a dangerous man. A murderer! And he had Mike. How long would it take to transport a police dog to the fair? Too long. She couldn't stand still. She ran out of the building.

She sped down the midway toward the lot where the vendors parked. Two officers were questioning the man at the hot dog stand. Another one scribbled on a notepad while the chicken wing vendor waved her arms toward the parking lot.

Chase put on more speed and was at the vendors' parking lot in less than two minutes.

She spotted Hardin/Harper right away at a big blue van four rows from where she stood.

Running as fast as she could, she sprinted for the vehicle. The toymaker opened the driver's door and hitched himself up into the seat. She was still a row away.

"Wait!" she screamed. "Wait!" She windmilled her arms.

He looked in her direction and reached for his handle to close the door.

"You forgot something!" Not true, but she had to stop him. She put on more speed than she'd known she had. Almost there.

That got his attention. He let go of the handle and waited for her to reach him, panting and breathless.

"What did I forget?" he asked.

"Let me catch my breath." She bent to put her palms on her knees while her lungs burned and heaved. The cold air didn't help her recover. She was disappointed that Mike wasn't there.

"I need to . . . ask you . . . something," she panted and coughed twice. She drew in the lingering odor of sweat and also that of the cigarette dangling from his surly lips.

He squinted at her, suspicious. "I thought you said I forgot something."

"I'm sorry. I had to . . . stop you." Her breathing was almost back to normal. "I desperately need to know something."

"Know what?"

A *thump*ing noise came from the back of his windowless van.

"What's that? Do you have an animal back there?"

"Huh? Yeah, that's . . . that's Wolf, my dog."

"Please tell me. I want to know. I have to know. I won't tell anyone you told me. The travel agent said you saw someone run out of the butter building."

"How do you know that?"

"Her partner, Holly, told me. It was immediately before Dr. Ramos went in."

"Not exactly. Maybe five or ten minutes before." He started the engine.

"That person could very well be the killer. Who was it?"

"I'm not talking to any cops."

"Can you tell me? I'm not a cop."

"I don't want to get involved at all, understand?" He still had one hand on the door handle. His fingers twitched impatiently, and his vehicle idled loudly. It needed a new muffler, Chase thought, almost choking on the black cloud of exhaust spewing from the rusty tailpipe. The thumping continued in the back of the vehicle.

"Yes, I understand. I said I won't say anything to them. I only want to talk to him, to know what that person saw when he was inside." Well, that and whether or not he'd murdered Larry Oake.

"It was that feller, that crazy one." He let go of the handle and made a circle beside his head, the universal symbol for *cuckoo*.

"Do you know his name?"

"Nope. There, I told you all I know."

"Thanks so much. I appreciate it."

"If someone comes around asking, I won't say I saw anything." He sneered at her. He transferred his cigarette to his left hand and took hold of the door handle with the same hand.

The thumping continued, but now she noticed a pattern. Three short knocks, three slow ones, then three more short raps. SOS! The message Mike had been texting her! He was in the van!

Chase grabbed the handles of the bay door and tugged.

"What the hell you doin'?" Hardin yelled.

"Dr. Ramos is back there! I know he is! Let him out!" She shook the handles, but the doors remained locked.

"Let go of my door. I'm leavin'. This fair has caused me enough problems. That foreigner. And the blonde. And now . . . now you."

She paused, confused by what Hardin had said. Chase changed tactics and grabbed the driver's door, still open.

The van started to roll. She hung on, jumped onto the

running board beside the driver's seat. "Stop!" she yelled over the sound of the loud engine.

He accelerated and shoved her with his left arm. The man was strong, but Chase clung to the door and started screaming. The cotton candy vendor, loading a pickup truck with boxes, raised his head.

"Help! He's a kidnapper!" she screamed. Maybe that wasn't the best tactic, since she was obviously not being kidnapped. "Help!" she continued to yell, hanging on tight. Hardin let go of the handle and pounded on her knuckles with his fist. She gulped down a scream, but still didn't let go.

The cotton candy vendor ran toward them, followed by two others in the lot.

The van sped up, heading toward the exit of the parking lot. Chase kept screaming. Hardin kept pushing her, trying to get her off his vehicle. Her knuckles slipped on the handle. If she gripped the edge of the door, she was afraid he would slam it on her hands.

They reached the gate. The brakes squealed. Chase grinned in relief, trying not to fall off as the van screeched toward the heavy metal gate that barred the way.

It was a solid metal affair, and if the van hit it, Hardin probably wouldn't be able to drive away. The vendors were inspected as they left the fair every day and today, the last day, was no exception. The gawky kid in the blue uniform came out of the small white guardhouse waving his arms.

"Slow down, sir. You were going too fast."

Chase jumped off as the van rolled to a stop. "There's

a man in the back." She was out of breath, could barely get the words out. "He's a kidnapper."

"The man in the back is a kidnapper?" the kid asked.

She pointed at Hardin. "*He's* a kidnapper. You have to get Dr. Ramos out of there."

"Hands on your head, don't move." Detective Olson was behind her, pointing a gun at Hardin.

Chase collapsed, hard, onto her knees. Olson didn't catch her this time.

TWENTY-EIGHT

C hase finally staggered into the arena. The Fancy Cat Contest was well under way. Anna flapped her hand, urging Chase to hurry to their stand.

When Chase got there, she looked her over. "You look . . . well, you've looked better."

"I'll tell you later."

She and Mike had been questioned and checked over by medics in the parking lot. They had bandaged her knees where she had hit the pavement and her hand where Hardin had banged it with his fist.

Mike had sat on the ground beside her. He was rumpled and his knuckles were raw from pounding on the inside of the van, but he didn't look too awful from his ordeal when he emerged from the back. He related some details to her. Hardin had gone to the clinic after packing up and told Mike he had something he needed to see and that it was in his van. Mike had thought he was going to show him the collar. But, when Mike stuck his head in the back door, Hardin had shoved Mike all the way in and slammed the door.

As they watched, Hardin was stuffed into the back of a squad car in handcuffs, yelling that he hadn't done anything and didn't know anything. Detective Olson climbed into the front seat to question him. Chase thought Hardin wouldn't tell Olson anything about who he had seen run out of the butter sculpture building.

One thing puzzled Chase. The patrolman who had read Hardin his rights had said he was under arrest for murder. *He* had killed Larry Oake? That didn't make a bit of sense. Then it dawned on her. He must have strangled poor Sally Ritten. But why?

When Chase ducked her head inside the squad car window and said she was showing Quincy any minute now in the Fancy Cat Contest, Detective Olson, showing his softer side, told Chase to go ahead and he'd get her official statement later. She had waved to Mike and limped off.

"Most of the cats are finished," Anna said, keeping her voice low. "It's almost our turn. Where have you been?" She sniffed. "I can't decide if you hair smells more like a locker room or a bar."

"I'll fill you in, I promise," Chase said. "I feel much better than I look . . . and smell. Although I'm still completely confused. At least I found Mike and he's all right. He should be here any minute." Quincy crouched on the stand where Anna had been steadying him with one hand while he watched everything that was going on, his whiskers twitching and his ears swiveling.

Since he was in full costume, Chase snapped his picture, then scooped him up. She laughed when he got a good whiff of her and drew his head back, his eyes narrowed and his ears flattened against his furry skull. He worked his nostrils in and out. It felt good to laugh.

Out of the corner of her eye, she saw Mike walk into the arena. He took a seat in the front row of the bleachers and gave Chase a wink. Her heart fluttered a bit.

The owner of the Maine Coon, outfitted improbably as a ballerina, complete with sequined lavender tutu and four satin ballet slippers, was returning the cat to his oversize cage.

Inger caught Chase's eye and waved from the bleachers. Chase held a hand out to her and pointed to their stand, asking if she wanted to join them. After all, she had designed the costume. But Inger shook her head. She pointed to Peter Aronoff and surprised Chase by making her way out of the bleachers to stand next to him and his father.

Patrice had shed her gauzy Madame Divine garments and wore blue jeans and a pink fluffy sweater. It very much matched the tutu Princess Puffball wore. The chubby cat also bore a cardboard tiara, covered with silver glitter, on her pretty head. From the nonchalant look in the cat's blue eyes, it was obvious she already considered herself the winner, if not the queen.

Daisy spoke into the microphone at her stand. "And now, Quincy, owned by Charity Oliver."

Quincy was fully dressed, thanks to Anna, little blue jacket snug on his round body, ox horns tied firmly, if lopsidedly, on his head.

"Do you want to take him?" Chase asked Anna, since she looked so ragged.

"No, he's your cat. You do it." Anna nudged the small of her back. "You don't look that bad."

Chase carried Quincy to the center of the semicircle formed by the contestants and put him on the judge's carpeted stand.

There were three judges. Chase figured there had to be an odd number to avoid tied votes. A stern woman and two men, one old with a crew cut, and one younger bald and jolly man, stared at Quincy, assessing. The stern woman tilted her head to the left, then to the right. The older skinny man bent over and squinted at the horns. The jovial one leaned back and smiled, clasping his hands over his substantial belly. He was the only one to give Chase's injuries a look.

Chase held her breath and kept her expression neutral, trying not to read anything into their faces or actions. The jolly man certainly looked pleased, but she couldn't tell about the other two. The jolly man would be the one she would want to play poker against.

After a few moments, the stern woman, still frowning,

nodded at Chase. She took that to mean she should return to their station, so she picked Quincy up and cuddled him, scratching behind his ears, as she walked back to their stand. His horns fell off and she stooped to scoop them up and stick them back on his head.

Peter and Ivan's handsome black cat wore a slick black cape and a black hood with extra large pointy ears. He made an adorable Batkitty. Or maybe, since he was owned by a man, he really *should* be called Batcat.

Other cats were outfitted as ballet dancers in tutus (two of them, one being the Maine Coon), firecats (three), and one had on a mermaid outfit, complete with wrapped back legs. That cat, a sassy Siamese, yowled over and over and looked miserable. The other Siamese seemed to be Neptune, in similar blue-green colors with a trident fastened to its back. The cat was trying hard to bite it off.

There were five orange tabbies dressed as Puss in Boots. That made her smile. She was right not to have picked that for Quincy's costume.

"Next," Daisy announced, "Shadow, owned by Ivan and Peter Aronoff."

What had Hardin muttered when she was clinging for all her life to his van? *That foreigner has caused me enough trouble.* How had she missed putting that together? The only person who sounded like he was clearly from someplace else was Ivan Aronoff. He was also cuckoo, as Hardin had pointed out. Chase frowned in thought. No, Hardin hadn't killed Oake. But she knew who had.

Chase stared at Shadow's stand. Both Peter and Ivan

were still there. Peter picked up his cat and took him to the judges.

Shadow behaved admirably, and Peter returned to their stand and tucked Shadow into his carrier.

"That's it," Anna said. "Quince and Shadow were the last two. Now it's time to hold our breath."

Chase had been doing that a lot lately. She fidgeted, trying to decide what to do about what she had figured out.

One of the police officers from the parking lot strode a few steps into the arena, looked around, and beckoned Daisy over to him. She hurried to the doorway. They bent their heads together, the large man leaning down to Daisy's level. After a few seconds, she jerked her head up and stared at him. He nodded grimly. After he said a few more words, she nodded, too, then came back to the contest.

The policeman looked behind him, into the corridor, then went to sit in the bleachers, on the first row, very close to the entrance. He should be able to catch Ivan if he made a run for it. But why would he run? No one here knew he was the killer except Chase. And what concrete evidence did she have? None. Just Hardin saying he saw someone who was probably Ivan leaving the building at the critical time. It didn't seem that Hardin had told the police what he told her, or ever would.

Daisy climbed the stand to the microphone and tapped it. Every single cat and half their owners flinched. "I need to make a special announcement. After the contest, no one is to leave the building. This is by order of the police. There has been . . . an incident and they want to question everyone here."

The huge space buzzed with startled exclamations and whispered words. It seemed that every single person stirred, either in their seats or where they were standing.

Daisy continued. "We'll finish the judging and award the prize, then, everyone, please stay here." She stepped down and nodded at the judges to continue.

The three judges put their heads together and conferred for the longest time. The crew cut man pulled a notebook from his inside jacket pocket and thumbed through a few pages. The woman consulted her phone. Chase assumed she had taken notes on it. The jolly man bobbed his head in agreement. Finally, the stern woman beckoned Daisy to the trio. She tripped across the floor, her frizzy hair bouncing, her eyebrows up expectantly. She was light on her feet, in spite of the heavy atmosphere. Daisy stood listening, gave two quick nods, then went back to the stand with the microphone. She refrained from tapping it this time.

"May I have your attention, please? The judges have reached a decision in the Fancy Cat Contest. Here are the results. In third place, Princess Puffball the ballerina, owned by Patrice Youngren."

Patrice, with a huge smile on her face, held her pudgy ballerina up so everyone could admire the frilly pink costume. Ms. Sharp, the prickly Picky Puss rep, marched over and handed a ribbon to Patrice.

When the clapping started, it was so loud that Chase looked around for the first time at all the spectators, perched on risers to one side of the competition area.

They filled every row, up to the top. She was surprised by the number of faces she saw. There were too many people there, she thought, for the crowd to be made up of just the friends and relatives of the contestants. It was clearly a popular contest. It was the last contest of the fair, and the contract for appearing on the cat food containers, plus a possible television ad, with royalties, were such high stakes—but would have been higher if the collar hadn't disappeared.

After the applause died down, Daisy spoke again. "Ladies and gentlemen, in second place is Shadow, dressed as Batcat." Shadow's owner was announced. Peter grinned and displayed Shadow as Ms. Sharp went to their stand and gave a red ribbon to Ivan. Chase wasn't sure how she felt about the show going on and a murderer winning a prize. If Peter was innocent of his father's crimes, she felt happy for him. Ivan, however . . . She had no happiness for him. In fact, anger was building inside her.

"And in first place, Quincy, as Babe the Blue Ox, owned by Charity Oliver."

The butterscotch cat's owner gripped him so hard, she was in danger of crushing him. Nevertheless, he purred loudly. Maybe he'd caught her infectious joy at winning the contest. Maybe he could tell he'd won and was happy about it. Maybe he liked being squeezed by his owner. The loud applause made him a bit jumpy, but he felt safe in his owner's arms.

After all, she was the one who fed him those delicious treats.
The other woman stroked him. He basked in the attention
and purred even more loudly, closing his eyes tightly in con-
tentment. The two women swelled with pride.

Inger smiled at Peter then ran over from the Aronoff's
stand to join them. Chase grabbed Inger's hand and raised
their arms in the air together, signifying that Inger had a
lot to do with the first-place win. Daisy handed the blue
ribbon to Anna, since Chase's hands were full.

"Where should we put this?" Anna asked Chase.

"Maybe in the shop?" Chase was distracted, watching
Peter and Ivan. Shadow was still out of his carrier. Ivan
held him and Peter admired their ribbon.

"Yes," said Inger. "In the front. I'll explain it to people."

"Be sure," Anna said, "that you mention who helped—"

A ginger furball leapt down, streaked past Chase and
Inger, and jumped upon the pedestal where the black cat's
carrier rested.

"Quincy!" Anna wasn't far behind, running to try to
catch him.

The ginger cat dove into the carrier and started pawing
the bedding, looking like a dog digging a hole, or maybe
a cat looking for a fresh place in the litter box.

Chase thought of that last one and was afraid he would
do his business in Shadow's carrier. She reached in and
pulled him out, knocking his ox horns off. It was a wonder they had stayed on while he'd streaked across the

room. Now, though, they fell to the floor. Anna swooped them up before anyone could step on them, although they hardly needed them now.

When Chase folded her cat in her arms, a dazzling sparkle caught her eye in the carrier. She reached in again and this time she withdrew what Quincy had been digging for.

It was the missing diamond collar.

TWENTY-NINE

Silence fell on the arena as, one after another, people noticed what she held.

Her hand, holding the precious object at arm's length as if it were contaminated, began to tremble. Showers of fiery sparks from the diamonds caught the bright arena lights and shot around the room. A few dabs of butter were wedged between some of the jewels. It hadn't been cleaned off since it had been taken from inside the sculpture, Chase thought. Quincy strained toward it, flicking his tongue out.

Ivan, more wild-eyed than ever, lunged for the collar, but Chase was quick enough to snatch her hand back against her chest. She narrowed her eyes and looked from one man to the other.

"You had this all the time?" she demanded, her throat tight with anger.

"No, no! I didn't know it was there," Peter cried. "Papa, what have you done?"

Ivan grabbed her arm, but she kept her grip on the collar. In a flash, Ivan threw Chase to the floor, banging her head and her right hand against the ground, trying to loosen her grip. Quincy jumped down. Chase flinched but didn't let go.

"Police!" Anna yelled, as loud as she could, which was pretty loud. She scrambled and caught Quincy, who had leapt away from the fray.

Chase shook her head in an effort to clear the stars spinning inside her skull. Ivan straddled her, clutched her wrist, and pressed, trying to get her to release the collar. Quincy, maybe having a change of heart, jumped from Anna's arms. He pounced and bit down, hard, on Ivan's forearm. The man yowled and rolled off Chase.

The policeman Chase had seen enter was there an instant later. He lifted Ivan off the ground and held him by both arms. Chase still had the collar. She slowly rose from the floor, rubbing the back of her sore head. Other officers stayed inside the door to the hallway, beckoning a dozen more uniformed police officers inside. She could barely see the tops of their heads, but she could easily tell which one was Detective Olson because he was a bit taller than the others.

Ingrid stood behind Peter, her hands clutching her horrified face.

"What's going on?" the policeman asked. He was a

large, stern-looking man of about forty with bristly dark brown hair, an acne-scarred face, and substantial jowls.

"It should belong to us," Ivan snarled. "The money spent on that thing should have gone to pay Peter. *She* should not have it." He tossed his head toward Chase on the word *she*.

The officer detached a pair of plastic strips from his belt and looped them around Ivan's wrists behind his back, ignoring what Chase held. Chase could tell Ivan was rubbing the officer the wrong way.

"How did it get in your carrier?" Anna asked.

Peter shrank back. "I didn't know it was there," he protested.

"How could you not?" asked Anna. "Didn't you bring your cat here in that carrier?"

Peter nodded. "Yes, but . . . I don't know. I didn't know it was there," he repeated.

"Did your cat notice it was there?" Chase stepped closer, putting her face in his.

Peter frowned and looked down at the cat, who sat crouched at the foot of the stand all this time. Peter picked him up. "That's strange. You'd think Shadow would have found it."

"Maybe he doesn't like butter as much as Quincy does," Chase said. Quincy, in her arms again, was now licking bits of it off the collar she still held.

"I hope none of those diamonds are loose," Anna said. "Maybe I'd better take it."

"Has anyone called Detective Olson over here?" Chase asked.

The policeman finally took a close look at what was in Chase's hand. "This is the missing artifact, isn't it?" the man said. He held out his hand, one arm on Ivan's upper arm, and Chase gave it to him. "I'll get backup right now." He slipped it into a paper bag and into a pocket one-handed. He waved toward where Olson stood, now surrounded by two dozen police. He took a whistle from his belt and blew it.

Chase watched Ivan. His eyes never left the collar as the man tried to summon more police.

"Why does your father have this?" Chase asked Peter. She wanted to hear someone else say it.

"I have no idea. I don't know how it got there." Peter looked genuinely puzzled.

Patrice came running over, carrying Princess Puffball. "That's him!" She pointed at Ivan. "That's the horrible man who threatened me!" Her eyes were wild. "He wanted me to give him the collar."

Ivan had wanted Patrice to give it to him, she said, after she stole it. He was the reason she'd put it inside the butter sculpture in the first place. "There's only one way it could have ended up in the carrier if you didn't put it there," Chase said to Peter.

Ingrid was giving Peter peculiar looks. He glanced back at her once, then quickly away.

"Yes, you're right." He looked at his father with sorrow in his eyes. "Papa? You took this? From the butter sculpture?"

Ivan had to have seen Patrice hide it there and gone to retrieve it.

"So what if I did? You should have it."

Chase could see the top of Detective Olson's head as he finally made his way through the throng toward them.

"But what else did you do when you took it?" Peter's voice shook and tears flowed down his face, scrunched in agony.

"All right," Ivan shouted. "I killed that man! He came in and saw me. I had to."

Gasps were heard from everyone crowding around the spectacle. Chase let one escape, too, at the unvarnished confession.

"Stand back, everyone," the policeman said. "You're not going anywhere," he told Ivan. "Everyone stay put until the detective gets here. No one is to move an inch."

They all watched as Detective Olson and six uniformed backup officers strode through the crowd toward Ivan. Ivan glared at everyone and hissed, showing his teeth. Chase thought he looked like an angry cat.

"That's him!" Patrice shouted again, stabbing her finger at Ivan, but staying a good distance away from him. Her mother, Mike's aunt Betsy, had made her way over and folded Patrice, cat and all, to her bosom.

Mike was right behind them. He went directly to Chase and put an arm around her shoulder.

"What's going on now?"

"Now we know who killed Oake." She leaned into him and watched Ivan.

When Olson reached them and confronted Ivan, the fight went out of the cranky old man and he submitted to a pat-down without further resistance. He kept his mouth shut, although he threw daggers at both Chase and Dr. Ramos.

Patrice repeated everything about Ivan's threats when he'd seen her with the collar, as one of the officers took notes.

Peter conferred with Inger briefly before following his father as he was taken out of the arena by two of the officers.

People were slowly beginning to leave the arena, one at a time, after being questioned by the police at the door.

Chase and Mike stepped aside, to the edge of the now-dwindling crowd.

"What just happened? I could see what I thought was a struggle, but too many people were in the way."

"Quincy and I found the diamond collar!"

"Where was it?"

"In Shadow's carrier. Ivan is the one who murdered Larry Oake."

"Are you all right?" he asked.

"Ivan tried to get it from me, but Quincy bit him on the arm. It was awesome. You should have seen it. I didn't get hurt much."

"How about out there with the van? You got hurt there, didn't you?"

"Not really. My hands are sore and a little bruised from Hardin pounding on my knuckles, but nothing too bad." They were a dozen yards away from where the guard held Ivan's biceps in an iron grip. "And I hurt my knees a little bit."

"What exactly did you do?" Mike took her hands in

his and inspected them, frowning at her bandages. His hands were warm. His own knuckles looked bruised. She rubbed a finger over them.

"I hung on to the car while he tried to drive away."

"If you had fallen off, you'd have been badly hurt."

Chase grinned. "But I didn't. How about you?"

"My hands are sore, too, from pounding on the wall of the van," he admitted. "Thank goodness you realized what was happening."

"We're quite the pair, with our injuries. But why did Hardin kidnap you?"

"I couldn't figure that out at first. I startled him earlier, on the midway. He was coming out from the aisle next to the butter building. He looked panicked—I didn't know why—but just ran away. After he took me to the van and threw me inside, he was raving about something he thought I'd seen. He thinks I saw him kill someone back there behind the booths!"

"It all started when Hardin saw Ivan run away after killing Oake."

"He saw him run from the building?"

"Yes. He told Sally, one of the travel agents, but then refused to talk about it, especially with the police."

Mike's jaw swung open. "Why? Why wouldn't he tell anyone what he saw?"

"He's a murderer who escaped from prison and changed his name. If the police found out, he'd be going back to prison. I'm not sure why he told Sally. He was probably trying to impress her. She was good-looking and was about the only person here that talked to him. She said she would go to the police if he didn't. I guess he thought it was worth harming both of us to stay out of prison."

"He thought it was worth killing for, Chase. He admitted to the police that he had strangled a woman behind the booths before they drove him away. Now I know it was the travel agent," Mike said. "He was raving that I had seen him kill her and that he would get rid of me, too."

"How can someone not care a bit about others? How could Hardin strangle her when all she did was tell people what he had told her?"

"He doesn't care about anyone. Just about himself."

"So there actually were two murders here. And two murderers." Chase shuddered violently and Mike squeezed her shoulders.

They rejoined the few people left on this side of the arena, Anna and Inger among them.

"Could we keep Shadow for a day or two?" Inger appealed to Chase and Anna as soon as she saw them.

"Inger," Anna said. "Do you know the Aronoffs?"

"I know Peter, mostly." She looked at her feet.

"How on earth do you know him?" As soon as she said it, Chase remembered how Inger had searched the homeless shelter and that the cook had mentioned a young man. She also remembered Ivan saying he and his son were homeless after Peter had lost his job with Picky Puss. "The homeless shelter?" Chase asked.

"Yes, I met him there, delivering our dessert bars. Peter is crazy about the Harvest Bars. I didn't want to say anything. It's too soon after Zack died. Isn't it? But Peter was so nice to me."

Anna put a hand on Inger's shoulder. She raised her chin up with the other hand. "Inger, you need to do what's best for you."

Chase wasn't sure Peter Aronoff was the best for her. Given her nutty on-again-off-again parents, though, it would be nice if someone else were looking after her. But maybe someone who wasn't homeless and whose father wasn't a murderer.

"Peter has a new job and they haven't been in the shelter for a couple of weeks, he said." She looked down again. "I talked to him today for a long time." She turned tear-filled eyes to Chase. "He's awfully upset about his father right now. He doesn't know what he's going to do about that whole mess."

"Did he know his father killed Oake?" Anna said.

"He thought his father knew where the stolen collar was, but he didn't really know about the murder. Not for long. He suspected but didn't admit it to himself."

"He should have turned him in as soon as realized what he had done." Chase wondered if he would be charged with obstructing justice.

"He did give the police an anonymous tip about the collar." Inger turned on Chase. "Would you do that?" Her words were impassioned. "To your own father? Could you really do that?"

Chase didn't know.

THIRTY

"Go, go!" urged Inger. "You'll be late." It was near closing time and only three customers lingered in the Bar None. Inger had been explaining the blue ribbon to them. She did it several times a day, but she said she didn't get tired of it. The picture Chase had snapped of Quincy in the Babe the Blue Ox costume was taped to the display case next to the ribbon.

Anna and Chase both felt it would be wrong to display the Picky Puss Cat Food bags in the shop, the ones featuring Quincy all dolled up in the diamond collar. Five different images of him, in various poses, graced the bags.

He had loved the photo shoot, Chase thought. Dozens of people fussed and fawned over him, and he purred nonstop. He even hammed it up when they shot the television ads. The one Chase liked best started with an empty metal bowl. You then saw Picky Puss kibble cascading into it. The camera panned out and left the kitchen, took the viewer through a living room and a front hallway, up the stairs, down a narrow hallway, and into a bedroom where Quincy lay in regal splendor on a gray silk cat bed, wearing, of course, the collar. Throughout the camera's journey, the sound of pouring, clattering kibble grew fainter and fainter. But when the camera—and presumably the sound, or maybe the smell—reached Quincy, his head shot up and he leapt out of the cat bed, reversed the route, and ended up chowing down in the kitchen.

The final product, which Chase had seen, but which hadn't aired yet, looked like one continuous shot. But it had been dozens of takes pieced together with fake partial rooms. Also, Quincy had refused to touch the Picky Puss food. Chase had brought some Kitty Patties with her, just in case, and the crew buried them beneath the dry food. Only then would Quincy enthusiastically dive in.

Chase looked at the clock behind the counter in the shop. "You're right, Inger. I'd better get changed. Do you need Anna to help out?"

"No, I'll clean out the cases. She's busy in the kitchen."

Inger radiated the glow of motherhood. Now that she was seeing Dr. Ingersoll and taking prenatal supplements, Chase and Anna worried about her much less. She was back living with her parents, but was moving into her own apartment in a week. She had gone out with Peter on official dates twice, but seemed to be cooling toward him. Or was that wishful thinking on Chase's part? Peter had Shadow with him in his own apartment now. Chase had kept him for three days, but Shadow and Quincy were not the best of friends. Quincy had kept Shadow pinned down under Chase's bed most of that time.

Inger had seen the therapist Mike recommended but had "graduated" from therapy after only a few sessions.

Chase took off her smock in the kitchen and put it in the basket of soiled linens. Anna was putting away the baking pans and utensils she had washed. Quincy was on counter patrol, inspecting for stray crumbs. Julie came in through the back door.

Chase paused a moment to take it all in.

Her shop. Her own shop. Hers and Anna's. She was living the life she wanted to live, making delectable treats that made people happy. And she had the best family and the best pet in the world.

"I only have a minute," Julie said. "Jay and I are on our way to a movie. Anna, you wanted to show me something?"

"I want to show both of you." Anna reached into her apron pocket and pulled out an envelope. "I got this today." She tossed it on the island countertop. The envelope was plastered with colorful stamps. The name in the upper left corner was Elsa Oake.

"Where is she?" asked Julie, picking up the envelope and extracting a sheet of paper.

"Read it," Anna said.

Chase extracted two photos from the envelope as Julie read:

Elsie and I decided we love Costa Rica. The place Larry rented is perfect. We've decided to buy it. We sent for Grey and want to stay here for a few months a year, or maybe year-round. Any time you want to come down and visit, we'd love to have you. Bring Quincy if you can.

"Let's see the pictures," Anna said. Chase showed them one of Lady Jane Grey against a jungle background, her leg securely fastened to a perch. The other was of Elsa and Eleanor—which was which was anyone's guess—on an impossibly white beach, surrounded by gentle waves from an aquamarine sea, backed by a matching cloudless sky, and swaying palm trees.

"Maybe we should visit," Julie said.

"With Chase's new website drawing in a record amount of business, we might be able to afford it."

When Chase had finally shown the website to Anna on Tuesday, after sending the remaining dessert bar photos to Tanner Monday night, Anna was thrilled.

"This is beautiful," she said, clicking through the pages. She grinned at Chase. "So this is why you took all those pictures."

Chase had had no trouble getting her to agree to pay Tanner from the Bar None account, which was nice and healthy after selling so much at the fair.

* * *

Mike talked about the last time they had been to this restaurant, when they had eaten outside a few weeks ago. It was much too cold tonight. The temperature had dropped twenty degrees since the day before. Besides, it rained, gently, all the way to Lord Fletcher's. The Wharf, the outdoor dining area, was closed for the season. It was November, after all. Chase remembered her disappointment that their time together hadn't been more romantic on that visit.

He said a few words to the maître d' and they were ushered to a table beside a large window. When the waiter brought the wine, he joked with Mike about the fact that, again, the Twins had had no chance of making it to the World Series. After a few one-liners, the waiter asked Mike, "What's the difference between dirt and the Minnesota Twins?"

Mike puzzled over it for a few seconds. "I give up.

"Nothing much," said the waiter. "They both always get swept."

The two men chuckled and the waiter left to put in their order.

Chase was happy to see Mike laughing. "You're in a great mood tonight."

"Not being a murder suspect will do that to a person." His deep, dark eyes twinkled in the soft candlelight. The waiter had poured them each a glass from a bottle of red wine that Chase suspected cost quite a bit more than she would pay if she were buying. Mike had insisted it was his treat tonight.

"Well, I never suspected you," Chase said. They clinked glasses and she sipped. "Mmm, this is yummy." The rain pattered against the window beside them and ran down in rivulets.

"I know you didn't." He sipped, too, then set his glass down and took both her hands in his. Both of them had healed quickly from their injuries, although Chase still shuddered when she thought about how close they had come to being killed. "I'm not sure I'd be alive right now if it weren't for you."

Chase ducked her head, embarrassed. "Oh, sure. Something would have happened."

Mike lifted her chin with a finger to look into her eyes. "You happened. You wouldn't give up, and you found me in the nick of time."

Yes, she had. She had to admit to herself she had saved his life. It was entirely possible that Frank Hardin would have killed him. She didn't want Mike to be grateful, though. She wanted something else from him. For the rest of the meal, they chatted easily, on the surface, about Quincy, about the parrot, Grey, whom Chase sort of missed, and about the Aronoffs. Inger was still seeing Peter, but not regularly. Inger became more confident with each passing day. Her baby was showing now, and she rubbed her tummy unconsciously when she was working behind the counter, out on the floor, or helping in the kitchen. She was turning out to be a competent baker with a good imagination for putting new ingredients together.

They also talked about the infinite, interminable wedding plans for Anna and Bill.

"It'll all be over by Christmas Day," Mike said.

"And not a moment too soon. If a 'simple' wedding is this complicated, I wonder how much energy an elaborate one would take."

Mike's answer was an enigmatic smile. The rain sprayed in a sudden spurt, clattering against the windowpane. "How's Julie doing with the new job?"

"She hasn't started yet. She gave notice last month and will begin at Bud's real estate firm in two weeks. She's so excited about it. For the moment, she's busier than ever, studying up on that aspect of the law every spare moment."

"She finds time to see Jay, doesn't she?"

"Oh yes. He says it's like she's walking on air, and she says it feels like she lost twenty pounds."

Mike snapped his fingers. "I keep forgetting to tell you, I weighed Quincy on the last day of the fair, before the contest."

"And?" Mike was smiling, so maybe this would be good news, Chase thought.

"He was down a half pound."

Chase knocked her back against her chair in astonishment. "With everything he ate? Everyone there was stuffing him."

"He also got a lot of exercise."

Chase nodded. Yes, he'd gotten out numerous times and had run the length of the midway with every escape, sometimes more than once.

That last burst of raindrops seemed to have been the final hurrah. She glanced out the window where the moon was peeking through drifting clouds.

"So he's not really fat," Chase said. "He needs more exercise."

Mike grimaced. "That might be splitting hairs. He could stand to lose another pound or two, but this is a very good start."

The doctor might not agree, but Chase decided that what Quincy needed was more exercise in the future. She fingered the silver-and-turquoise ring that Anna had given her. It was finally resized and she didn't have to worry about it falling off, unless she started losing weight. She didn't think that would happen any time soon.

"What ever happened with Dr. Drood?" Chase asked. "I felt sorry for him, after I calmed down over the way he acted. He was out of his depth."

"Yes, he was. His name was left on a referral list inadvertently. It's off now, so that should fix the problem of calling him up to sub. My friend insisted on paying part of what I paid Drood, since he felt responsible. He wasn't, of course. Anyone could have made the same mistake. His credentials, from when he was active and had his own practice, were good."

Chase didn't ask Mike if he'd paid Dr. Drood for a whole day at the fair. She knew the answer.

After they ate, they donned their coats and scarves and strolled onto the wooden deck to watch the moon send its stripes onto the water. The rain had stopped completely now and a half-moon was still playing peekaboo through ragged fringes of clouds. A slight breeze blew across the deck, the air fresh and dry after the shower.

Chase shivered slightly and Mike put his arm around

her shoulders. She had such a warm feeling about the meal she had just eaten, but the strange thing was, she couldn't recall what any of the dishes had been. They had all been flavored by Mike's smiling, dancing eyes and his soft, expressive lips.

He must have felt the same way, because he held her tighter and tighter, until they were embracing face-to-face. It felt so natural to look up at him and to finally—at long last—kiss those lips that had been tempting her for so long. They felt decidedly something more than grateful. So much better than she'd been imagining. Tender, delicious. The kiss went on and on . . .

RECIPES

HARVEST BARS

1 box of either carrot cake or spice cake mix
1 15-ounce can pumpkin pie filling
powdered sugar or toasted pumpkin seeds

Preheat oven to 350 degrees.

Stir the box mix and the can contents together. The mixture will be stiff.

Spread into greased 9 × 13 baking pan.

Bake 20–25 minutes, until toothpick inserted in center comes out clean.

Cool completely on wire rack.

Slice into desired size.

Either sprinkle with toasted pumpkin seeds or dust with powdered sugar. If using the powdered sugar, do this just before serving.

Store loosely covered at first.

Wrapped in plastic and refrigerated, these will keep for several weeks.

GO-GO BALLS

½ cup water-packed canned tuna fish (or
   salmon)
4 ounces light cream cheese
2 tablespoons dried catnip (or more)

Drain the fish. If using salmon, be sure to take out the bones and skin. Flake the fish in a bowl and add remaining ingredients, all with a fork.

Form small marble-size balls by hand and store refrigerated in an airtight container.

Makes about 30–32 balls.